A Splendid Boy

a novel

~

Melanie Martin

FLANKER PRESS LIMITED
ST. JOHN'S

Library and Archives Canada Cataloguing in Publication

Martin, Melanie, 1975-, author
  A splendid boy / Melanie Martin.

Issued in print and electronic formats.
ISBN 978-1-77117-532-6 (paperback).--ISBN 978-1-77117-533-3
(epub).--ISBN 978-1-77117-534-0 (kindle).--ISBN 978-1-77117-535-7
(pdf)

  I. Title.

PS8626.A77257S65 2016   C813'.6   C2016-902089-4
                                                    C2016-902090-8

PRINTED IN CANADA

This paper has been certified to meet the environmental and social standards of the Forest Stewardship Council® (FSC®) and comes from responsibly managed forests, and verified recycled sources.

Edited by Robin McGrath   Cover Design by Graham Blair

FLANKER PRESS LTD.
PO BOX 2522, STATION C
ST. JOHN'S, NL
CANADA

TELEPHONE: (709) 739-4477   FAX: (709) 739-4420   TOLL-FREE: 1-866-739-4420
WWW.FLANKERPRESS.COM

9 8 7 6 5 4 3 2 1

We acknowledge the [financial] support of the Government of Canada. *Nous reconnaissons l'appui [financier] du gouvernement du Canada.* We acknowledge the support of the Canada Council for the Arts, which last year invested $153 million to bring the arts to Canadians throughout the country. *Nous remercions le Conseil des arts du Canada de son soutien. L'an dernier, le Conseil a investi 153 millions de dollars pour mettre de l'art dans la vie des Canadiennes et des Canadiens de tout le pays.* We acknowledge the financial support of the Government of Newfoundland and Labrador, Department of Tourism, Culture and Recreation for our publishing activities.

For my father, who never believed I couldn't.

Shout loud the praise of Newfoundland,
Our gallant volunteers,
We hail our fellow countrymen
With loud and hearty cheers;
For in that drive they played their part
And proved what they could do,
And lost their lives to save the flag,
The old red, white, and blue.

Those gallant sons from Newfoundland
That day they showed their might,
Their regiment full 800 strong
Were foremost in the fight;
While some lay wounded on the field
Whilst more brave lads lay dead,
Those fearless youths from Newfoundland
They boldly marched ahead.

They marched up to the German lines
Where shot and shell did fly,
Where many's a brave young volunteer
Gave up his life to die;
But yet undaunted they pushed on,
Up nearer to the foe,
To find them well prepared that day
To lay our regiment low.

The July Drive
Author Unknown
Collected by MacEdward Leach

one

DANIEL BERESFORD RAN HIS FINGERS OVER THE CORNER OF the crisp, white envelope, carefully tracing the outline of the crest. His eyes locked on to the stately caribou, its antlers wide and strong. It stared back from its bright claret bed surrounded by the wheat-coloured laurel wreath in the shape of a crown.

Brave. Courageous. Defiant.

Maybe he had those qualities once, but not anymore, though he had been proud to wear this symbol and paid a heavy price for it, too.

He could guess its contents. "On this thirtieth day of June, on the eve of . . . thank you . . . sacrifice . . . bravery . . . your country . . . never forget . . ." He'd received the same letter for nearly fifty years now. He practically had it memorized, though this one had come much earlier than usual.

Daniel turned toward the window, pulling at the sheer material, once white but now yellow and stiff with age. It was a fine day. The sun glistened on the water, making the entrance to St. John's harbour look like it was covered in diamonds. He chuckled. Diamonds, all right. With the hundreds of tons of shit pumped into the harbour every year, it was far from diamonds down there.

But life was deceptive.

Daniel pushed the letter into the centre of the table and shuffled his way to the sitting room, slumping into an old green recliner. Why couldn't they just forget about all that nonsense now? It was a lifetime ago. Hell, it was two lifetimes ago. Through the picture window he watched the neighbourhood kids riding their bikes and teasing each other as they played hopscotch without a care in the world.

Job done.

Daniel's eyes wandered back to the table where the letter sat goading him. It was an invitation to the annual Regimental dinner on the thirtieth of June. They invited him every year, even though he'd never attended one. He didn't want to go to their damn dinner and he didn't want to hear their glorious version of what they *thought* had happened over there.

Daniel rubbed the deep crater running down the left side of his leg. There was no comfort today. He pulled himself up, his finger catching in the hole in the armrest where it was worn down to the wood. His leather-bottomed slippers scuffed along the faded linoleum. Sometimes those twenty steps to reach the kitchen were like climbing Everest.

He sat at the table again. It was just as well to open the bloody thing, because he'd been in a foul mood since it arrived about two months ago.

"Oh, shag it." He picked it up, but it slipped from his feeble grasp.

His fingers were once long and slim but were now so gnarled by arthritis it looked like he was permanently poised to hold on to something—a cruel irony, since he had little feeling left in the tips. He examined the uneven scar running along his palm, a rigid white mass of raised tissue that went almost to his wrist. After dropping the letter a third time, he whispered a raspy curse and picked up a butter knife. He sliced the paper clean across and unfolded the letter.

March 30, 1981
Dear Mr. Beresford:

July 1, 1981, marks the 65th anniversary of the Battle of the Somme, in which so many men lost their lives. To commemorate the fallen, and all those who fought there, the British and Canadian Governments have planned a special joint pilgrimage to the North of France for all who are able to attend. Various day trips include visits to Vimy Ridge and to the communities that are home to Newfoundland's caribou monuments: Gueudecourt, Monchy-le-Preux, Masnières, and Courtrai. The ceremony of remembrance will be held at Beaumont-Hamel at 4:00 p.m. on July 1, followed by a Veterans of the Great War Reunion Dinner hosted that evening in Amiens.

The trip runs from the 27th of June to the 5th of July and includes return airfare, accommodations at Le Prieure Hotel in Amiens, meals, and ground transportation to the various sites. You may bring a family member or personal care attendant.

Please contact the Royal Newfoundland Regiment office in Pleasantville by the 30th of May to confirm your attendance. As a veteran of the First World War and one of the last Blue Puttees, I hope you will consider attending this special pilgrimage intended to pay tribute to you and your comrades.

Sincerely,
Lieutenant Colonel Alan Williams
Royal Newfoundland Regiment, First Battalion

Daniel blinked and laid down the letter. His eyes darted over the page again, at the community names staring back at him as if they were normal places where people lived and worked. He didn't remember them that way at all.

He'd thought about returning to France once, when he was much younger, and he and Phonse had talked about it a few years ago, but that was just two old men talking about what-ifs. It didn't mean anything. They weren't serious about it, and anyway, Phonse was sick now.

They'd paid him to go once. Once was enough.

He looked down at the letter again. That was a hell of a trip for someone his age. They didn't expect much, did they? Fly them all over so a few politicians could get up and say their fancy speeches like it means something. The war was supposed to mean something, too. The war to end all wars, or so it was said. His eyes drifted to the window and the modern city outside, but his mind flashed back to images of craters, barbed wire, and blood, a mental scrapbook of a war-torn landscape he wanted to close forever.

The phone startled him. "Hello."

"Mr. Beresford. It's Marilyn Greene, Phonse Whelan's daughter." She hesitated. "I'm afraid Dad passed away last night."

"Oh," he said.

"It was peaceful. He went in his sleep."

"I see."

"I wanted you to know. I know how close you two are." She paused. "Were. Been through a lot together, you two," she said.

Just a war and a lifetime of feelings nobody else understood.

"Hmm," he muttered.

"You meant a lot to him, Mr. Beresford. I'm not sure how he would have survived all these years without you. So, thank you."

"I'm sorry for your loss, Marilyn," he said.

"Thank you," she said.

"Goodbye."

There was an awkward silence as he waited for her to hang up.

"Oh, and Mr. Beresford?"

He coughed. "Yeah."

"He had a message for you."

"Yeah? What was that?"

"He said you should go."

The words echoed in his ear. Of course, Phonse had received the same invitation.

"Hmm. Did he, now?" He looked out the window just as a steel-grey Canadian Navy ship passed through the Narrows and into the harbour.

"Yes. And I think he's right."

"I'll take it under advisement."

She chuckled. "Okay. Take care of yourself, Mr. Beresford."

Thanks," he said, and hung up the phone.

Well, then, Phonse was dead, and he was the last of them now. The last of his generation. The last of the good old boys from Middle Tickle. The last Blue Puttee. That was a lot of lasts. He thought about his great-uncle, who once rejoiced upon hearing of the death of the eldest woman in his community. His father said he danced a jig on the gallery and yelled at the top of his lungs, "Yahoooo! The old bitch is dead—I'm King of the Harbour!" But he felt little glory in being the last living member of the Royal Newfoundland Regiment who served in the Great War.

Since returning from the war, his life had been an abyss of loneliness, and his friendship with Phonse had filled a void. Just knowing Phonse was out there had been comforting. Many times Daniel prayed for the end and was disappointed every morning when he opened his eyes to the brown water spots on his bedroom ceiling.

He had no preference toward heaven or hell. By his calculations, he'd done his fair share of good and evil, depending which way the pendulum swung, and he'd be judged in accordance. But every day he drew a breath meant watching the world from that old armchair plagued by the slow march of time. Now his last friend, his last brother-in-arms, was gone, and he was alone.

Daniel scuffed a few feet to the cupboard and picked up a small glass. He reached for the whiskey bottle below the counter, and a feeble hand shook as it unscrewed the cap. The amber liquid wobbled out of the bottle and splashed into the glass.

Daniel raised it toward the ceiling. "Here's to ya, old boy, wherever ya are. Don't let the bastards get ye, Phonse, don't let the bastards get ye."

They'd been saying that to each other for nigh on sixty years now. On the morning of July 1, 1916, before the whistle sounded, signalling it was time to go over the top, the last thing both men heard was Private Mattie Dwyer yelling at the top of his lungs, "Don't let the bastards get ye, lads, don't let the bastards get ye!" Unfortunately for Mattie, the bastards got him.

Daniel downed the whiskey in one gulp, and it burned deep in his gut. The alcohol hit him hard, and he teetered on the edge of his memories. It had been at least five years since he'd pulled out his precious box. It held a part of his life he most wanted to forget, and another part he wished he had more of to remember. He poured another and another. There were people who drank to forget. He drank to remember, and the pain of remembering was far worse than any hangover could bring.

Daniel dragged his feet down the hall and inside his bedroom. Manoeuvring around the faded wooden dresser, he hesitated in front of the closet door. He straightened his bent body and patted along the top shelf until he felt the smooth wood of the ditty box. It was tucked good and tight against the back wall. He should have just kept it on the floor. Why had he pushed it back so far?

He clicked his tongue, contemplating several scenarios to get it down. Each involved climbing on furniture, which in some semblance of soberness he knew was unwise. He could fall and break a hip, or worse yet, die. Most days that was a welcome thought, but not now. Now he wanted to go through the box and read his letters . . . and see her.

One last time.

He spied his cane hanging on a hook inside the closet and clapped his hands together. He held the shaft and used the handle like a gaff to slide the pinewood box, with its dovetail joints, toward him. Pleased with his own resourcefulness, he carried it to the coffee table in the sitting room and sat down to wipe the dust off the lid with a navy blue handkerchief he hauled out of his pants pocket.

His breath was shallow, and beads of sweat formed over his brow. He looked down at the box Aunt Beatty had given him shortly after he had returned. It had belonged to his cousin Peter, who hadn't returned from the war. The rusty lock resisted his attempts as he turned the key. He grunted as pain shot through his wrist and up his arm as he wrangled with it. The sound of a click echoed, and the lid loosened. He lifted the top of the box and hesitated, opening it just a crack. His service picture was on top, followed by the letters and postcards and, underneath it all, the picture of her.

He eyed the smart-looking young man in the sepia-coloured service picture staring back at him with a face full of hopes and dreams. The number 493 was printed on the bottom right-hand corner. Daniel had been the four hundred and ninety-third man to enlist in the Newfoundland Regiment in 1914 and one of the First Five Hundred. He was one of the lucky ones, or so he'd been told many times. He was often left to wonder by which scale this luck was measured.

He sighed. There was no raw courage left in these old bones now. He laid the picture next to the box and made the trek to the kitchen. The only remedy for this was more whiskey.

Daniel sat back on his perch and poured another drink. Deciding it best not to waste half an hour with his less than capable fingers, he fiddled with the thin string, which held the stack of letters together. He slipped the first letter out and opened it.

A knock at the door startled him, and he cursed.

"Mr. Beresford?" a woman's voice called through the door. "Are you there?" The rapping continued.

Who the hell was that? He didn't get visitors. He laid the box down on the table, taking several seconds to make his way to the window. He peered through the curtains and noticed a silver car parked in the driveway.

"Mr. Beresford?"

"Go away."

She rapped faster this time. "Please, will you let me in? My name is Penelope Ashford. Please, I'd like to ask you some questions."

"Jesus Christ," he muttered, before barking, "Go away! I don't do interviews."

"I'm not a journalist. It's not that kind of interview. Please, Mr. Beresford. Lieutenant Colonel Williams said you might talk to me."

"Did he, now? Well, he shouldn't have. I don't talk to anybody."

He heard her laugh through the door.

"Yes, he said that, too. But I've come a long way. Will you just see me for a few minutes, if nothing else?"

He edged closer to the door. The soft voice was mid-twenties at best and the British accent unmistakable. Devon? Dorset?

"Oh, and Mr. Beresford?"

"What?"

"I really need to use the loo."

"The what?" he grumbled.

"Oh, sorry. Right. Your, ah, toilet."

He glanced at the box on the coffee table and back to the door. He should put his treasures away before letting her in. He started for the living room, but she knocked again.

"Please, Mr. Beresford. Just five minutes?"

He teetered as he considered how long it would take him to get the box back in the bedroom closet and himself over to the door.

"Mr. Beresford?"

Goddamn it, she was persistent! Didn't she realize how long it took an old man to get around? He cast one final glance at the box. With a dismissive hand gesture, he moved toward the door. She wouldn't be here long. He unlocked the deadbolt and swung the door open. The woman who stared back at him was no more than a child. His eyes travelled from her black walking shoes and up her spindly legs to her pale face. She smiled and blinked wide blue eyes at him. A mass of strawberry blonde curls settled around her face.

"The loo, huh? I haven't heard it called that in a long time," his raspy voice muttered, and he stepped aside to let her in.

"Thank you, Mr. Beresford. You're a lifesaver." She hurried into his kitchen, wheeling a large black bag behind her. She set it down and clicked a button, lowering the handle into the case.

"That's some kit bag you got there, missus. You've come a long way?" He closed the door.

She grinned. "The accent gives me away every time."

"Colonel Williams seems to know an awful lot about me."

"Are you two friends?" she asked.

"Never met 'im."

"Oh, I see." She shifted her feet and frowned. "Pardon me, but I do need your toilet." She pointed around the kitchen with her finger.

"Oh, right. That way." He directed her. "Second door on your left."

She smiled. "Thank you, I won't be a tick."

The British had the queerest sayings, didn't they?

He remained by the door as she scurried down the hallway, his eyes never leaving his beloved box perched on the coffee table.

When she reappeared, he surprised himself. "I suppose you'll be wanting a cup of tea, now, will ya?"

Her eyes widened. "I was only going to aim for a glass of water, but tea would be quite nice."

"I thought you British only drank tea," he said. "If you wants water, you can have water. Less work for me."

She threw her head back and laughed. "We do, but quite frankly I didn't think you'd let me stay long enough for a cup of tea."

Neither had he. He turned away and trudged into the kitchen so she couldn't see the corners of his mouth turn up.

"Sit down there and I'll get the tea."

"That'll be lovely, Mr. Beresford, thank you." She sat in one of the two chairs at the small table.

"Call me Danny." He filled the copper kettle with water from the tap and turned on the stove element. "My friends call me Danny." His last friend had called him Danny. There was no one left to call him anything, now.

When he turned around, he was shocked to find her standing right behind him with her hand extended.

"Well, Danny, let me introduce myself properly. I'm Penelope, but my friends call me Penny."

He took her tiny outstretched hand and looked into the bright eyes staring back at him. He blinked and pulled his hand away, turning back to the cupboard to dig out a bag of biscuits. Young people unnerved him. It was like they had no concept of how terrible the world was. Either that or they thought the bad things wouldn't happen on their watch.

The kettle whistled, and he placed tea bags in each mug, filling them with boiling water.

"There's sugar in that dish there." He pointed toward the centre of the table. He shuffled his way over with two mugs of steaming tea. His right hand was up to its old tricks, shaking more than usual today, and he spilled a few drops on the floor. She didn't ask if he needed help, and he appreciated that. He was old, but very stubborn.

"Is there milk in the fridge?" she asked, just as he took great effort to sit. Without answering, he started to rise again, but she had reached the fridge and placed it on the table before he had a chance to answer.

She was a clever one. He'd have to watch her. A smile crossed her lips as she poured the milk into her tea. And right proud of herself, she was, too. He picked up the bag of biscuits.

"Here, have one." He pushed the bag in her direction. In his day, the women all had some shape to them, but the young ones today were nothing but skin and bone.

"Oh, ta." She reached in the bag and pulled one out, popping it into her mouth.

"Take two. You could use a bit of fattening up."

She coughed as she swallowed. "You think so?"

He nodded, and she laughed, reaching for another.

All right, Penelope . . . Penny." He stopped and raised an eyebrow. "First of all, how did you get such an ungodly name?"

She chuckled. "I thought I was the one here to ask the questions."

"Well, I don't have as many questions as you do." He nodded toward the large coiled notebook she'd just taken from her bag.

She held her hands up. "Fair point. My mother just liked the sound of it, I guess." She shrugged. "My turn."

He sipped his tea.

"You have a very interesting story from your time in the First World War. Do you want to tell me about it?"

He shifted in his chair. "Not really, no." She didn't hang about much. "Why not?"

"It was a lifetime ago. It doesn't mean anything now. Not sure it ever did."

"You don't believe that, do you?"

"I do, yes. And if you know that much, you know the rest, so what more do you want from me?"

"Didn't you ever want to tell your story?"

"*My* story?" His eyes widened, and his voice croaked. "It wasn't *my* story. It was all our stories. We were all in the middle of that shithole together!" Sixty years later and thinking about the war still got his ire up.

He sipped the hot tea. "It isn't my story." His voice was calmer this time.

"You saved lives, Danny."

"We took as many. And it was all for nothing, because they turned around and did it again twenty years later." He snorted. "At least I won't be here to see it the next time around."

"You think there'll be a next time?"

"You're a fool if you think there won't."

They stared at each other for some time.

"I can see Colonel Williams was right." She closed her notebook and sighed. "But it was worth a try. I truly enjoyed meeting you, Danny. At least I can go home and tell my family I met a Blue Puttee today. You have quite a reputation in British military history." She stood.

"What are you writing about, anyway?"

"I'm interested in why people joined the war. I know there are all kinds of reasons, but I'm fascinated with that sense of honour, that noble pride, that obligation."

He stared at her. "You think that's why I signed up?"

"I don't know." She crinkled her nose and turned her head to the side. "You tell me."

"It wasn't for any of those reasons you just said. We killed and maimed and waded in water, shit, and blood. Millions died." His voice shook. "What was noble about that?"

She sat down with wide, staring eyes. "Why did you join?"

"I had to get away."

"From what?"

He left her at the table and dragged his feet to the living room to retrieve his prized possessions. In a matter of minutes, this stranger was about to pull the most painful details of his past out of him, and he was resolved to relive it one last time. He returned with the box and laid it on the table.

"Oh, it's exquisite." She ran her hand over the carved anchor on top of the old ditty box and looked at Daniel with her head cocked to the side. "I thought you were with the Regiment."

"I was."

"But that's a ditty box. They were usually only issued to seamen."

She knew her stuff. "Yes, that's true. It was my cousin Peter's. He was a naval reservist."

"I'm sorry, Danny."

"What are you sorry for?" He thought it was ridiculous when people said they were sorry for things beyond their control. Her cheeks reddened, and a pang of guilt stabbed at him.

"Nothing to be sorry about, Penny."

Daniel lifted the cover. The letter he'd taken out earlier was on top. He laid it aside and reached to the back of the pile.

She touched his arm. "Danny, are you sure about this?"

"I thought you wanted to hear my story."

"Oh, I do. Very much." She placed her young hand on his old, weathered one and smiled.

He cleared his throat and laid a photograph in front of her. "She's the reason I enlisted."

Penny raised her eyebrows. "Oh, dear," she said, "was she that terrible?"

Daniel shook his head. "No," he said. His eyes grew wet. "She was the love of my life."

two

August 1914
Middle Tickle, Newfoundland

"YOU'RE DOING REALLY WELL, DANIEL." SHE SMILED AT HIM from across the desk. Her eyes sparkled in the soft glow made by the lantern. "But," she said, getting up and coming around to his side, "see this word?" She leaned against him and pointed at the cream-coloured page of an old book she was using to teach him.

"Yes," he replied. But he couldn't see anything. She smelled sweet, like the inside of the candy jar that sat on her father's store counter, and clean, like windblown clothes flying high in the salty breeze. Her warm breath caressed his neck, and his pulse raced.

She ruffled his hair. "There's no D sound in 'mother.'" The word hovered over her lips.

"Well, I know that can't be right, because that's how everyone says it," Daniel said.

She laughed. "I don't say it that way." She watched him for the briefest of seconds before he hauled her down into his lap. She squealed, curling into him.

"Only because you're a proper English lady," he said. She arched forward until their lips met, and he gasped at the warmth flooding through him. When they broke away, her cheeks flushed a rosy pink over her flawless skin, and when her grey eyes eventually met his, they reminded him of smooth, weather-beaten rocks he collected off the beach. He tangled his fingers in her long, black hair. Even after all this time, he found it difficult to believe she was his.

A thud sounded outside, followed by voices, and he broke their embrace.

"It's nothing," she said.

He frowned, but she laughed, kissing his apprehension away. When her lips covered his again, lighting a fire where they touched him, his mouth relaxed, taking in everything she offered. Tucked away in the shadows of this small room, barely lit by the kerosene lamp on the desk, they had the next few hours to themselves.

He straightened at the faint echo of footsteps on the wooden floor. "Emma, someone's here."

"They'll go away." Her hands roamed and caressed as she trailed kisses up his neck.

He swallowed hard, his eyes flickering toward the door. He couldn't ignore the approaching footsteps pounding in his ears. Or was that just fear pumping blood from his racing heart?

"What if—" he started, but she stopped him with a gentle kiss.

She smiled. "Daniel, no one would ever come back here."

Try as she might to hide it, her English accent was still strong, and it always made him smile. Her eyes sparkled as she cupped his face with her hands and kissed him much deeper this time. He groaned, relinquishing his fears, unable to hold back any longer. No responsibilities, no worries. And no guilt.

The rusty handle clicked, and light spilled into the small room, slamming him back to reality.

"Emma?" Her father's deep voice jolted through him like the after-shock from an earthquake.

"Father!" She jumped out of Daniel's arms and stood, smoothing her dress. Her hands fluttered over her flushed cheeks, and she looked wide-eyed at Daniel, who now stood next to her. Edward Tavenor's bulky frame filled the doorway.

Emma had always believed, on the rare occasion they spoke of it, that her father would just need some time to adjust to their relationship. On some level Daniel wanted to believe it, too, but always thought it was more likely the opposite was true.

Emma's wide eyes were locked on her father now, and, judging from the look on the man's face, he was going to need more than a few hours to adjust.

"Mr. Tavenor, I can explain." Daniel paused, his mind racing. What was he going to say? There was obviously more going on here than her teaching him to read, though it had started that way. No, the truth was in order now. But what could he say? *I love your daughter.* He hadn't even told her yet.

Tavenor raised his hand at Daniel, a silent gesture to stop whatever was about to come out of his mouth, and his cool gaze shifted to his daughter. Daniel recognized the look in the man's eyes. The "not living up to expectations" look was one he knew all too well.

"Emma, what are you thinking?" The weight of his stare hung heavy. Daniel felt Emma shrinking next to him. He wanted to rescue her from drowning in her father's disappointment, just as much as if she were floundering in the harbour. It wasn't right. She hadn't done anything wrong, besides love him.

She did love him, didn't she? She'd never said so.

Daniel was used to being yelled at and had even had his fair share of beatings, but he didn't know what to do with all the silence. Father and daughter stared at each other, and Emma's heavy breathing was like cannon fire in the still room.

When she spoke, her voice was clear and unwavering, cutting through the thin air laced with the smell of fear and uncertainty. "Father, I love him."

Daniel's head snapped in her direction, but she stared straight ahead. He glanced back at Tavenor, whose blue irises were so icy, Daniel shivered as if the chill from a northeast wind had just blown through. A brief glint of sadness flickered there, and he knew it was sadness for Emma, for her revelation.

She loved him.

He didn't care what else happened to him tonight. He turned toward her and smiled. "I love you, too, Emma, more than anything." He took her hands, squeezing them as he peered into her beautiful eyes. His happiness was overshadowed by the ominous presence, firmly anchored in the doorway, as Tavenor loomed over them.

"Sir—" he began, but Tavenor held his hand up again.

Daniel's breathing quickened. He was six feet tall and fairly filled out for his sixteen years, but Tavenor had at least another three inches on him. He noticed for the first time how the seams of the man's suit coat stretched over his broad shoulders. The buttons on the crisp, white dress shirt were one deep breath away from popping open. Daniel puffed up his chest, adrenaline surging through his veins.

The coldness melted from Tavenor's eyes, and he smiled at his daughter. "I know you think you love him, Emma, my sweet girl, but you're young. You don't know what love is." His voice was as soft as a worn wool blanket.

"I'm far from a child, Father, and I know I love Daniel." She was confident, almost defiant. He shouldn't be shocked. The girl knew her own mind—he'd seen it time and again—but as he looked between father and daughter now, it was hard to tell which one commanded more authority.

"Don't you think it's time Daniel went home? His mother will be wondering where he's gotten to, and we wouldn't want her to worry, would we, love?"

That was a low blow.

Anger bubbled inside him as a smirk settled on the man's face. Daniel closed his eyes, trying to keep his temper in check, but he couldn't control the contempt in his voice.

"Since when do you worry about my—"

The door clicked as it closed, and Tavenor's footsteps faded.

He took a deep breath and pulled her into his arms. "I'm sorry."

"Why are you sorry? This was my fault. I should have told him sooner."

"The way he looked at you. The disappointment in his eyes. In you." Daniel shook his head. "It's because of me." He didn't like Tavenor very much, but he still felt guilty.

"Daniel, no." She lifted his chin with her finger until he met her gaze, and she kissed him. "It's done now." She kissed him again and nuzzled her cheek against his neck.

"Emma, I don't think he's just going to accept this."

"Come on, Daniel. The worst is over."

He kissed her lips and felt her smile as he did so. She opened the door and tugged at his hand, pulling him into the main store area. She was slender and graceful as she navigated through the store, her shiny black hair cascading in waves down her back. Tavenor stood waiting behind the counter.

"You want to become a fisherman's wife, Emma?"

"Suits me just fine." She squeezed Daniel's hand, and he looked at her. *Marriage!* Well, of course he hadn't thought quite that far ahead, yet, but it sounded like she was already saying yes. His heart thudded.

"And how do you propose to take care of my daughter?"

Daniel's eyes narrowed. "Fishing, sir, just like my father has always taken care of us. It's not a lot, but it's a living. An honest one."

"And how's that going for your father?"

The last two seasons had been too wet to cure the fish properly, making it impossible to get a decent price for the substandard grade they had produced. Tavenor had extended his family extra credit, which his father hadn't been able to pay back—yet—though it wasn't for lack of trying. Then there was the business with Richard. Daniel swallowed hard.

Before he could say anything else, the door to the small shop opened, and Harry, the postmaster, stood in the doorway.

"Afternoon, Mr. Tavenor, Miss Tavenor." He nodded in Daniel's direction, his eyes lingering on their clasped hands. "Daniel."

Daniel's anger bubbled as Harry continued staring at them. His questioning look said it all. What was the merchant's daughter doing with the likes of him? It wouldn't take long for the whole community to hear about it, either. Harry Scanlon saw more people in a day than the priest did all year for confession.

"What is it, Harry?" Tavenor's tone was low and even.

"Telegram, sir."

"Lay it there on the counter, Harry. I'll see to it later."

Harry coughed. "I think you'll want to be reading it now, Mr. Tavenor, sir. It's from the governor's office in St. John's." He walked over to Tavenor and passed him the folded message.

"The governor?" Tavenor raised his eyebrows and accepted the yellow parchment, unfolding it as he narrowed his eyes downward.

"Yes, sir."

Three pairs of eyes watched the deeply etched lines of Tavenor's forehead as they crinkled.

"Father, what is it?" Emma tightened her grip on Daniel's hand.

Harry's eyes fixed on the pair once again in a curious, assessing stare. Daniel glared at the man and moved closer to Emma. At least when Harry recounted this tale in one of his many gossip sessions at the post office tomorrow, there would be no question as to what he saw.

Tavenor contemplated the telegram for a few more seconds before laying the paper on the counter. "England has declared war on Germany."

"What does that mean?" Harry looked bewildered, though, in fairness, he'd looked like that since entering the store.

Daniel smirked. "It means nothing for us. Sounds like England's problem to me."

Tavenor ignored him. "Thank you, Harry."

"Thank you, sir." Harry nodded and placed his cap back on his head, stealing one last glance at Daniel and Emma before exiting the shop.

Tavenor folded his arms across his chest and surveyed Daniel. "It has everything to do with *us*." He pointed back and forth between himself and Emma. "Emma's mother resides there."

"Is Mother in danger?" Emma dropped Daniel's hand and moved closer to her father.

"I don't know, darling. I really don't know."

Daniel moved a step closer and placed his arm around her shoulders. "What can I do?" he asked.

She faced him, and he saw fear in her eyes. He tried to think of something to say, but it was hard to ease another's pain. Hadn't she tried so hard to do the same for him only a few months ago?

"I think it's high time you were on your way, Daniel." Tavenor walked out from behind the counter and stood next to his daughter.

Tavenor made a career of dismissing people, and they responded to his commands. Keep the merchant happy, Daniel had always heard the old folks say, but at what cost?

Daniel stiffened at the man's proximity but ignored him, rubbing Emma's shoulder. He met her gaze. "Is that what you want?"

She nodded. "It's getting late, Daniel, you go on home. I'll be fine."

He felt a stab of disappointment in his gut. He longed to console her as she'd done for him after Richard's death, but Tavenor loomed over her, pushing Daniel out the door with his stony stare. He would go, but only because she wanted him to, and not before he said goodbye. Properly.

"I'll see you tomorrow." He leaned in and kissed her cheek. She nodded and touched his face with a tender caress he felt hours later.

Tavenor opened the door and reached his arm out in an exaggerated gesture, encouraging Daniel's departure. The evening had taken quite an unexpected turn, all right. He couldn't help but wonder what would have happened otherwise. He had little choice but to leave her there.

He stepped outside Tavenor's shop onto the narrow bridge leading down to the dirt road and turned back to steal one more glance at Emma. Tavenor's large body took up the full of the doorway, blocking his view. Daniel bit his lip to keep his anger at bay.

"Good night, Daniel. Oh, and tell your father we have some business to discuss." Tavenor slammed the door, and the wood just brushed the tip of Daniel's nose.

three

August 1914
Middle Tickle, Newfoundland

"SIT DOWN, JACK, YOU'LL WEAR THE PAINT CLEAN OFF THE floor." Mary Beresford's husband paced in front of the wood stove. She emerged from the pantry using her apron as a bowl to hold potatoes. She counted out nine large ones and hesitated, laying the ninth to the side.

"I'll have to go see him. See if I can reason with him." He snorted. "Not like there's any reasoning with the bastard. I just need enough credit to finish out the season. We'd be out of this mess by now if—"

She wheeled around with a small knife in her hand, pointing it like her finger. "Don't speak of it. Five months is not enough time to mourn Richard! You got him a berth on that godforsaken schooner."

Her husband grimaced, as if the knife had just sliced him to the bone.

"Oh, Jack, I'm sorry." She covered her mouth and gasped. He didn't need any reminders of how Richard died any more than she did. There was no way any of them could have known what cruel fate would befall their boy, and all the others, or they would never have let him go.

Her husband sank onto a rickety wooden chair next to the wood stove where several pots simmered. Wool socks and a few pot cloths were folded over a piece of rope strung in a half-moon shape on the wall behind the stove to dry. Jack stared through it, his eyes fixed to the wall. She laid the knife down, wiped her hands in her apron, and went to him, placing her arms around his shoulders. The lines around his face were drawn as deep as the crevices in the rugged cliffs surrounding Middle Tickle. He'd aged since her brother Tommy had come to their door last April with the terrible news.

There had been a quiet knock, which in itself was unusual. Nobody knocked in Middle Tickle. It wasn't as if there were any strangers around. Everyone in the harbour was a friend or a family member, welcome day or night. Thinking back on it now, it was a kind of foreboding, a warning something was wrong.

She had turned around from the counter with dough-covered hands and smiled at her older brother, who stepped out of the dark porch and into the doorway of the kitchen.

"Evenin', Mary."

"Tommy! What are you doing all the way down in Middle Tickle at this hour?" Before he could answer, she called out in no particular direction. "Jack, Tommy's here. Come down and pour him a grog."

She picked up a fistful of flour, rubbing her hands together, plying the sticky dough off her fingers. Drying her hands in her apron, she hurried over to the tall man slouching in the doorway. She hugged into him, but his arms stayed by his sides. She pulled away and saw his down-turned mouth. He hesitated, scooped his hat off, and held it in front of him with shaky hands.

"Come in and have your supper. I can't send you back to Eileen hungry, can I?" She chuckled and returned to her dough. She still ordered her brothers around—an unbreakable habit left over from childhood. Their mother had died giving birth, and she was the only girl left to help her father raise seven boys. She had no choice but to run the household, even if she was only ten years old.

"Mary," he whispered.

"Jack and the b'ys got a fine haul in the snares on Saturday, so we're having rabbit stew. Sit down. Don't mind your boots."

"Tommy, come in. What's all the gaff down yer way?" Jack scratched his stomach as he walked across the kitchen toward his brother-in-law. "Didn't figure you for down this way today. Some gale of wind out there."

Jack disappeared into the small pantry and reappeared with a bottle of shine and two small glasses, placing them on the table. He turned around to look at his brother-in-law. "Come in, b'y, out of the way. You're making the place look untidy."

Mary's brother let out a small wail before breaking into full sobs, covering his face with his hands.

"Jesus. Is it Richard?" Mary's heart beat wildly in her chest, and she covered her mouth.

Her brother nodded, his sobs filling the room.

Jack caught her when she fell.

Every now and again the emptiness she felt the day she learned Richard was one of seventy-seven men from the SS *Newfoundland*, who froze to death on the ice, sneaked in and held her hostage. Fortunately, Richard's body was returned, so they had a funeral and were given a chance to mourn him. She often thought of the families of the eight men whose bodies fell into the water and were never found.

The mothers and wives of those poor men never got to say goodbye. It was every fishing family's worst fears, their loved one's final resting place being the cold North Atlantic, their souls left to wander aimlessly through the afterlife, much like the living, unable to reconcile their loss.

She came from a long line of fishing folk, and the old people never had any illusions about seafaring life and its danger. They knew death lurked just beneath the water's surface. The seal hunt had long been a rite of passage, separating the men from the boys. It was hard, danger-ous work, but it was necessary to supplement their meagre existence, especially in poor fishing seasons. And for the last three years, each was worse than the one before. Bad weather and wind prevented the men from getting out of the harbour. Lots of rain meant whatever they caught didn't cure well, and Tavenor said he couldn't get much for it. Perhaps it was true. It was nobody's fault. It was just how it was.

Jack had asked Tommy to get a berth for Richard to go to the ice that year. He had connections through his wife's family, the Breens, who were somehow related to the Keans. Richard was more than up for it. He was excited about the prospect of making enough at the hunt to square things with Tavenor. He was adamant the Beresfords would start the next season in the black, for the first time in more years than any of them could remember.

She stifled her grief. It was never easy to lose your own flesh and blood, but to endure was the only way. She couldn't tell you if it was cold or warm the day Tommy delivered the news. She had little memory of the day itself. The physical memory was buried deep, but the feelings refused to leave. If she put them in a boat and set it adrift, they would find their way back to her. On those days there was nothing to do but sit in the rocking chair and conjure up precious ghosts.

"Don't go like that." She nodded at his clothes as she peeled the last potato. Apart from shedding his rubbers and gloves, Jack still wore the dark green work pants and the grey wool sweater he had donned at four o'clock that morning before his small boat steamed out of the harbour.

"Put on your church clothes. Don't give him the satisfaction of looking down on you any more than he does now." She dumped the peeled potatoes into the large boiler on the wood stove.

"It's useless, Mary. I can tell you right now, he don't care." He looked down at his pants. "And he sure as hell don't give a tinker's damn about me clothes."

"Jack, he's human, ain't he?" She walked over to her husband and rubbed his shoulders. "And I care about your clothes." She pecked his cheek and couldn't remember the last time she had kissed him. "It won't be that bad. It's your pride that hurts, but pride won't put grub on the table." She squeezed his hand and scurried into the pantry.

Daniel latched the outside door behind him. He was still reeling from what had just happened. Edward Tavenor never missed an opportunity to make someone in his family feel unworthy. It was nothing new. He'd treated his father that way for as long as Daniel could remember. He frowned. Then there was this war business, which had upset Emma. He supposed it was natural she was scared for her mother, but it wasn't like the woman was enlisting in the British Army. Frankly, he couldn't give a damn what happened in England. When was the last time the British did them any good?

His mother laid the last plate down and smiled at him. "Hi, sweetheart. Where have you been?"

Without responding, he asked, "Where's Father?" He plopped down in the rocking chair opposite their kitchen table and leaned forward, his elbows on his knees, his chin resting on folded hands.

Her smile faded. "Out." She studied him for a moment. "You're far too young to look like you've got the weight of the world on your shoulders, Daniel. What's wrong?"

He locked eyes with her for several seconds, mulling over how much to tell her. "England has declared war on Germany."

"Well, lucky for us we don't live in England or Germany." She squinted at him before laughing. "Surely that's not what's got you so worried, is it, my love?" She walked over to him and brushed the hair off his forehead.

Daniel looked into his mother's kind blue eyes. She always knew when something wasn't quite right with him. "No."

"What is it?"

"Tavenor knows."

Her face hardened. "I told you not to trust that girl, Daniel, let alone carry on with her."

Steam hissed from the pot, bubbling away on the stove, and she crossed the room in two strides to rescue it from boiling over. The lid clattered to the floor as she recoiled, shaking her burned hand back and forth.

Daniel jumped to his feet and ran to examine the burn. "Jesus, Mother, watch what you're doing."

"What I'm doing? I'm not the one carrying on with the merchant's daughter! And now she's landed you in it good and proper."

Daniel snatched a cloth from the sideboard and doused it in the bucket of cold water they kept in the porch. A red welt was already forming, and he wound the cold cloth around her hand.

"Emma didn't tell him. She wouldn't do that. She knows what he's like."

He wrestled with her hand as she fought him off. "Stop moving. This will help." He finished winding the cloth around and held her hand, staring at her sullen face. He didn't like her insinuations. "You don't trust her at all, do you?"

"Well, how did he find out?"

"He came back early from his supply run and found us in the back of the store."

"Oh, sacred heart, ye weren't—"

"No! It was nothing like that, but it doesn't matter. As far as he's concerned, she shouldn't speak to me or even breathe the same as air as me." He threw his hands up in the air. "I'm just a lowly fisherman's son, with no prospects, who will never be good enough for his daughter!"

The colour drained from her face.

He laughed. "You can't be surprised. To him, we're good-for-nothings."

She glared at him. "It's not that, Daniel. I'm well aware of how Edward Tavenor sees us."

"What, then?"

"Your father went to see him."

His stomach churned. "When?"

"About an hour ago."

Daniel cursed under his breath just as the outside door slammed, and his father barrelled into the small kitchen.

"What have ye done, boy?" He grabbed his son by the arm and swung him around.

"Jack—" his mother started, but Daniel cut her off.

"I love her."

"Listen to this, Mary, he loves her." His father mocked him. "Love? You know nothing of it. If you did, you'd know you can't love her kind."

Daniel leaned toward him. "You're as bad as him!"

"As bad as Tavenor? I doubt that very much."

"He says we can't be together."

"Oh, well, we're agreed on one thing. Ye can't be together, Daniel, because he'll never allow it. He'll make your life a living hell." He nodded in his wife's direction. "Did you know about this?"

She pursed her lips and dropped her eyes to the brown canvas floor.

"Jesus, Mary, and Joseph, what's the world coming to? It's not bad enough there's a war on the other side of the ocean, but you're after taking up with the merchant's daughter." He pushed his son away and held his hands up in the air. "Do you know what you've done? We're finished. Ruined. You stupid boy!"

Daniel's father slammed the door behind him. The picture of the Virgin Mary, hanging from the nail his grandfather had tapped into the wall sixty years ago, crashed to the floor and shattered. His mother collapsed into the rocking chair, her shoulders heaving. He put his arms around her. In the five months since they'd lost Richard, it was the first time he'd seen her give in to her grief.

This time it was all his fault.

four

August 1914
Middle Tickle, Newfoundland

"FATHER! DANIEL!" BILLY, THE YOUNGEST MEMBER OF THE Beresford family, bolted into the kitchen with wild eyes. The porch door swung wide open in his wake.

"Jesus, Billy, b'y, calm yourself down and go close that door," his father said as he popped a crust of bread in his mouth and swigged the last of his tea.

"B'ys, you better get down to the wharf. That old bastard Tavenor is down there with some men from La Scie, and he's taking our boat!"

"Billy, mind your mouth!" his mother yelled, shooting a worried look at Daniel and then his father.

"I'm sorry, Mother." Billy's blue eyes were wide, and his head swung back and forth between Daniel and his father. "Ye got to get down there!"

Daniel locked eyes with his father before they both scrambled out the door. Daniel hadn't seen his father move that fast in years. He might be twenty years his junior, but he couldn't keep up to the man as he ran toward his wharf.

"Afternoon, gentlemen." Tavenor's leg was up on the gunwale of his boat, and he leaned forward with one arm propped on his knee. Daniel recognized the man standing next to Tavenor as one of his cronies from La Scie named Savoury. The other fellow, tying their boat to Tavenor's, looked like a Taylor, but he couldn't be sure.

"What the hell are you at, Tavenor?" Jack yelled, breathing hard. Their footsteps echoed on the wharf as they came to a halt before the men. "What do you think you're doing with my boat?"

"Slow down there, Jack, and catch your breath," said Tavenor. "You wouldn't want to have a heart attack." The other men laughed.

The fellow named Savoury tossed his cigarette over the side and jumped from Tavenor's boat into theirs, to help his friend.

Tavenor ran his hand along the boat's smooth side. "She's my boat now."

"You can't do this," Daniel shouted, stepping forward.

"Be quiet, Daniel," his father said, hauling him back. "You can't take my boat, Tavenor. How else will I feed my family and pay you what I owe?"

"Well, now, see, I've given that some thought, Jack. This boat will just about square you with me. You won't have to worry about that any-more." He glanced back at the other men. "Tight enough, boys?"

"Yes, sir," Savoury said, as he lashed the last knot, fastening the Beresfords' small boat to their larger one.

"Don't do this, Tavenor. If you take her, I'll be left with nothing."

"Oh, you're resourceful, Jack, you'll come up with something. Sure, you can fish with your wife's crowd down the shore."

"I can never make the kind of money with them that I could make on my own."

Tavenor turned away.

"Please."

Daniel closed his eyes. His father's plea sliced through him. He worked so hard, but the terrible conditions over the last few years were nobody's fault. The fact that Tavenor had no heart, well, there wasn't much to be done about that, either. Daniel knew he'd antagonized him by carrying on a relationship with Emma. As bad as things were, Tavenor had had no intention of calling in his father's debt before yesterday.

"Stop!" Daniel stepped in front of his father. "Please, Mr. Tavenor, we both know why you're doing this."

"Do we, son?" Tavenor held Daniel's gaze and threw his hands up in the air. "It pains me to do this, Jack, but I've got bills to pay, just like everyone else. Unless, of course, you've got another suggestion."

"Please, sir." Daniel swallowed hard. "Don't do this."

"Stop it, Daniel," said his father. "It's bad enough I have to beg. I won't have you begging for me. Go on up to the house."

Daniel's fists were clenched by his side, and he remained fixed in place. "No, Father, this isn't right! You know why he's doing this. This is because of me. I can—"

"No!" His father took him by the shoulders and drew in a long breath. "You've done enough."

His father's soft tone caught him off guard. He was angry with Daniel, who had made all their lives more difficult the minute he fell in love with Emma Tavenor. And make no mistake, he loved her. He'd loved her from the moment she showed up in Middle Tickle three years ago, with her raven-black hair and her cool grey eyes. Never in a month of Sundays did he think his feelings would be reciprocated. That was a surprise. Just thinking about her now made his stomach flip-flop. He thought back to yesterday and how he felt when she'd declared her love for him.

Billy barrelled down the wharf, skidding to a stop in front of Tavenor's boat. "That old bastard's trying to take our boat, ain't he?"

Daniel lifted his eight-year-old brother and held him in mid-air as his arms and legs flailed. The young boy uttered a string of curse words at Tavenor that could have put a sailor to shame.

The two men with Tavenor grinned. Tavenor straightened up and chuckled. "Those are big words for a little fella like yourself." He turned to Daniel's father. "I took you for a God-fearing man, Beresford. What are you teaching your children?"

Billy continued to curse and spit despite Daniel's hold on him. "Me father says you're an old bastard, that's what he taught me."

Tavenor's accomplices laughed.

"Is that right?" Tavenor smiled at Billy and looked sideways at Jack. "Well, he's entitled to his opinion, I suppose. Don't guess he's the first to think that." Tavenor shrugged. "Probably won't be the last, either." He wiped his hands on his pants and looked around. "Well, boys, we ready?"

"Yes, sir."

They jumped back into Tavenor's boat as the engine revved to life.

"Daniel, take your brother up to the house while I finish this."

"But—"

"Go!"

He laid Billy down on the wharf but kept a firm hold on the boy's arm. "Come on, Billy."

"But Daniel, we can't leave."

"Come on. You heard him." Daniel stole one more look at Tavenor before stepping off the wharf.

Tavenor's lips curled. He was enjoying every bit of their humiliation.

Emma must have been like her mother, because there was no way she had any of that heartless son of a bitch in her.

Beside him, Billy breathed deep in his restful sleep, and Daniel envied the young boy. Daniel had been upstairs ever since coming up from the wharf. He didn't have the heart to sit across from his father at the supper table and bear the weight of the man's stare. He didn't want to see the disappointment in his eyes, or the desperation. Instead, he had been a coward. His whole family was being destroyed because he loved a girl who was not his equal.

Just his luck he had to fall in love with Emma Tavenor.

He didn't know what time it was, but it was dark. He heard voices in the kitchen and strained to hear the mumbled conversation. He crawled out of bed and lifted a bowed floorboard to hear what was going on below.

He heard Mr. Pad's raspy voice. Daniel enjoyed the old man's visits and loved to hear his vivid descriptions of the old days in Middle Tickle and the people who were dead and gone. Mr. Pad himself was pushing eighty.

Daniel lay flat on the floor with his ear to the wood.

"I wanted it to be different for my kids, Pad. I never wanted them to be caught up in this Christly cycle of debt. But this fishing racket never changes. You live and die by the merchant's hand. Will it ever be different?"

Glasses clinked. "Pigs might fly, Jackie, b'y, but they are unlikely birds all the same."

"Yes, b'y, I suppose you're right."

Mr. Pad had a great love of music and always sang a song or two after having a few drinks. The man's gravelly voice drifted up through the floorboards.

"On St. Patrick's Day, the seventeenth,
From New York we set sail;
Kind fortune did favour us,
With a sweet and pleasant gale.
We bore away from Americay,

The wind being off the land;
With courage brave we ploughed the wave,
Bound down for Newfoundland."

When he'd finished his song, Mr. Pad bid Daniel's parents good night. The door closed, and his mother's rocking chair squeaked a song of its own.

She sniffled. "He can't take the boat, Jack."

"We owe him the money, fair and square. That blackard can do whatever he wants, Mary."

"Sweet merciful God."

"Save your prayers, Mary, He's not listening. I got me doubts if He ever did."

"Jack! I'll not have blasphemy in this house. It isn't God's fault."

"No, you're right, it's that son of yours up there in the bed who thinks he's high and mighty enough to have the merchant's daughter, that's whose fault it is."

"It's not his fault, either, Jack. It's nobody's fault." His mother's voice cracked. "The next thing you'll be saying is it's poor Richard's fault for dying."

Hearing his brother's name was like a stab to the heart. He would never get used to not seeing him perched in the corner at the kitchen table, smiling his big, toothy grin, winking and making that clicking sound through the side of his teeth.

He would give anything to be able to talk to his brother now. Before Richard died, Daniel had confided in him about his relationship with Emma and his concern about her not only being Tavenor's daughter, but also a Protestant.

Richard had chuckled in his easygoing manner. "Sure, what odds do it make, Danny, b'y? If you loves her and she loves you, it don't make no difference about anybody else."

There wasn't a man in the harbour, including Tavenor, who could make Richard feel any less of a man. He oozed charm and wit, and after an encounter with him, you'd believe he was lord and master, not a simple servant. Why didn't anyone else see the world the way he had? Daniel shook it off and focused on the conversation in the kitchen.

"What will we do?"

"I don't know, Mary, I don't know."

The chair legs scraped across the floor, and his father's heavy footsteps thudded on the stairs. His mother sniffled again and released a thin, helpless wail. Daniel eased himself up off the floor and leaned against the chimney, which was still warm from the dying embers of the fire.

On the other side of the wall, the bed creaked as his father settled in for the night. A few minutes later his mother trudged up the stairs and paused outside his door. He held his breath, praying she wouldn't come inside. He couldn't face her yet. After a minute her footsteps faded down the hall, and he sighed. He reached for Richard's old sweater, fastened his cap in place, and headed down the stairs, careful to avoid the step with the creak in it.

Daniel scuffed his feet over the beaten path, kicking at rocks along the way. A breeze rippled across the glassy black water, and a full moon hung over Middle Tickle harbour, lighting the path as bright as day. Puffs of smoke floated from the short brick stubs on the housetops, and a scattered light still shone in some windows.

A faint light was visible in Tavenor's shop window, and the door was unlocked. Daniel held his breath, not quite sure what he was going to say. The door clicked as it closed behind him. He leaned against it for a few seconds, gathering his thoughts.

Tavenor appeared in the doorway of the office at the back of the shop with a glass in his hand. "I can't seem to get clear of the Beresfords this night." He took a long sip of amber liquid. "I'm tired. Go home."

The man disappeared inside the small room. He sounded a bit tipsy, which could complicate things in an unpredictable way.

Daniel walked across the shop floor into the office, remembering the last time he had been here, and sat down across the desk from Tavenor. If he started off on the wrong foot, they wouldn't get anywhere. As much as he despised the man, it was time to do some begging of his own.

"Please, don't do this to my family."

Tavenor sighed. "Daniel, your father owes me a lot of money. I can't carry his debt any longer."

"But you're doing this because you're angry with me, which isn't fair to the rest of them."

"Daniel, it's nothing personal. It's business." Tavenor took a sip of his drink. "And I'm a businessman."

Daniel could think of a few other things he was as well. He swallowed his anger.

"So you had to take her today? You made that decision all of a sudden this afternoon?"

Tavenor shrugged. "It's been coming for a while."

"Give us some time. We'll work it out. I'll go next spring." He thought about his mother. Even if they had to live in a tarpaper shack, she would never let him go to the ice. But he owed his family this much. "At least give us until then."

The two men locked eyes for a second, and Daniel was sure he saw a flicker of sadness there.

"Richard's death was—" Tavenor stopped. "A tragedy. I wouldn't wish that on any family."

"But Father deserves to have his boat taken away? Now *he* has nothing, *we* have nothing! The only thing he knows how to do is fish. How do you expect him to make a living without a boat?"

"You've got kin. You can go to the Labrador with one of your mother's brothers. All you crowd stick together."

"That's not the same as owning your own boat, is it?"

"Well, it's too late for that now."

"How can you do this to us after all that has happened? I've lost a brother and they've lost a son trying to pay you back. If anyone should be resentful, it should be us!"

"I know your father is desperate, Daniel, but sending you here to plead his case and bringing your dead brother into it, well, that's a new low."

If Daniel's father knew he was here now, he'd string him up. The man didn't have much, but he was proud. Tavenor's words hung in the air, and Daniel's face grew hot. He clenched his fists as he sized up the man sitting across from him. The British merchants were bad enough, but the ones from St. John's, who made their fortunes on the backs of families like his, made his stomach turn. He and his father, like fishermen all over rural Newfoundland, worked long days, in dangerous conditions, and turned everything over to the merchant at the end of the season, hoping they'd made enough to make it through another year. They never did.

And Tavenor? He sat in his house high on the hill, ordered a few supplies, marked in his account book, and drank tea from china cups. He hadn't known a day of hard toil in his life. All the anguish he'd repressed over Richard's death poured through him until he felt like he was floating in blackness. "Why do you despise us?"

Tavenor opened his mouth, but Daniel kept going.

"You have nothing but contempt for all of us." Daniel gestured behind him, toward the houses running along the harbour. "You profit from our back-breaking labour, but you begrudge every piece of twine and every bag of sugar marked down in that little book of yours. We're honest, hard-working people. Good enough to make you money, but not good enough to treat as human beings. Not good enough for *you*!"

Tavenor swigged the last of his whiskey. "I want more for her than to be a fisherman's wife. And if you weren't so selfish, you'd want that, too. That life is not for her."

He opened the bottom drawer, producing a brown jug and another glass. He half-filled it and held it out to Daniel, who stared straight ahead, ignoring the offering.

After a few seconds, Tavenor shrugged. "Suit yourself." He downed Daniel's share and refilled his own glass before putting the jug back in the desk drawer. "You think I don't understand. I understand all too well, Daniel." Tavenor stared at Daniel. He ran a hand through his hair and opened his mouth as if to say something else, but stopped.

"I can't let it happen. I won't let it happen."

The two eyed each other from either side of their mountainous impasse.

"After today, you have even less to offer her than you had before, and that wasn't much. Go home, Daniel, and forget about my daughter. Worry about finding someone to fish with, the lot of ye, because that's the only hope you've got left, now."

"Whatever about me, don't do this to my family. Please. We can work out some kind of deal."

"Go home, Daniel." Tavenor leaned back in his chair and stared down at his account book.

Desperation flooded through Daniel's body and seized his heart, squeezing it until he thought his chest would explode. He was drowning in a swell of emotion as he stood up and turned toward the door.

He swung back to face Tavenor and slammed his hands down on the desk. "Billy was right. You're a real bastard. You don't deserve a daughter like Emma. I may have nothing to offer her, but by God, she's far better off with me than she is here with you!"

Daniel stormed out of the office and across the store. He grappled with the door, his thumb slipping off the handle as he fumbled with it.

"Maybe we can find some middle ground."

He stopped, letting the door go. Soft footsteps crossed the shop floor and stopped. The smell of whiskey was strong.

Whatever the compromise, he could be sure his family would still lose somehow, but right now he had little choice but to hear the man out. He would probably have to sell his soul to the devil, but Daniel was willing to do anything to save his family.

"End it with Emma. Tell her you don't want to be with her any-more."

He wheeled around. "What?" His brow furrowed, and his mouth gaped. "You can't ask me to do that. Besides, she'd never believe me."

Tavenor laughed. "It doesn't have to be true, Daniel. It just has to be convincing."

"Hurting people seems to come easy to you, Mr. Tavenor, but it doesn't to me." He turned his back on Tavenor and opened the door.

"You haven't heard the second part of my proposal."

Daniel paused, his hand welded to the handle.

"End it with Emma and your father can have his boat back."

The words reached out and strangled him.

"And I'll clear his debt."

Tavenor had him, and he knew it. Daniel turned around to face the man, who lifted the glass to his lips and raised his eyebrows.

"This was your plan all along, wasn't it?" Daniel asked.

"It couldn't have been easy for you to come here tonight. I admire your commitment to your family, as I'm sure you can understand mine." He sipped and shrugged. "It's a good deal, Daniel. Take it."

"You want me to walk away from the one thing I love most in the world!"

Tavenor rubbed the stubble on his chin. "Sometimes men have to weigh out their options and make tough decisions, Daniel. It's called being a man. Take myself, for instance. I had to weigh out what was more important, money or ensuring my daughter's future. I've made my decision. Now it's time for you to make yours. What are you going to do? Walk away from Emma, and not only does your father get his boat back, but his debt is clear and your family is in a better situation than they've ever been."

Daniel's body shook. Tavenor knew Daniel had no choice but to choose his family's future. The gleam in the man's eyes said as much.

"Everyone wins but me and Emma," Daniel whispered.

"You can't blame a man for trying to save his family, can you, Daniel?" Tavenor grinned and raised the glass in salute. "This is what they call winning the battle but losing the war, lad."

"This will crush her."

"Emma's young and impressionable. She'll get over it. There's a whole world waiting for her out there." He turned away from Daniel and headed toward the office. "I'll give you a week to make up your mind."

Daniel stepped into the stillness of the August night. The wind was down, and the water was as smooth as glass in the harbour.

five

August 1914
Middle Tickle, Newfoundland

MEET ME. HE LOOKED AT THE NOTE EMMA HAD GIVEN TO Billy for the hundredth time and stuffed it in his pocket. She wouldn't insult him by writing more.

He mulled over his conversation with Tavenor as he walked. The man had him over a barrel. There was no way to get his father's boat back that didn't mean giving up the one thing he loved most, and he alone had caused this. It was true, he couldn't be held responsible for the accumulating debt of the last few years, but the events preceding Tavenor taking the boat were his fault. If his unhappiness would save his family, he had no choice but to live with that. His stomach tightened. It wasn't just his unhappiness on the line, though, was it?

He kicked the grass, reluctant to make his way to their spot near Flatrock Pond where she waited. She was perched on a rock, her dark hair blowing in the breeze, dipping a bare foot in and out of the pond as the water lapped against her makeshift seat. There was something graceful about the way she moved her head to the side, unaware of being watched.

Daniel stepped through the wall of trees, weighed down with so much dread he ached to his fingertips.

"Daniel!" Her face lit up, and she ran into his arms and kissed him. "I thought you weren't coming."

His heart raced as he returned her kiss, his mind flickering through the last two years of these rendezvous. What if he came clean and told her everything? She would hate her father, which had its advantages. She might marry him right away, and they could live with his family until they had enough money to build a small house of their own. But no boat meant no income. How could he build a house with no money?

He ran his hands through her hair and breathed in her sweet smell, savouring her with an intensity she matched. He seared the memory deep in his mind until he couldn't stand the thought of it and pulled away.

Her cheeks were flushed, and her eyes danced with excitement. She frowned. "You look so serious."

She kissed his hand. "What's wrong, Daniel?" She placed her hands on his chest and studied him. "Is this because of my father?"

He didn't answer.

She giggled. "If so, Daniel, don't give it a second thought." She leaned in and nuzzled his neck. "I told him last night I've made my choice, and there isn't anything he can do about it."

Daniel swallowed a large lump in his throat. "And how did he take it?"

"Well, he was humming this morning at breakfast, so I would say pretty good." She laughed an innocent laugh, oblivious of the lengths to which her father had gone. She trailed kisses along his neck, and a shiver passed through him.

He tore himself away and breathed deeply. "Maybe your father's right, Emma."

"What?" She pulled away.

"We're from two different worlds."

She smiled. "You know I don't care about any of that, Daniel."

His eyes watered, and he squeezed them shut. He must try harder. He opened them and stared straight into her love-filled eyes.

"I can't provide for you the same way your father has all these years. I don't have much." He shook his head, trying to find the right words. Overnight, he'd gone from having a decent share in his father's haul to having nothing at all. "In my world, the teaspoons aren't silver, they're stained and bent."

"What are you trying to say, Daniel?"

"Emma, look at you. You're beautiful. You can talk circles around everyone in the harbour. You're smart." He had her attention now. He pointed at her dress. "Your clothes come special order from England." He put his hands in his pockets and looked down at the ground. "I'll never be able to give you those things, Emma. I can't even read!"

"Daniel, don't talk like that. Do you think I care about dresses from England? I'd be happy in a flour sack."

That was true. For all her fancy upbringing, she'd never lorded it over anyone in the harbour. She was generous, too. He'd been in the store more than once when she "forgot" to mark down a bit of sugar or flour in the account book.

"And considering England is at war, I expect shipping dresses isn't high on anyone's priority list these days." She laced her fingers with his. "And Mother will be fine. Father said he would telegram her today and make arrangements for her to come home straight away on one of Mr. Bowring's boats. Everything will be fine, and we'll all be together again soon. I can't wait for Mother to meet you."

He couldn't imagine Mrs. Tavenor, a born and bred English lady, wanting to meet him, nor being happy about it, either.

Emma reached up and linked her arms around his neck. "Don't you see, Daniel? All I care about is you." She leaned in and kissed him. When she drew away, she smiled and raised one eyebrow. "And we'll keep working on the reading. You're doing well."

She placed his hands so they cupped her face and peered deep into his eyes.

"Emma, if you stay with me, you'll become a fisherman's wife. It's all I know how to do. And you . . ."

"I what, Daniel?"

"You can't tend to a fish flake. It would be a waste. Emma, you deserve more out of life than I can give you." He looked away. The more he talked, the more he realized his father and Tavenor were right. He could never ask her to adapt to his way of life. Would she even know how? He thought back to her father's words.

No one can blame a man for trying to save his family.

She would hate him for breaking her heart, but there was too much at stake.

"I love you for saying that, as if it mattered to me. Whatever you do, I'll be right alongside you."

She took a step closer and kissed him. "You can teach me everything I need to know. As long as we're together, everything will be fine."

Emma was making this impossible. He wrapped his arms around her, wondering what to do next. She felt so good. He closed his eyes, and they stood there for what seemed like hours. He knew what he must do. It was inevitable, but a few more days couldn't hurt.

Daniel leaned against the gunwale of the twenty-foot skiff his brother had built before his death. Richard had learned the art of boatbuilding from their grandfather, a master craftsman who had built dozens of vessels in his lifetime. He'd earned a reputation as one of the finest boatbuilders on the island. Even big merchants out of Harbour Grace and St. John's paid to have one of Jack Beresford Sr.'s creations, which were nothing short of a marvel, since the man couldn't read or write.

He died long before Richard's masterpiece, the *Mary Anne B*, named for their mother, ever glided through the waves.

Daniel spent countless hours cutting wood with Richard, measuring, and sanding. His brother had so much patience. Rarely did he abandon a piece and start again, but it had happened a few times. He would accept no less than perfection and fitted the pieces together with precision like a puzzle only he could solve. He'd built a few dories before, but the *Mary Anne B* was his finest work, his last work. And now she was tied up at Edward Tavenor's wharf.

An emptiness had settled over their house since yesterday, and it wasn't just the circumstances around Tavenor taking what was left of their livelihood. It was that he had taken *this* boat. It was Richard's boat and their last link to him. There was a hole in his chest, and it wouldn't heal until the *Mary Anne B* was home where she belonged. He glided his hand along her side, admiring Richard's workmanship, and made a silent promise to the boat, and to his brother, that she would be home and tied up to the Beresfords' wharf before week's end. Then there would be another hole in his chest, but he couldn't think about that now.

"What in the Jesus is *she* doing tied up here?" Frankie Drover called down over the side of the wharf.

Daniel looked up and saw the quizzical look on his best friend's face. "The old feller wants to do a bit of work to the wharf, and Tavenor offered to keep her here for a while."

He didn't have the heart to tell the truth, not even to Frankie. If he said it out loud, it would be true.

"Christ, b'y, you could have kept her down to ours," Frankie responded.

"Shorter steam from here," Daniel said.

"Suppose so," Frankie replied. "Still, something not right about her being here," he muttered.

Daniel winced. Frankie had no idea just how true that statement was.

"So, Danny, me and the b'ys been talking."

"Yeah? 'Bout what?"

"About going to St. John's to sign up for the war."

Daniel heaved a bucket of water over the side and squinted up at Frankie. "The war? What do you want to do that for?"

Frankie screwed up his face. "Sure, why not?"

"The war is a world away from us, Frankie." Daniel filled the bucket again and heaved it over the side with a splash. "I'm sure they don't need the likes of us over there, complicating matters."

"Them's the ones lookin' for us, Danny. They wants all our able-bodied seamen. Uncle Alf and Mr. Hennessey left a few days ago. Father said they're part of the naval reserve. Have been for years. But they're looking for men for the land, too. What do you say?"

Daniel stopped what he was doing and stared up at his old friend. Frankie must have taken it as a sign of interest, as he kept going.

"Alls I know is they're looking for fellers to sign up. Phonse says we should go see what all the fuss is about. They says we probably won't even leave St. John's. His father said they're just training men to say they're doing their part for king and country."

"King and country?"

"Yep."

Daniel placed a boot up on the thwart and leaned on it. "England ain't my country, and King George ain't my king. And he ain't yours, neither, Frankie Drover."

He tossed the bucket in the fo'c'sle and climbed up the rungs of Tavenor's wharf, which was in pristine shape. With every day that he climbed up the rungs of his father's wharf, he expected the beams to collapse and float out to sea where all things went to die. Last winter he and Richard had cut enough wood to replace the cribbing, which held the stagehead in place, just one of many projects lined up when this season ended. After he mentioned he would make a start at it this summer, his father shook his head and said if he wanted his help he'd ask for it.

"I wouldn't mind gettin' away for a few months. Me and you and Phonse in St. John's? Oh, my son, what a time we'd have." Frankie rubbed his two hands together with glee. "How about it, Danny?"

"I don't know."

Frankie rolled his eyes. "Oh, you don't want to be leaving the missus behind, is that it?"

Daniel unwound the painter and pulled the rope tight before securing it again. He strained through gritted teeth. "What are you on about?"

"No need to be shy about it, I knows all about ye two." Frankie gawked at Daniel through a row of crooked teeth and laughed. "Tavenor's daughter? Now, then, there's a catch, buddy. Lucky man, I says."

Daniel threw the end of the rope down on the wharf and walked up the landwash with the eager Frankie in tow.

"Frankie, there's nothing going on between me and Tavenor's daughter." A dull ache crept into his bones.

At least there wouldn't be by next week.

Frankie ran behind, struggling to catch up. "That's not what young Billy told me."

Daniel chuckled. "And what did he get out of you for that piece of news?"

Despite feeling sorry for himself, he marvelled at his younger brother's skills. He'd never be stuck for a dollar in his lifetime.

"A cigarette." Frankie shoved his hands in his pockets and shrugged.

"Well, Billy's good at spinning yarns, Frankie. I figure he got more for his bargain than you did."

Frankie's face fell. "You mean it's not true?"

"Nope." Another tug at his heart.

"Well, I guess there's nothing stoppin' you and me and Phonse from goin' to St. John's for a few months." Frankie slapped him on the back. "What do you say?"

Daniel supposed it couldn't hurt to go hear what the recruiters would say.

"Come on, b'y, it'll be a lark! We'll be home by Christmas. Maybe we'll even bring home a little darlin' from St. John's."

He winked at Daniel and sprinted up the grassy embankment toward the Beresfords' house.

The last thing Daniel wanted was a darling from St. John's, but a few months away from Middle Tickle might be the very way to get his mind off the one thing he couldn't have.

June 1981
St. John's, Newfoundland

"Two days later, we boarded a train for St. John's and joined the Regiment," Daniel said.

The light had almost faded, sending Signal Hill into the black, and Daniel's kitchen was dark. He stood up and turned on the light switch.

Penny dabbed at her eyes with the tissue. "You didn't say goodbye to her?" She took a sip from her cup and made a face, laying the cold tea down.

"What would I have said?" Daniel asked, coming to rest on his chair again.

"Oh, Daniel." She stifled a sob. "She must have been heartbroken."

"We both were." He reached into the ditty box and took out a simple gold band. He laid it in his palm, tracing the rim with his finger.

"Was that for her?"

He nodded and breathed deep. "This one is mine. Men didn't usually wear wedding rings in my time, but during the war I came across a few fellows who did. They said it was to remind them of who they'd left at home, so I bought two and I gave the other to her. She said yes, but we didn't make it to the altar."

Penny's eyes widened. "When did you see her again? Did she come to St. John's? Did you see her before you shipped out? Her father sounds so controlling, though. How did he even let her leave Middle Tickle?" Penny placed her hands on the table and stared at him with her big, brown, youthful eyes.

Daniel rubbed his eyes and laid his hands in his lap. "I think that's enough for tonight, Penny. This old man is tired."

"Oh, of course, Daniel. I'm sorry. I just—" She stopped. "This is your life, not just some made-up story. I should be more respectful."

"Come back tomorrow. I'll tell you the rest then." His voice was gruff.

"Really?"

He nodded.

Daniel's sleep was restless, as was the case after he stirred up the dust of old ghosts. Sometime in the early hours of the morning, thunder rumbled in the distance. He shot up in the bed in a cold sweat, fear flooding his body. He blinked a few times, his eyes adjusting to his surroundings. A sliver of light shone through the open window, lighting up his tiny bedroom. He took a deep breath, allowing himself to sink back into the comfort of the soft bed. The air was clean, and he was dry and safe. There were no shells exploding outside his window. No one was shooting at him.

Daniel turned on his side and slid his hand under the pillow. His finger touched the tattered corner of the photograph he'd tucked there before he went to sleep. He stared at the wall. Sixty-five years ago, the moon shone just as bright and he was wedged between Frankie and Phonse, their backs against a trench wall. The smell of rot and death was everywhere, and he held on to this photograph, waiting.

Waiting to go over the top.

six

ON THE OTHER SIDE OF THE OCEAN, MRS. PURCELL LAID THE invitation down and looked out the window of her study. Pilgrimage. Interesting choice of word.

Somehow she'd always envisioned a pilgrimage as something peaceful for the soul. Nearly sixty-five years had passed since the Battle of the Somme. Sixty-five years of life and loss. Some days the emptiness was still as vast, the wounds just as deep. She didn't need a piece of paper to remind her.

Would a pilgrimage bring her peace after sixty-five years?

She had placed the invitation and additional information about the trip back in the envelope and left it on her desk. It wasn't hidden, but she hadn't discussed it with anyone, either, which made it all the more infuriating this morning when her daughter mentioned it.

"Surely you're not entertaining the idea of going, Mother," Amelia had said.

They were in Mrs. Purcell's study, and Sam, her butler for over thir-

50

ty years, was pouring tea. They shared a knowing look. Her daughter had been rifling through her mail.

"Well, I hadn't ruled it out entirely." That was a lie. She had most definitely ruled it out, but she'd had second thoughts since last week.

Amelia sighed. "Honestly, Mother. At your age? Do you think this is wise?"

Mrs. Purcell picked up her cup and winked at Sam, who returned her cagey smile as he exited the room.

"Well, you see, dear, the Red Cross called last week," she said. "As I am the last living member of the Voluntary Aid Detachment, they wish to honour me for my work near the front in 1916."

Amelia smiled and squeezed her hand. "And deservedly so, Mother, but if they want to honour you, shouldn't they do it here in England? After all, you are eighty-four years old." She laughed. "Not that you act like it. Besides, do you think it's wise to revisit all those old memories at your age?" Her eyes clouded.

Amelia's misgivings over the trip weren't unfounded. Too many times throughout the years she had retreated to dark and lonely places, and her family wondered if they would ever reach her again.

Mrs. Purcell didn't want any awards for her service—that was the furthest thing from her mind—but the more she thought about it, the more she warmed to the idea of going back to France. It might be good for the soul to visit a grave or two. Maybe, after sixty-five years, a pilgrimage was in order.

The shrill ring of the telephone broke her thoughts. A few minutes later, there was a quiet knock, the door to her study opened, and the butler appeared.

"Mrs. Purcell," he said, "the telephone is for you. It's a Miss Wilson."

Her daughter shot Sam a look, which he ignored. Mrs. Purcell frowned at her daughter. "Hmm, Sam, I'm unfamiliar with that name," she said, "but put her through."

"Mother, let me—"

"Shall I tell her you will ring her back?" Sam asked, interrupting Amelia.

Mrs. Purcell raised her hand in Amelia's direction. "No, Sam, it's fine, I'll take it."

"Very well, ma'am," he said, nodding toward the telephone on her desk. "When you're ready." He stepped out and closed the door behind him.

"Hello."

"Hello, Mrs. Purcell. This is Sarah Wilson. Thank you for taking my call," the girl said with a slight laugh. "You're a difficult woman to reach."

"Really? My dance card is pretty empty these days, Miss Wilson." She frowned, looking up at her daughter, knowing she was only difficult to reach if those around her didn't want her to be reached. She hated being managed.

"What can I do for you?" she asked.

Sarah paused. "I'm a graduate student in history at King's College in London, and I'm writing an historical account of women who served in the Voluntary Aid Detachment during the First World War. I was hoping you might agree to do an interview with me."

Mrs. Purcell paused. "That was a long time ago," she said. "I can't imagine I could be much help to you, my dear."

"You have a fascinating story, Mrs. Purcell," Sarah said. "You served at a casualty clearing station near the front, which in itself is remarkable."

She could hear the excitement in the young scholar's voice.

"Those were some very dark times in my life, Miss Wilson, in all our lives, for those of us who were there. I've spent a lot of my life trapped in the past. With what little time I have left, I'd like to focus on the future."

"Are you ill?" Sarah asked.

She chuckled. "Oh, no, nothing like that, but at my age it could be any day, you know."

"I understand, Mrs. Purcell. But you served near the front on July 1, 1916, on the opening day of the Battle of the Somme, and it's just so . . . surreal. Heroic. Your story deserves to be told."

Another pause. "I wasn't a hero, Miss Wilson," she said.

"You joined the war to help people, to take care of the sick and dying. And you went to the front, right to the heart of the conflict. In my book, that's brave."

"I had my reasons. They were mostly selfish at the time."

"Could I come down to visit you? We could talk for a while. If you feel at any point it's too much, we can call the whole thing off."

"It would probably be a waste of a trip," Mrs. Purcell said.

"I'm willing to take that chance." Sarah paused. "If you are."

"All right. Come on down tomorrow."

"Thank you, Mrs. Purcell. I will see you tomorrow. Any particular time?"

"You've got a fair jaunt ahead of you if you're coming all the way to Devon in the morning. Whenever you arrive is fine. I'll be expecting you."

She hung up the phone and met Amelia's eyes. The two women stared at each other for a minute before Amelia threw her hands in the air and said, "You win, Mother. But mark my words, nothing good can come from all this reminiscing about the war."

Mrs. Purcell grinned and embraced her daughter. "Oh, Amelia. Not everything that came out of the war was bad." She kissed the top of her head. "I got you, didn't I?"

Sarah drove her red Citroën up the long, secluded drive toward Mrs. Purcell's house, though to call it a house was an understatement. She parked next to a fleet of other vehicles and straightened her long, flowery skirt as she got out. The whole estate was impressive, but so too was the fact that an original family member still owned it. Mr. Purcell had married well. England had experienced great economic difficulty in the years following the First World War, as did the world, and many families were forced to sell off their large homes. The traditional feudal system, which had supported this way of life for hundreds of years, had faded away. Some families walked away from these big properties, no longer able to afford the privileged life the English gentry had enjoyed for generations.

Sarah's eyes scanned the colourful gardens on either side of the large estate—or was it a manor? Given she grew up in a cramped, two-bedroom flat in London, she was not well-versed in architectural terminology and the types of structures the aristocracy called home. The land around the old brick house was well-manicured and typical of most English-style country gardens. Rows of hedges, all the exact same shape and size, and foliage of various shades of green, lined the brick drive and pathway leading to the double entrance. Before Sarah could reach for the black, wrought iron door knocker, a thick wooden door swung open. A stout, middle-aged man stood before her in a dark suit.

"Miss Wilson, I presume."

"Yes." A butler? Sarah's mouth gaped a little. She hadn't expected such formality, but it was key to these old English families. He fit the part well.

"Do come in. Mrs. Purcell is waiting for you in the library." She recognized the voice as the man who had answered the phone yesterday. He stepped aside to allow her entry into the large foyer.

Sarah lifted her sunglasses, her eyes darting around the grand entrance. A round mahogany table was situated in the centre of the room. A colourful arrangement of carnations and lilies sat on top in a tall crystal vase. A wide, red-carpeted staircase wound its way up a wall lined with portraits. Sarah's gaze lingered on each of them, and she wondered if they were past inhabitants of the grand home.

"This way, Miss Wilson." The butler led her to the right and into a large room filled with bookcases.

Thick drapery was pulled back to reveal a wall of windows showcasing the side of the property. Sarah gasped at the beauty. Flowers of every colour and size grew there, and a brick pathway leading to a pond was situated in the centre of the estate. Tall, wispy trees framed the pond with, a swing hanging from one. It was the perfect setting for an old English love story, and she expected to see Mr. Darcy put his arm around Elizabeth Bennett at any moment.

"It is breathtaking, isn't it?" a woman's voice sounded behind her.

"It's exquisite, yes," Sarah said, wheeling around to find a slender woman with grey hair cut to rest above her shoulders standing next to the fireplace.

She was expecting to see a plump, stooped-over woman suffering from terrible arthritis, but Mrs. Purcell was anything but. She stood tall and had an air of sophistication about her, not in an elitist kind of way, just intelligent and reserved. As Sarah shook the woman's hand, she noticed her unusual grey eyes. She had been a real beauty in her day.

"I'm Sarah. I'm honoured to meet you. Thank you for seeing me."

"And you." Mrs. Purcell sat in one of the wingback chairs, motioning for her to sit in the other. "How was the drive down?"

"Beautiful. I don't get out of the city nearly enough." She spied a dark wooden box on a side table next to Mrs. Purcell's chair. "I'm so happy you changed your mind about talking to me."

"I'm not sure I have, just yet." Mrs. Purcell smiled and leaned forward, reaching for the service laid out in front of her. "Tea?"

Sarah nodded. "Yes, thank you." Her shoulders shrank a little as she reached for the cup Mrs. Purcell held out. "Have you changed your mind?"

"I guess we'll find out," Mrs. Purcell said as she sat back in the chair. "It depends on what you want to know."

Sarah smiled and pulled a notebook out of her large purse. "Let's start with something easy. Did you always know you wanted to be a nurse?"

"No." She crossed her feet at the ankles. "And I wasn't a nurse. I was a VAD."

Sarah looked up from her book. "Sure, but they were one and the same, weren't they?"

Mrs. Purcell shook her head. "Don't let a nurse catch you saying that." She laughed. "Most of the VADs came from well-to-do families, while most of the trained nurses were working-class. The VADs saw it as their duty to do their bit for the war effort, but they weren't interested in studying nursing as a vocation."

Sarah cocked her head to the side. "Was class much of an issue?" She had read a few academic papers dealing with class issues during the war, but hearing it first-hand from someone who lived it was something else entirely.

"Hmm. Sometimes, yes." Mrs. Purcell took a long sip of her tea. "People often feel threatened by what they don't know or understand." She pushed away something invisible on her pant leg. "As VADs we were trained in the basics, but we were often reminded our role was to assist nurses. We cleaned wards and prepared bandages, did laundry, and some of us cooked. A fair number of nurses were just happy for the help and didn't dwell on the distinction much."

Sarah jotted down the woman's comments.

Mrs. Purcell chuckled and tilted her head in Sarah's direction. "Though I always had the feeling they got great satisfaction when we were on our hands and knees scrubbing the floor."

"Was it all domestic work?"

"Oh, no, we cared for the soldiers in other ways. We wrote their letters home and read to them." She swallowed hard. "Sometimes we just held their hands until they died."

Sarah scrawled some shorthand in her coiled notebook. "Were you ever ridiculed by nurses because you were well off?" Sarah looked past Mrs. Purcell at an impressionist painting covering a large portion of an adjacent wall.

"I did my best to hide it for as long as I could." She gave a thin-lipped smile. "But eventually they realized I was upper-class, as it were."

"That must have been hard for you. To be ostracized because of who you are."

A flicker of sadness appeared in Mrs. Purcell's eyes, and Sarah paused. The last thing she wanted to do was dig up bad memories for the woman.

"I mean, it's just so unfair." Sarah shook her head. "It shouldn't matter what anyone's background is. Millions of people were forced into this situation, fighting next to each other in the bloodiest war the world has ever seen." Heat rose to her cheeks. "Why should it matter who you were or where you came from? It was an equal playing field of terribleness. Don't you think?"

Mrs. Purcell stared straight ahead for the longest time before turning to Sarah. Her eyes glistened.

"Ah, but the world didn't quite work that way, dear girl." She shrugged. "I'm not sure it does now, either. Some are mistreated due to elevated social standing, others for their lack thereof." She flashed a brief smile. "But it's nice to hear the younger generation get riled up about it. It gives me hope for the future."

The faraway look returned to the woman's eyes. Sarah's mind raced. Time to move on to a lighter topic and away from the serious stuff for a while. She leaned forward and tucked her hands under her legs.

"I guess fraternizing with the soldiers was out of the question."

Mrs. Purcell's eyes fluttered. "Oh, yes, it was forbidden, though more than one woman came home with a husband."

Sarah laughed. "Who could blame them, with all those handsome young men in uniform? They would be pretty hard to resist. It was such a tragic period in history, but such a romantic one, too, don't you think?"

Mrs. Purcell looked at her hands. "You weren't there," she replied. "Your generation has never lived through a global conflict, so you have no idea of the cost." She looked away.

"What about you? Did you meet Mr. Purcell over there?"

Mrs. Purcell slid the top off the box next to her and pulled out a pile of letters. On top of the stack of letters was a sepia-coloured service picture of a soldier. She brushed her thumb along the photo with a wistful look in her eyes.

Sarah examined the tall, handsome man in the uniform. "Did you meet during the war?"

"No, we knew each other before."

"He looks so young."

"He was only sixteen when that photograph was taken."

Sarah blinked in surprise. "I can't imagine any of the boys I knew when I was sixteen being mature enough to go to war."

"It was a life lesson." She locked eyes with Sarah. "In more ways than one. The war forced us all to grow up quickly."

Sarah chewed on the end of her pen. "How old were you when you went to France?"

"Seventeen."

Her eyes widened. "I thought you had to be at least twenty-three to serve abroad."

Mrs. Purcell nodded. "But just as they needed men and would take them where they could get them, they needed us to take care of the wounded." She folded her hands. "I called in a couple of favours."

"He was from here in Plymouth as well?"

Mrs. Purcell smiled. "No, he was from Newfoundland."

Sarah raised her eyebrows. "But you said you knew each other before the war."

"Yes, we did."

Mrs. Purcell leaned forward and poured more tea into both their cups. "You see, I spent a few years in Newfoundland with my father. We met there and fell in love."

"Remarkable." Sarah picked up her notebook again. "So, you both decided to volunteer for the war effort together?" Her eyes lit up. "Were you married during the war?" She chuckled. "And you said the war years weren't romantic."

"I had no intention of serving, and if circumstances had been different, I'm not sure he would have, either."

Mrs. Purcell's eyes drifted to the wall of windows looking out onto the estate. "But I had to find him. It was my fault he enlisted, and I wanted to make it right." She made a sound somewhere between a laugh and a cry. "So, you see, Miss Wilson, a hero I am not."

Sarah closed her notebook. "I'm sorry. I've upset you. Perhaps I could come back another day."

Mrs. Purcell sat with her cup in her hand, staring out the window. Sarah tucked her notebook back in her bag and stood, but Mrs. Purcell touched her arm. The woman's eyes were glassy.

"To answer your question. No. We weren't married during the war. We weren't married at all. The man in the picture isn't Mr. Purcell. This isn't the story you came for, Miss Wilson, but after all these years, I think it's time I tell it to someone." Mrs. Purcell reached into the box and removed a white handkerchief with letters embroidered in the corner. A thin gold band fell into her hand.

Sarah sat down on the end of the chair. She had a feeling she was on the cusp of something far bigger than she had come for.

seven

August 1914
Middle Tickle, Newfoundland

E MMA WALKED ALONG THE WINDING PATH AROUND MIDDLE
Tickle. Two-storey saltbox houses poked out of the peaks and val-
leys of lush green grass like ornaments on a Christmas tree. Even
though she'd only lived in the community for the last three years, it was
home. She squinted up at the sun beating down on the white sheets flapping
on the clotheslines. A salty breeze wafted up from the flake-lined beaches.
Salt cod was the main trade in the outport, and Oliver Grey, her grandfather,
had been the merchant responsible for the area for more than thirty years.

The goings-on in the O'Reilly garden caught her attention as she
passed. The eldest girl, Margaret Jane, was up to her elbows weeding the
garden, and her two younger brothers were chasing each other and had
left the gate open, and now the sheep were in. Mrs. O'Reilly was chasing
the boys, cursing them up in heaps.

Middle Tickle was a beehive of activity in the summer months, and
so different from her grandfather's estate back in England, where she
had spent the majority of her youth. While the men fished, the women

and children ploughed the soil and planted gardens on the land behind the houses, if there was room enough, or out on the grassy embankments overlooking the ocean. The women and children were also responsible for covering the fish when the rain pelted down, and for making the same trip to uncover it when the sun came out. The fish flakes were spread with dried cod, a process where the fish sat in the sun, skin on one side, and large pieces of white, flaky flesh on the other, covered in big salt granules, which kept it from going bad.

The curing process took weeks and was weather-dependent. If it was a rainy summer, as it had been the last two years, the fish wouldn't cure well. If it was too warm a summer, the fish could turn pink. The only remedy then being to salt it again, but if it became smatchy or sour, it couldn't be sold except for West Indie cullage. Each family collected its catch, and it was shipped to market, through her father, who now ran the Newfoundland branch of Grey's Trading Firm since her grandfather's passing. The fish was shipped out in the fall to the West Indies, Spain, and Portugal, where dried codfish was a staple, and through a trading relationship that spanned centuries.

It was late morning, and Daniel and his father were usually back by now. She wondered how they had been fishing since their boat had been tied up at her father's wharf most of the week. When she asked her father about it, he told her to ask Daniel, but she hadn't clapped eyes on him in days.

She ran her hand along the tall grass as the Beresfords' wharf came into view. She'd never been bold enough to visit his home or the family's fishing premises before. She bit her lip, debating whether to turn around and go home. He had been so distant the last time they saw each other, and the things he said about her father being right bothered her.

He must stop worrying about their different social backgrounds. She wasn't bothered by it in the least, but she was worried that he was so down on himself. Fishing wasn't an easy business, and he worked hard. She didn't give a damn where her clothes came from, or anything else, as long as they were together. And as for her father, well, he was in no position to judge, now, was he? Where would he be if he hadn't met her mother? Not running Oliver Grey's business in Middle Tickle, that's for sure.

She sauntered down the steep hill leading to the wharf. Billy, Daniel's ten-year-old brother, stood on a wooden box at the splitting table. His deft hands sliced through the silver skin with straight cuts, dividing the white flesh into equal parts. He tossed the unnecessary bits over the side of the wharf, the clean fillets in another tub, and gutted his next victim in one fluid motion.

"Hello, Billy."

He looked up at her without stopping his work. "Hello."

"All by yourself this morning?"

Barrels of fish encircled the young boy, and the smell of innards turned her stomach. She tried to ignore it.

He wiped the sweat off his brow with his forearm and continued. "Yep, gonna be that way for a while, too."

"Do you mind if I wait here for Daniel?"

"You'll be waiting a while, then, missus."

Billy squinted through the sunshine, instinct and practice moving his hands. He didn't appear one bit concerned that with one stray movement he could injure himself.

He was a curious child, Emma thought as she smiled. "You expect them to be gone awhile?"

"Well, Father and Uncle Tom will be back in a few hours. There's no telling when Daniel will be back. Christmas, he says."

She laughed. "Christmas?"

Daniel had always said that, next to Richard's, Billy's sense of humour bested them all.

"But Father says it'll be longer."

She waited for the rest of the joke, but the young boy carried on about his work as if she weren't there.

"Billy, where is Daniel?"

"On his way to St. John's."

"Why?"

He sliced another fish open and repeated the process. "Daniel joined the Newfoundland Regiment, and he's going to fight for England."

She grabbed her chest as if Billy's splitting knife had flung itself into her heart. "He can't be. He can't join the army. He's not even old enough!"

Billy shrugged. "None of 'em are. Daniel, Frankie, Phonse, they're all gone. Daniel says I'm the oldest man in the harbour now, Miss Tavenor, and it's up to me to watch over everyone."

She placed a hand over her mouth as her breath caught in her throat. Why had he done this? And how could he have left her without even saying goodbye? Her head swam with confusion, and her knees buckled. She stared at Billy, blood and innards oozing from his small hands as he continued his work, unfazed.

"Hey, missus, you all right?"

The smell of rotting guts and salt water overwhelmed her, and she ran to the edge of the wharf and threw up. She held on to the thick wooden beam for support, squeezing her eyes shut. When she opened them, she saw her reflection in the calm water as seagulls squawked overhead. She stared, waiting for his reflection to appear next to hers, but all she saw were fish guts and entrails floating in a red sheen.

"Didn't tell you he was leaving?" a voice sounded behind her.

She twisted around to find Daniel's mother standing near Billy.

Emma shook her head. Mrs. Beresford beckoned her forward. "Come on, child, let's get you off the wharf."

"I don't understand."

"I don't suppose you do."

"How could you let him go?"

"Let him?" Mrs. Beresford's eyes widened. "I couldn't stop him."

"I could have."

Mrs. Beresford reached for her shawl, which had slipped off one shoulder. "No, girl. Not even you could have stopped him."

Emma ran her hands through her hair. "Why would he choose this?"

"Choice is a funny thing, Miss Tavenor. Sometimes you have no choice. Sometimes you have to make choices. I have one dead son, and a son on his way to fight in a war on the other side of the world because of choices."

"I have to stop him!" Emma grabbed the hem of her skirt and ran up the wharf, stumbling on a gap in the wood.

Mrs. Beresford caught her before she fell. "It's done, girl. You'll not change his mind."

"I have to try!"

Emma tore up the main road out of Middle Tickle, toward the train station three miles away. She would talk him out of this craziness. They could get married and stay with her Aunt Ethel in St. John's until they got on their feet. Daniel was resourceful and would find work, and she could teach.

Her hair whipped across her face and she pushed it away, running hard until her lungs burned. Excitement filled her, and she ran faster. She would get on that train with him right now, with nothing but the clothes on her back, and go to St. John's. They could live their lives without interference. As she sprinted around the corner, the small station appeared with at least a hundred people gathered around it.

As if on cue, a puff of smoke blew from the train's stack, signalling its departure. Emma pushed her way through the crowd. The whistle sounded, and the train chugged to life. The sound got louder as it picked up speed. She ran beside the train cars, searching faces, desperate to see him.

The train was full, and several boys waved, blowing farewell kisses to their mothers, sisters, and sweethearts. Excited voices rang out through the open windows as they hung over the seats, talking and laughing. Her eyes darted from face to face. She spotted him, seated alone, by the window. Only his profile was visible, but it was enough to make her heart skip a beat.

"Daniel!" she yelled.

His lips were fixed in a straight line, a grim expression on his face. The train's tremendous roar and the raucous party on board drowned out her voice.

"Daniel!"

She screamed his name over and over as she ran beside the train, but it raced away, taking him with it. Her vision blurred, forcing her to stop. She leaned forward, hands on her legs, trying to catch her breath. She looked up as the train rounded a rock cut and fell out of view. An intense emptiness swelled inside her, as though Billy had sliced her open and spilled her soul into the sea.

June 7, 1981
Plymouth, England

They were both quiet for a few moments. When Mrs. Purcell finally looked over at Sarah, the young girl was dabbing at her eyes with a tissue.

"I can't believe he left without saying goodbye." Sarah's voice quivered. "He was going to war. He might never have returned. How could he not have said goodbye to you?"

Mrs. Purcell straightened the handkerchief across her leg, smoothing it repeatedly. "I spent some time wondering the same thing, my dear, and I was angry with him, too, for a long time, until I learned the truth."

"The truth?" Sarah asked.

"It wasn't his fault. He didn't want to say goodbye to me that day, or any day. He didn't want to say goodbye at all."

Sarah raised an eyebrow. "I don't follow."

Mrs. Purcell leaned forward and poured more tea in both their cups. "Daniel did the only thing he could do."

eight

June 1981
St. John's, Newfoundland

"COME IN OUT OF THE RAIN, CHILD."

Penny gasped, shaking the rain from her coat. Her strawberry blonde curls whirled around her head, and she struggled to lower the black, mangled umbrella as she entered the small porch.

"Good morning, Daniel. Heavens, it is awfully windy out there."

Daniel took the umbrella and shoved the flap back down, closing the door behind her. "These are useless here in Newfoundland, my dear girl." He tossed it in the corner of the porch and moved into the kitchen. "Come on inside."

"And the fog, well, I could hardly see the road," she said over the whistle of the kettle.

"Caplin weather," he said, as he made his way over to the table with two steaming cups in hand. He knew she'd be back this morning, just as she'd promised, and this time he had made a little effort. A plate of raisin buns his neighbour Joan had given him a few days ago sat in the centre of the table next to a tub of Good Luck Margarine.

"What's caplin weather?" Penny asked, reaching for a bun.

Daniel sat down across from her and lifted the thin curtain, nodding toward the window. "This is."

She laughed. "How did you sleep?"

He stirred the creamy Carnation milk into his tea and laid the spoon down next to his cup. He'd been more honest with this stranger than he had been to anyone in decades. "Not well."

"I guess we stirred up some old memories yesterday, didn't we?" She patted his hand a few times.

"You could say that."

"Daniel, we don't have to continue if it's upsetting you too much."

"Can't leave a story half-finished. That's as bad as a life half-lived."

She smiled, and her big blue eyes told him what he already knew. She wanted to hear every word. "Now, where were we?"

September 1914
St. John's, Newfoundland

In St. John's, all the activity was centred around the harbour. Fish was off-loaded at nearly every available wharf, and steamers and schooners came and went at all hours. Bernard Morey had secured them a room with his eldest sister, Sade, who had lived in St. John's for almost forty years after she left Middle Tickle to go into service for the Comptons. Bern was from La Scie, a larger community about ten miles from Middle Tickle, and was a little older than Daniel. He was distant kin of Daniel's mother's family, and his older sister was married to Phonse's uncle.

Sade's house was small, and the four of them were crammed into a double bed, which they tried to make the most of by putting two at the head of the bed and two at the foot. Bern had assured Sade they'd be out of her hair in no time, but she enjoyed their company. If anything, it filled a void left by her husband's passing a few months previous.

On the harbourfront this morning, they'd heard some men talking about a recruitment meeting at the Church Lads' Brigade Armoury planned for seven o'clock that evening. Bern asked Sade for directions, but by the time they reached Queen's Road, they only had to follow the crowd, which seemed to be heading to the same place. The buzz of excitement was electric. Daniel took his cap off as he passed through the great arches of the CLB and stepped inside. At least a hundred men milled about. He followed behind the others and sat between Frankie and Phonse at the back of the hall. He spotted his cousin, Peter Squires, with a few older men from La Scie, and the two nodded at each other in acknowledgement.

"They must be the recruiters over there." Frankie pointed at three men in tailor-made suits and bowler hats standing around a table with a wide ledger open in front of them.

"Not much gets past you," Daniel said to Frankie, but grinned at Phonse.

Phonse Whelan was a few years older than Daniel and Frankie but had knocked around with them since they were children. His grandmother raised him after his mother went mad and threw herself off Idleman's Point. Her husband's schooner banged up on the rocks outside the tickle back in 1905, and she was never the same. Mr. Pad had told Daniel, the one time he asked, that it was a terrible scene. He said everyone in the community could hear the men's cries for help, but it was an angry sea and the waves were too high to reach them. When they did, it was too late. The seven men on board had perished.

Daniel looked to the front and sized up the men Frankie had pointed out in their fancy suits. Only two occasions required men to wear suits in the outport—marriage and death. His father didn't even own one. He'd borrowed a suit coat from his brother when he got married and hadn't returned it. Daniel hadn't even known this until they'd buried Richard in it.

The tallest of the three, a bulky man with a salt-and-pepper beard, stepped in front of the crowd. He wore an old-fashioned frock coat over a colourful vest. A small swivel clasp on the vest button kept his watch chain in place. Sure, he looked like he could be the king himself.

The man cleared his throat. "Good evening. My name is Mr. Outerbridge." He pointed to the table. "And these men with me are Mr. McGrath and Mr. Cashin."

They nodded their heads in the general direction of the crowd. The boys craned their necks, and a few whispers circulated before the hall fell silent.

"I am proud to see so many young men here this evening prepared to fight for their country, and let me tell you, your country needs you now more than ever."

A low murmur swept through the armoury.

"The governor of our fine colony, Sir Walter Davidson, has issued a challenge to you brave Newfoundlanders." Outerbridge paused, surveying the crowd.

Frankie looked at Daniel. "Jesus, do all the crowd in St. John's talk like that?"

"Imagine what they'll think when they hears us," Daniel said.

Frankie shook his head. "There's no way we sounds half as strange as them."

Outerbridge continued. "Germany poses a threat to our freedom, our very civilization, and that of the world's."

The murmur in the crowd was a little louder this time.

Outerbridge raised his hand to silence them. "This war has been forced upon us, but don't be foolhardy enough to think because we live on the other side of the ocean we are exempt from its effects. We must come together, as a band of brothers, with Britain and her allies, to overcome this threat to our very existence."

Daniel cast a sideways glance at Frankie, whose anxious grin had disappeared.

Frankie raised one eyebrow. "What's he sayin'?"

"At this time the Empire needs her strongest resources, and we are no exception. Prime Minister Morris has promised to raise a regiment of five hundred men for land and a thousand more for sea. We offer these resources with great pride, knowing we have some of the finest able-bodied seamen to walk our fair shores. As I stand before you, scores of British soldiers are assembling to drive the Germans back where they belong. Together we will defeat them!"

The rumblings through the crowd got louder again.

Outerbridge smiled and opened his arms up wide. "And who better than the boys from Newfoundland, whose superior naval abilities have been the backbone of the British economy for hundreds of years?"

A loud cheer erupted, and the boys stood, shaking their fists, signalling their allegiance. Outerbridge had extolled their virtues and constructed their significance to a war a world away.

"You can count yourselves among the thousands of brave young men who have come forward to fight for king and country!"

Young men poured out of their seats and raced to the back of the hall. Daniel noticed Ambrose Toms and Bertie Foss race toward the registration table, and a mock fight started over whose name would be the first one recorded in the recruiting ledger.

Daniel leaned toward Frankie, who stared straight ahead. "Still up for it?"

But Frankie's enthusiasm had vanished. "I don't know, b'ys. This don't sound like much fun."

"It's not supposed to be fun. They're fightin' a war," Phonse said.

"I never thought about that part of it." Frankie shrunk into the chair, turning his cap over and over in his hands.

Phonse slapped him on the back. "Come on, Frankie, what about the adventure?"

His cousin Peter appeared. "Hi, Danny, you signin' up?"

"I'm thinking about it."

"Make sure you tell 'em you're eighteen."

"Why?"

"They can't take you unless you're eighteen."

Frankie breathed a sigh of relief. "Thanks be to Jesus." He stood up. "Let's go."

Daniel pushed Frankie back down in his seat. "Sit down."

"You're not eighteen," Daniel said to Peter.

"I know!" Peter laughed. "But I've always been a good liar."

"We're good liars." Phonse elbowed Frankie in the arm and grinned. "Aren't we, Frankie?"

"No, not me." Frankie shook his head. "Mother always knows when I'm lying."

"Well, it's a good thing your mother's not up there," Phonse said, and the boys erupted in laughter.

Even Frankie curled his lips for a second.

"Ah, don't worry, Frankie." Peter pointed toward the table. "Father says there's that many men signed up, the Germans will be drove home by Christmas."

Daniel nodded at his cousin before looking at Frankie and Phonse. "I figured as much. But at least we can say we got to St. John's, hey, b'ys?"

"That's good enough for me." Phonse stood up, beckoning the boys to follow.

"See ya, Daniel," Peter said, as he mock saluted his cousin before bounding toward the recruiting line with his buddies.

"Yeah, see ya."

Daniel turned his attention back to Frankie, who stood in the aisle between the chairs, refusing to budge any farther. "Come on, Frankie, this was your idea."

Daniel held his arm out as an invitation to follow Phonse and, in the end, shoved Frankie forward.

"And what are your skills, young man?" Mr. Cashin asked as he beamed up at them.

Phonse spoke up first. "We're fishermen, sir, and the finest kind."

Phonse grinned at Frankie and Daniel. Frankie was grim.

"More seamen. Marvellous!" Cashin replied.

"I think I've had enough of the sea life for a while, sir, if it's all the same to you. I'd like to volunteer for the land," Daniel said.

"Don't you think you'd be better suited for the naval reserve, lad?" Cashin asked, folding his arms.

Daniel stood six feet tall and was strong and lean like his father's side of the family. He was broad-shouldered, and his arms were muscular from the daily regimen of hauling nets and lifting heavy barrels of fish. He was young and fit and wouldn't have much difficulty with the intensive training required to become a soldier.

"He'll never tell you, sir," Phonse said, grasping Daniel's shoulders from behind. "But he's first-rate with a rifle. Shoots to kill every time."

"Well, it sounds like you're a fine candidate, son." Cashin placed his pen on the line and asked, "Your full name?"

"Daniel Patrick Beresford."

"Home community?"

"Middle Tickle."

"Next of kin?"

"Jack and Mary Beresford." Daniel almost cringed at the sound of their names. He had caused them so much grief. It would be easier, for everyone, when he was gone.

"Height and weight?"

"Six feet, sir, and one hundred and sixty-five pounds."

Cashin glanced up at the three boys. "You're a different breed out around the bay, aren't you? Altogether big strapping lads."

"Hard work, sir," Phonse said.

Daniel shot him a look, and Phonse shrugged, but Cashin seemed oblivious to the offhanded comment.

"Do you have any ailments to disclose?"

"Don't think so, no."

He looked up and scrutinized Daniel. "And your age?"

Steady. Keep looking him in the eye.

"Eighteen, sir," he said without hesitation.

Cashin paused, and Daniel stared straight at the centre of the man's eyes. It looked like an honest exchange between two men, each measuring the other for his integrity, a quiet respect, even. But for Daniel, remaining focused meant the difference between leaving and staying. He stared, without flinching, at the two black dots. Joining the Newfoundland Regiment was his ticket out of Middle Tickle, to forget what he couldn't have, and to escape the cruel punishment of seeing Emma every day. It also meant freedom for his family.

He couldn't afford to flinch. As the seconds ticked by, his pulse quickened.

When Cashin moved his pen across the parchment, Daniel was slow to let the air out of his lungs. He recognized a few bits of the cursive loops, but like most boys his age in Middle Tickle, he left school when he was nine or ten to fish with his father. He was clever enough in a general way, but the three R's had never come easily to him, and there wasn't much need for formal education in his line of work. He knew how many quintals of fish they made each season and the merchant's price. That information was crucial to their survival and about as much as he needed to know.

Cashin turned the ledger around and handed Daniel the pen. "Just need your signature right there." He pointed to the bottom of the ledger.

When Daniel hesitated, Cashin said quietly, "Or just mark an X there, lad."

A few months ago, he could barely write his own name, but Emma had helped him learn some of the basics he had forgotten when he'd set aside his schooling to fish with his father. He leaned down and scrawled his name across the line. Cashin took the pen from him, and the two men exchanged a nod.

"Thank you, Daniel. Your Regimental number is 493." Cashin pointed at the man seated next to him. "Welcome to the Newfoundland Regiment. This fine gentleman here will provide you with all the details of where to report for training."

nine

October 3, 1914
St. John's, Newfoundland

DANIEL FELL IN LINE BETWEEN FRANKIE AND PHONSE AS THE Newfoundland Regiment marched from their white tent camp in Pleasantville. Five hundred and thirty-nine of them, kitted out in khaki uniforms, marched up Kings Bridge Road and past St. Thomas's church, its bells tolling for them as they passed by. Without guns, and their uniforms lacking, they were a marvellous sight all the same with their knitted caps, their long greatcoats, and their blue puttees.

Left, right, left, right.

It was a typical October day in St. John's. Blankets of fog lingered just beyond the hilltops, waiting to roll in, and a light drizzle fell. Scores of people cheered, and youngsters ran beside them as they marched four to a row, a dust-coloured sea flowing toward St. John's harbour and the vessel waiting to take them to England. People called them the First Five Hundred. The first of the Regiment to go to war. Over a hundred men had shipped out a month before with the Royal Naval Canadian Volunteer Reserve, but little had been made of it.

The dun wool of his uniform made Daniel's skin itch, but he marched straight on past hundreds of people yelling out how smart they looked.

"This sure is a lot of fuss for seeing us off," Frankie murmured, keeping perfect marching time. "We'll be home again in a few months."

Left, right, left right.

"For king and country!" someone shouted as they passed.

Daniel gritted his teeth and kept his eyes forward. He hadn't joined out of a sense of duty. It was just easier than staying behind in Middle Tickle. Frankie and Phonse were caught up in some great patriot game, and it sounded like the whole country was on board.

Left, right, left, right.

What he thought about every day was Emma. That hadn't changed. Thankfully, in St. John's there was so much to occupy his time. Army training was rigorous, between the drills and the physical training and shooting. Sometimes he fell into his cot at the end of the day like a corpse, so exhausted he woke up in the same position he'd fallen asleep in. Some evenings he knocked around with the boys, but even after several weeks, the pain of leaving Emma behind was still raw.

Father Flanagan had written him a few weeks ago on behalf of his mother. She knew he would want to know Tavenor had kept his word. Like her, he went to the only trustworthy person who would read the letter, but also keep his confidence—the Regiment's chaplain. Emma had taught him a few words before he had left, and he was determined to master the alphabet before he returned. He might even write to her one day, to show her how much he'd learned.

Just this morning, before they packed up, Private Wells entered the barracks with a postal sack over his shoulder. "Mail's here."

He emptied the sack on the table. Excitement buzzed when the mail came, and men dropped whatever they were doing and gathered around, waiting for their names to be called.

"Matthews, Hynes, Beresford," Wells called as he shuffled through the envelopes.

Daniel retrieved the envelope and examined it. He frowned, turning it over a few times. If there was a letter inside, it was short. He ripped it open, and his heart stopped beating. It was a photograph of Emma. She stood in front of a tall fireplace, her hands folded in front of her. Her dark hair was pinned up high with some loose pieces cascading down her back. He closed his eyes, remembering her smell.

He ran his thumb along the side of her face. She was as beautiful as ever, though her eyes were sad. Was he the cause? He turned the photograph over, only to find a few lines written on the back. He would ask the chaplain what it said later. For now the photograph was enough.

"What you got there, Daniel?" Frankie asked.

"Nothing, b'y, another letter from me mother."

He tucked the photograph in his breast pocket next to the Bible they were all issued and the handkerchief his mother had embroidered for Richard. Now he had something belonged to the two people he loved most in the world.

The photo was safe inside his pocket as he marched.

Left, right, left, right.

A cool, light mist sprayed in his face as he followed his comrades down Prescott Street toward St. John's harbour. The SS *Florizel* came into view, steam billowing from her stacks. He was comforted by the thoughts of spending a few weeks on the vessel. She had come to the assistance of the SS *Newfoundland* during the great sealing disaster, and she had carried Richard's body back to St. John's. Daniel swallowed hard. If Richard were still alive, he'd probably be standing right next to him now.

People lined the streets, cheering and waving, and "It's a Long Way to Tipperary" echoed in the air. A marching band, made up of the Church Lads' Brigade, the Catholic Cadets Corps, and the Methodist Guards, led the Regiment toward Furness Withy Company's pier, where the vessel waited. Daniel marched between his childhood friends and, for a brief moment, wondered what they were all doing. All Frankie could talk about was the great adventure they were going on and all the places they would see. But they were training to go to war.

To go to war. Had any of them considered what that meant?

They arrived at the waterfront and separated into their respective sections, marching on board single file. Next to the gangway, several men in dark suits and hats shook hands with the soldiers as they boarded. Daniel recognized Mr. Cashin and Mr. Outerbridge from the recruiting meeting in St. John's. Some uniformed men held umbrellas over the two men closest to the gangway, and as he got closer, Daniel heard them identified as Governor Davidson and Prime Minister Morris.

As his black, polished boots stepped onto the gangway, one of them held out his hand and looked Daniel straight in the eye. "How does it feel to be one of the First Five Hundred, young man?"

Daniel stared back. The tone of his voice and the pride in the man's eyes stopped him. Daniel's heartbeat quickened, but he didn't speak.

"You're doing your country a great service."

He must have been the governor, since he spoke the king's good English.

"Thank you." Daniel hesitated and added, "Sir."

His chest puffed a little as he continued up the gangway. He couldn't imagine under any other circumstances in his sixteen years that he would be in the presence of the governor and the prime minister of Newfoundland, or that they would be wishing him well.

Life was a funny thing.

They assembled on the top deck, and the commanding officer granted them permission to fall out and stand along the starboard side to wave at friends and family. Daniel wedged between his buddies and leaned against the railing. The rough wood was slick with remnants of sea salt combined with the moisture falling from the sky. All around him, men waved and blew kisses at the crowd gathered below. Wives and children called to the men, and the band struck off with "God Be With You Till We Meet Again."

The low drone of the ship's horn sounded just above him, and Daniel flinched. In the front row, a white handkerchief waved back and forth. His stomach somersaulted, and he focused on the cloth, his eyes drifting to the hand waving it, hoping beyond hope it was Emma. She had sent him a photograph that very day. Maybe she was in St. John's.

Disappointment flooded through him as his eyes fell on the short, blonde woman holding it. Standing here in the middle of hundreds of men, Daniel felt very alone, and a sudden wave of grief threatened to overtake him. His knuckles whitened as he grasped the railing, driving a splinter into the heel of his palm. It was better this way.

There was no one here for him now. There would be no one waiting for him.

"Where in the name of Christ's paddles is everyone going to sleep?" Frankie asked as they crammed inside the small passenger vessel that regularly sailed between St. John's, Halifax, and New York. She was built to hold about 180 people and was occasionally used for sealing, but there were over 539 men on board for this trip. And a dog.

"Sure, it's only for a few days." Phonse nodded at a group of officers from St. John's. "And by the looks of that crowd, who never set foot on a boat before, they're going to spend most of their time on deck." He tilted his head to port. "Easy access to the side, if you catch my meaning." He laughed.

"Jesus, Phonse, it's more than a few days. It's at least two weeks!" Bern said.

"I hope you didn't join the Regiment expecting all the comforts of home," Daniel said.

Frankie's eyes widened, as if he hadn't considered conditions might be less than desirable. "Can't be any worse than them tents we had down in Quidi Vidi. Sure, half of them blew apart in September."

Somehow, they all squatted inside the hull of the ship and hunkered down for their first night. It was the next day before the *Florizel* left St. John's harbour to join a convoy waiting for them off Cape Race. Within twenty-four hours they learned a much bigger vessel was meant to transport them to England later in October. However, fears of German submarine attacks were rampant, so the British Army had ordered an earlier departure date to steam with the Canadian convoy in their journey across the pond. The original vessel, the *Letitia*, couldn't reach St. John's in time, so the governor had accepted the Bowrings' offer of the little SS *Florizel*, part of their Red Cross Line, for use in wartime service.

A series of ships' horns blew, each with a distinctive sound, and Daniel followed Frankie, Phonse, and Bern out onto the deck. As their vessel rounded Cape Race, twenty ships were moored, waiting for them to join the Atlantic convoy.

"Now, she's a ship," Bern said. He fair drooled as his eyes fixed on the large hull of the SS *Cassandra* as they came astern and joined the convoy.

Excitement filled the air as the men pointed and waved at the other soldiers and exchanged pleasantries. The smile disappeared from Frankie's face when the band aboard the *Cassandra* struck off with "O Canada" followed by "The Maple Leaf Forever," the sound soaring over the waves like a seagull.

"What the devil?" Bern asked.

"It's Canadian," Phonse said.

Frankie huffed and pushed away from the railing, disgusted with the distinction. "They think we're Canadians?" he asked.

Daniel laughed and slapped him on the back. "Don't take it so personally, Frankie."

"That's all right," Phonse said. "They'll all know once we get there we're Newfoundlanders, don't you worry. Hey, b'ys?" Phonse looked around, and a collective roar sounded on deck.

The vessel was two days into the journey when the heavy seas came on. As she rolled from side to side in the heavy swell, it was easy to pick out the landlubbers. They hung on to the ship's rail for dear life, heaving their guts out over the side every few minutes.

Frankie elbowed Daniel and pointed. "Look at that, luh."

Second Lieutenant Harold Winter was struggling to stand on the ship's deck in the swell. His feet were planted on the deck, his hands glued to the railing, and he was stiff as a corpse.

"And he's an officer," Bern said, snuffing out his cigarette. "I got to follow the likes of him into battle. Some chance."

"Sure, being an officer don't mean nothing, Bern. Just means they got more money than we do."

The boys scoffed and murmured their agreement.

Phonse slapped Bern on the back and laughed. "Well, if we do have to go into battle, I'd sure as hell follow him before I'd follow you."

A large wave crashed into the boat, and Second Lieutenant Winter lost his grip on the rail and fell backward onto the deck. Frankie and Bern burst into fits of laughter.

"If he can't stand up on a boat, he sure as hell isn't going to be able to stand up to the Germans."

Frankie made a show of walking to the railing to throw his cigarette butt over the side in the heavy swell. He passed the officer, scrambling to get up off the deck, without offering assistance.

A voice boomed from behind. "Gentlemen, I believe one of your men requires assistance."

Daniel turned around and stared into the scowling face of Captain O'Reilly. "Is that how you fellows mean to conduct yourself on the battlefield? Leaving a man in distress when you are more than capable of lending a hand? Is that what we taught you? Perhaps we've erred.

Maybe you're not at all ready to serve with this Regiment and behave like proper soldiers."

O'Reilly stepped forward, and Daniel could smell the cigarette smoke off his breath. Winter had finally legged himself up off the deck and smoothed out his uniform before heading toward them. The boys straightened up.

As Winter approached, an awkward silence fell over them all. The young officer cast his eyes downward. Daniel worked hard not to fidget.

"You see a soldier in distress, you help," Captain O'Reilly said, reaching into his pocket for a packet of cigarettes.

"It's all right, sir. I'm fine," said Winter.

"Of course you are, Second Lieutenant, but that's not the point, is it?"

"Suppose not," he replied.

Captain O'Reilly lit a cigarette and started walking away from them.

Frankie leaned toward Daniel. "Yes, I allow if it was one of us crawling around on our hands and knees they'd be over to help us up. They'd be making fun, that's what they'd be at."

The captain turned back and stared at Frankie. "Your name, soldier?"

Daniel flinched.

Frankie straightened up again. "Private Drover, sir."

"Well, Private Drover, the only *us* and *them* you should be worried about is this Regiment, our British comrades, and those bloody Germans we're going to defeat. Do you understand me?"

"Yes," Frankie said.

The captain turned on his heel and marched away, yelling some kind of profanity at another group of soldiers a few feet away.

Daniel spoke up first. "Daniel Beresford, sir. And this is Frankie Drover, Phonse Whelan, and Bernard Morey." The boys all nodded.

"I'm Harry. Nice to make your acquaintance." He reached his hand out to Daniel. Phonse and Bern followed suit. Frankie was the last to come forward; he mumbled something under his breath, ending with "needing to take a piss," and left them all there on the deck.

"Sorry about that," Daniel said.

"It's all right." Winter gave a slight smile. "I guess you noticed I'm not much of a seaman."

If ever there was someone green in the face from seasickness, it was Second Lieutenant Harold Winter. Daniel felt sorry for him. Truth be told, Daniel had been sick a time or two on the water himself, but Winter was downright miserable. Rumour had it he wanted nothing to do with joining the Regiment in the first place, but had little choice. He was married to Leonard Outerbridge's daughter, and Outerbridge was not only a close friend of Governor Davidson but was instrumental in recruiting, training, and building the Regiment. Of course, Outerbridge made Winter an officer to ensure he was as far from the front as possible, according to the rumour mill.

"I'm sure I looked a right sight to you boys. You've probably been in a boat since you were twelve years old."

Daniel looked at the others and shrugged. "I was eight."

"Nine," Phonse said.

"Five," Bern said.

They all looked at him.

"What? Father needed the help, and me two older brothers was gone away."

"Next thing he'll be telling us he had his first girl when he was ten," Phonse said, elbowing Daniel.

Bern smiled. "Eleven."

Daniel's eyes drifted past his buddies to the great expanse of horizon, which seemed to stretch forever. Well, at least to England. He moved to the railing, leaving the boys behind him, laughing and insulting one another. Joining the Regiment was one way to see the world. It was his only way. St. John's was like a foreign place with its motor cars and shops. It was a bustle like he'd never seen before. He could only imagine what England would be like.

He reached into his pocket and took out Emma's photograph. The black and white tones made it hard to pick out her finer features, but he still knew the exact colour grey of her eyes and the exact shade of black of her hair. He was happy to have the picture, even though it hadn't done her justice. He would have to rely on his memory alone, which was fine. There was nothing about Emma Tavenor he could forget, even if he wanted to.

"Is she your girl?" Winter asked. He stood next to Daniel, his hands gripping the ship's rail, and chuckled. "Not taking any chances," he said referring to his tight grip.

Daniel laughed.

"She's pretty." Winter nodded toward the photo.

"Even more so in person," Daniel said, not taking his eyes off the picture.

Another wave hit the boat, and Winter stumbled, but Daniel caught him by the arm. "Widen your legs out to line up with your shoulders, and let your body move with the swell. Like this." Daniel stepped away from the rail, and Winter watched him as he stayed planted to the ship's deck, but moved his hips side to side with the sway of the vessel.

Winter spread his legs apart, still looking pretty stiff. "Yeah, that's it," Daniel said. "Now, let go of the railing."

Winter hesitated. "Oh, I don't know about that yet."

Daniel laughed. "Give it a try."

Winter took one hand off, followed by the other, but stayed close to the rail. He swayed from side to side and smiled. "It's kind of like dancing."

Daniel shrugged. "I suppose so, yes. Hope you've had better-looking dancing partners than me, though."

The two laughed. Another big swell came on, and Winter grabbed the railing. He winked at Daniel. "I think I'll practise when it's a bit calmer out there." He reached in his pocket and took out two cigarettes, handing one to Daniel.

"Is she a good dancing partner?" He nodded toward the photograph Daniel still held tight.

"Don't think I'll ever find out," Daniel said.

"Oh, come on. It won't be that bad. By all accounts, we'll be home again in a few months."

Daniel turned over the photograph, staring at the words and angry with himself for not knowing what they said. "Harry?"

Winter took a hard pull on his cigarette. "Yeah." He blew a long puff of smoke out.

"Could you tell me what that says?"

Winter watched him for a second before looking at the back of the picture. "Daniel, Carry me with you. All my love, Emma."

"Thanks," Daniel said, shoving the picture back inside the breast pocket of his tunic.

"She'll be waiting for you when you get back, make no mistake." Winter tossed what was left of his cigarette over the railing and stepped away.

If they were going to be home by Christmas, he had two months to figure out what he was going to do. Where would he go? Could he return to Middle Tickle? He imagined everybody knew he'd enlisted in the Regiment by now. He couldn't help but wonder what that son of a bitch Tavenor thought when he heard the news. A fisherman wasn't good enough for his daughter. Was a soldier?

ten

February 1915
Middle Tickle, Newfoundland

EMMA SAT ON THE STOOL BEHIND THE COUNTER AND STARED OUT the store's window. The bells tied to the door top jingled, breaking her daydream. She looked up, hopeful. Six months had passed since Daniel and the others had left. At first she prayed the rumours were true and they would all be back by Christmas, but reality was beginning to set in. Daniel wasn't coming back, at least not any time soon.

"Oh, hallo, Mrs. Broderick."

"Hello, Emma." Mrs. Broderick held on to her head scarf as she struggled to close the shop door against the wild February wind, pushing her inside. "Blowing a gale out there today." She smiled and laid a small change purse down on the counter. "Are you feeling all right, dear? You look pale."

Emma smiled half-heartedly. "I'm fine, thank you, Mrs. Broderick. Just a bit tired."

Truth was, she wasn't sleeping much at all.

"Take care of yourself." Her eyes took on a sudden sadness. "We haven't got many young ones left here now. Most of the boys have signed up. The harbour feels empty, I tell you. Emptier than my tea can." She shook her head. "St. John's, sure, that's a world away. I've never even been there, never mind England. I don't know what to make of it, meself. All the talk down on Alfie Brown's stage is that our boys are needed." She tapped her finger several times on the store counter. "Well, they're needed here."

The thought of Daniel in St. John's had been bad enough. Emma didn't need reminding he was training to fight in a war. There was something wrong about this. She couldn't understand how he would rather go off and fight in a war than stay here with her, where they were safe from all of it. How had she not realized his feelings for her had changed?

She blinked a few times. "What can I do for you, Mrs. Broderick?"

The woman opened her change purse and unfolded a twenty-dollar bill. She slid it across the counter. "I think this should more than square my account." She beamed. "Our Pius sent it to me."

Pius was Mrs. Broderick's eldest, whom Emma had never met. He'd been living somewhere in Canada for a long time and must have done well for himself, since he sent his mother money several times a year.

Emma looked underneath the counter and noticed the ledger was missing. She held up one finger. "I'll just go get the ledger. I'll be right back."

"I'll marl around and pick up a few things," Mrs. Broderick said, as she headed to one of the long shelves of dry goods lining the back wall.

Emma was glad for a few minutes to compose herself. She slipped into the office and took in a long breath, using her sleeve to dab her eyes. She spotted the ledger on the desk with her father's other account book beside it and a bottle of whiskey on top. She retrieved it, along with a pen and inkwell, and returned to the store just as Mrs. Broderick laid her items on the counter.

She opened her grandfather's old leather-bound ledger. The accounts were all handwritten in her tidy, cursive writing. Daniel once said her handwriting was beautiful, even if he didn't understand what it said. She flipped the heavy, yellowing pages and knew the Beresfords' page sat adjacent to Mrs. Broderick's. She closed her eyes and breathed deep, refusing to look at it. Reminders of him were everywhere today. She added the sum of money to the woman's account and recorded today's supplies: sugar, loose tea, flour, and some molasses. She placed the items in a small box and wrapped it up with brown paper before bidding the woman good day.

As she began to close the ledger, something caught her eye and made her open it wide again. She stared at the name on the page, wishing the act alone could make Daniel appear. She didn't even know how to contact him, and even if she did, what was the point? If she wrote him a letter, he'd have to get someone else to read it, and she didn't want anyone else reading out loud the things she wanted to say to him.

But it wasn't the name that stopped her. It was the zero, with a line through it, indicating no monies due. There was no mistaking her father's scratches, but it didn't make any sense. Daniel's father couldn't have cleared his debt unless he'd come into money all of a sudden, which would have been the talk of Middle Tickle. She closed the ledger and sat down on the stool, tapping the pen against the hard leather cover.

A few months ago, Jack Beresford's boat was tied up at her father's wharf for the best part of a week with no explanation. A few days after, Daniel left for St. John's without even saying goodbye. Now the Beresford account was square. Something was definitely amiss. Emma buttoned up her sweater and stepped out into the chilly evening air.

The weathered wood of the Beresfords' front porch creaked as Emma stepped onto it. The white paint had blistered and peeled off in small sections of the old two-storey saltbox, and it was in desperate need of a good scraping and painting. She knocked on the dark green wooden door as an orange tomcat rubbed against her leg. Mary Beresford opened the door and stared at Emma for a few seconds, and the old cat sauntered in. She sighed, gesturing for Emma to enter. She closed the door and brushed past her on her way to the kitchen.

Emma blinked as her eyes adjusted to the dark porch and she followed the woman inside.

Daniel's mother pointed to the rocking chair. "Have a seat."

Mrs. Beresford crossed the room and retrieved two cups from a cupboard above a short counter. Emma's eyes landed on the white hand-embroidered cloth on the kitchen table. The fabric wasn't long enough, and the table's legs were exposed. Four posts stuck out underneath the cloth like scraggly branches on a dead tree. She thought about her mother's large mahogany table, made somewhere in South America, in their dining room at home. Dark, polished wood with hand-carved legs that seated as many as ten people sat unused.

The chairs around the Beresfords' table were different colours. Two were white, and the other two were rusty brown. Emma sat in the fifth chair, a rickety old rocking chair, which couldn't come all the way forward. Only five chairs, she thought, and they had eight mouths to feed. She glanced around the room again, wondering where the others ate.

Mrs. Beresford disappeared into the pantry and reappeared with some loose tea. She removed the steaming kettle from its perch on the wood stove and filled the cups with boiling water. One of the cups had a faded pattern of red roses on it; the second, which she gave to Emma, was much brighter, with pink flowers.

A large buffet and hutch sat in her own dining room filled with bone china. The dainty teacups, with their matching saucers, were always saved for guests.

"I have no sugar, Miss Tavenor. Will molasses do?" She lifted the container off the table, showing it to her.

"Please call me Emma. Of course, molasses is fine. It's better, really."

Emma had never had molasses in her tea, but she nodded in agreement and watched as the thick, brown liquid fell to the bottom of the cup like an anchor.

"Aren't you having some?" The woman had mixed Emma's tea but left her own black.

She shook her head. "I'll let the lads finish what's left."

Mrs. Beresford picked up the cup and cradled it in her hands as she sat on one of the brown chairs. She turned the cup around as she lifted it to her lips. As Emma sipped from hers, she noticed the rim of Mary's cup had a large chip in it.

Daniel's words haunted her. *I can't expect you to live like this.*

"We aren't like you, Emma. We don't have very much," Mrs. Beresford said, as if reading her mind.

Why did everyone have to keep reminding her of their differences? Was this why Daniel had left? Emma's face grew hot, and she bit her lip.

"I know, Mrs. Beresford, but I don't care about any of that."

"It's not that simple, Emma. There are people who care very much about it."

"You mean my father?" Emma sniffed and waved her hand. "He would have made his peace with it, eventually."

Daniel's mother opened her mouth to speak, but lifted the cup to her lips instead, turning it just ever so much before it reached her lips.

"I do not know why he just left, but I would like to fix it," Emma said, her voice cracking. She swallowed. "If I could just talk to him, I am sure I can get him to return home."

Mrs. Beresford shook her head. "He left to save his family, don't you see? *You* can't fix this." Her bitter laugh said everything else her words did not. *Because this is your fault.*

Emma's heat skipped a beat. "Save you from what?" Even as she spoke the words, she knew Mrs. Beresford was about to explain the great mystery of the family's new-found wealth, which had everything to do with Daniel's rapid departure from Middle Tickle.

"We owed your father a great deal of money. With several bad seasons in a row, we just couldn't get ahead." She hesitated, her mouth moving as if to find the right words. "Jack arranged for Richard to go the ice. The extra money was supposed to clear our debt with your father."

Emma closed her eyes. Daniel had grieved in her arms for weeks after Richard's death, but not once did he tell her any of this. She didn't realize Richard had gone solely to pay her father back. All these months, Daniel must have blamed her father for Richard's death. Hated him, even. Maybe deep down Daniel blamed her, too. An emptiness settled over her. Make no wonder he left. How could he have stood to look at her all those months?

"Fishing is the only way Jack can make any living at all, but your father took the boat."

The woman's words sank in. That's why their boat was tied up at her father's wharf. Her hands shook as she laid her teacup on the sideboard, not trusting herself to hold it any longer.

Mrs. Beresford took a deep breath and met Emma's gaze. "Your father would have never let you two be together, Emma. Surely you must realize this. And let's just say your father made it easier for Daniel to make this decision."

Emma's brow furrowed. "I don't understand."

"They had an arrangement. After Daniel left, your father returned the boat and forgave the debt. We don't owe him one red cent."

The room spun, but somehow she stood and staggered toward the door. It all made perfect sense now. Daniel's brother died trying to make enough money to pay her father back. Her father knew Daniel would do anything to save his family from financial ruin. He had taken the Beresfords' boat and persuaded Daniel to leave Middle Tickle before he'd return it.

Emma hurried outside, stumbling over a loose board on the Beresfords' gallery. She caught the railing and leaned over its side. The sickly sweet aftertaste of the molasses lingered in her mouth.

Emma stood in the window and looked up at the sky. The stars were bright, and she wondered if Daniel could see them from wherever he was. Pain stabbed through her arms like shards of glass, poking and prodding, until she found it hard to breathe. She held the last reminder of him in her hand—the handkerchief he had given her before he left.

They had been curled up at the pond one afternoon when she told him she was worried something would happen to him while he was fishing.

"Don't be so foolish." He kissed her neck. "Sure, what's going to happen to me?"

She twisted around to look up at him. "Anything at all. Can you even swim?"

"Oh, yes, I'm a champion swimmer. Come to think of it, I should give up this fishing racket and swim for a living." He rolled his eyes and laughed. "What good is being able to swim out there? Where would you swim to?"

She swatted him in the arm. "I'm serious, Daniel. What would happen if you got caught in a gale and the boat capsized?"

"Emma, if we got caught in a gale, being able to swim wouldn't help us out too much." Her eyes filled.

He hugged her tight. "You worry too much." He reached into his pocket and pulled out a handkerchief. "Here."

Emma took it in her hand and examined the piece of white linen. It was very fine material with the initials DB embroidered in thick navy blue stitching in the top right-hand corner.

"The stitching is beautiful, Daniel. Who did it for you?"

"Mother. When we were born, she did one for each of us."

It was just as fine as any of the ones Emma's mother had come from Paris. "It's really good. Where did she learn?"

"When she was a young girl, she was in service for a few years in Harbour Grace. An old English missus taught her to stitch while she was there."

"I can't keep this." She reached out her hand to return it to him. "Your mother made it for you."

He covered her hand with his own and closed her fingers around it. "You keep it. That way you can carry me with you."

He kissed her fingers and pulled her into a warm embrace.

She held the handkerchief as close to her chest now as she had then. Nothing could quell the ache in her heart as she lay back on her bed.

She noticed a box wrapped in plain brown paper at the foot of the bed. She sat next to it, inspecting the London postmark. Had her mother sent her something? It was rather unlikely, since she hadn't so much as heard from her in over two years. She undid the twine and ripped open the paper. Emma lifted layers of tissue paper to reveal a beautiful, emerald-green dress lined with cream-coloured trim. Underneath were two more dresses neatly packed together.

Her hands shook. She gathered the dresses in a heap and stormed out of the house, down to the wharf, not caring if anyone saw her. She tossed the whole lot over the head of the wharf and turned around to face her house. A faint light glowed in her father's room.

"I don't want your dresses," she yelled at the window. "They won't make me happy!"

Emma sat down on the end of the wharf. The water was smooth as glass, and the light from the full moon divided the harbour. Maybe her mother's happiness hinged on material things, but hers did not. The only thing that could make her happy right now was if Daniel Beresford came home this very minute. After what she had learned this evening, she knew that wasn't going to happen. He had too much to lose to come back to Middle Tickle. All this time she had thought he had left her, but he had left because of her.

She made her way back to the house and upstairs to her room. She climbed in bed and pulled the covers up around her. She smiled and closed her eyes. It would take some time, but if he couldn't come home to her, she would go to him.

eleven

February 1915
Edinburgh Castle, Scotland

"So, why are these better than those Canadian guns we had?" Phonse looked over his newly issued British Lee-Enfield rifle, turning it over in his hands several times.

The Regiment's shipment of Canadian Ross Rifles had showed up on the Reid Newfoundland Company's express train about twelve hours after they had set sail for England, but were shipped to them after the fact. Not long after, the Ross Rifles were swapped out for the British Lee-Enfields, which was all part of the British standard-issue kit.

The boys were cleaning their rifles for the second time that day. In training they had learned the firing mechanism was famous for getting dirt and grit caught inside, causing the rifle to jam up or misfire. It didn't take much convincing to get into a cleaning routine. The last thing a soldier needed was a jammed rifle when he needed it most.

Daniel laid the magazine and the clip down on the table and inspected the rifle carefully.

Frankie shrugged. "Well, of course the British ones are better," he drawled before rolling his eyes. "They're British."

It hadn't taken long before the air of British superiority blew their way. The boys had become easy targets with their blue puttees, a distinctive piece of dress, which heralded their difference and fast turned them into a target of ridicule. Tired of being treated like poor colonials, they shed them just as quickly for standard-issue. At least when they all stood together now, it was harder to tell the difference at a simple glance.

Phonse shot Frankie a look as he picked up his rifle. "They're as good as any, and we need good rifles to do this job."

Daniel had thought a lot about the job since they arrived in Scotland, but there were no signs the Regiment was going anywhere yet.

"And why couldn't we have kept our uniforms?" Frankie looked down at his standard-issue British uniform.

"You're here to fight, Frankie. I don't suppose it matters much what you wear," Phonse said.

Frankie tilted his head as if he was pondering this for a minute. "I suppose. But I liked our blue puttees. If I got to run at some German bastard and kill him, I want him to know I'm different from the others. I'm not just any soldier. I'm a Newfoundland Regiment soldier."

The boys all raised their eyebrows at Frankie's burst of patriotism.

"Jesus, the governor should send you home to recruit, my son. With a speech like that, you'll empty the bays in no time." Bern started to laugh, but it fast turned into the barking cough he'd had for weeks now.

When they first arrived from Newfoundland, the Regiment had been stationed at Pond Farm Camp on Salisbury Plains in England, a tent camp with no floors. The heavens opened up one day in November, and the rain continued for weeks. Pools of water sat on top of the mud, and it was always cold and damp inside the tents. Their clothes were rarely dry, and they often joked about knowing what soggy doughboys felt like. When news came of their transfer to Scotland in December, they were happy enough to go. There was a lot of shuffling around with ten weeks in Fort George and then on to Edinburgh Castle, but at least they were dry.

If Newfoundlanders were bothered by the cold and damp, it must have been bad. They'd all had bouts of sickness, but Bern had the worst of it. Daniel hoped the warm, dry quarters they were enjoying since arriving in Scotland would eventually ease his friend's symptoms.

"Afternoon, boys." Second Lieutenant Winter appeared next to them.

They scrambled to their feet, but Winter furrowed his brow and looked over his shoulder as he lowered his hand.

"Afternoon, sir," Daniel said for all of them.

Little had been seen of Winter since they got off the boat in Plymouth, but recently he'd been assigned to their platoon of fifty men. Frankie had never properly apologized for his behaviour on the crossing over, but Winter was a gentleman and carried on as if it never happened.

Bern went back to cleaning his gun, unaware of the attention his long, wheezy breaths drew from the men around him.

"By Jesus, you got the consumption, Bern, make no mistake," Phonse said, shoving the cleaning rod up and down through the barrel of the gun.

The boys laughed, but Phonse was serious. "What? Me grandmother said if you got the consumption you were as good as dead."

Winter shook his head and chuckled at Phonse. "You got the Pond Farm Particular, Bern. The dampness has settled on your chest. Should go away now that we're in dry quarters." Winter rested a foot on a stack of sandbags and leaned on his leg. "But in all seriousness, there have already been a few casualties from the weather."

"I told you. It's the consumption," Phonse muttered.

The boys laughed again.

"Any signs of shipping out of here?" Frankie squinted in the late afternoon sun.

Winter shook his head. "No word as of yet."

"Doesn't look much like we're going home, either." Phonse clipped the magazine back in place.

Winter sat against the makeshift table the boys had cobbled together and took a package of Woodbines out of his pocket. Frankie watched Winter light the cigarette as if the man had just sat down to a five-course meal. They'd been waiting for some packages to come from home, but they hadn't arrived yet. Frankie had run out of cigarettes more than a week ago, which served him right. He smoked more than he ate these days.

Winter held the package out to Frankie in offer. He was reluctant at first but took it, muttering a low "thanks" under his breath.

"Second Lieutenant!" A voice boomed behind them. "These are not your mates. They're your men. You should be inspecting their rifles, not loitering about sharing cigarettes."

Winter stood to salute the red-faced Major Ashdown.

Frankie cursed under his breath as he tossed the unlit cigarette down. All the boys stood to attention and saluted Ashdown.

Winter hesitated. "These men are doing a fine job cleaning their rifles and their kit, Major," he said with much less force than he should have.

Ashdown smirked. "I'll be the judge of that." He stepped closer to Frankie. "What is your name, Private?"

Ashdown was from Manchester, and his accent was thick. Daniel had marvelled at the various British accents at first but had gotten better at picking them out. Ashdown was a real son of a bitch who got his jollies from belittling them as often as he could.

"Drover, sir," Frankie said.

"Private Drover, is that mud on your boots?"

Frankie looked down. Sure enough, they were filthy. Again. His eyes met Ashdown's, and the two men stared at each other.

"I asked you a question, Private." Ashdown edged closer yet, until their noses almost touched. "Is that mud on your boots, Private Drover?"

Frankie looked down, lifting his leg up to examine one foot, and then the other. When he was finished, he looked up at Ashdown and without blinking said, "I believe so, sir."

There was a flicker of disbelief in Ashdown's eyes at Frankie's nonchalance. "You believe so. It's a yes or no question, Private. Either there is mud on your boots or there isn't. Which is it?"

It was one of those moments where the silence was stifling, and Daniel was thankful for Bern's loud wheeze. Bern tried to hold it in until his face turned red and he erupted into a coughing fit, giving the whole encounter an air of humour that made the situation dangerous for all of them.

Eventually, Phonse couldn't stifle the laughter.

"You find this amusing, lads?" Ashdown snarled at them.

"No, sir," Daniel said.

He cursed Frankie, who kept pushing his luck when it came to the British officers. He had no respect for them and was constantly getting himself in trouble. Daniel respected the hierarchy of the army itself and understood why it existed. It was just too bad these know-it-alls, who didn't know as much as they thought they did, were in charge, but he knew better than to draw unwanted attention to himself. That would make his time here even worse.

"Come on, lads. Get it together. Your superior officer is speaking to you," Winter said, his eyes wide.

"I'm sorry, Harry—" Bern started, and Winter winced.

Ashdown's face contorted to the point where the boys thought he was going to have a stroke.

"*Harry?*" Ashdown turned to Bern. "Who the flaming hell do you think you are, Private? Harry? This is Second Lieutenant . . ." Ashdown trailed off. When Winter said nothing, Ashdown closed his eyes and sucked in a breath.

"What is your name, Second Lieutenant?"

Winter's eyes widened. "Harold Winter, sir."

Ashdown got right up in Bern's face. "This is Second Lieutenant Winter, your superior! Not Harry."

Harry took a step back. "Sir, we're all from—"

"Second Lieutenant Winter. See to it these men get a lesson in respect." Ashdown surveyed each one of them.

His face was beet red, and a vein in his temple throbbed like it had its own heartbeat. There was a deep look of disgust in his eyes, too. Daniel swallowed hard. Ashdown turned on his heel and stomped off, muttering under his breath. "This is what happens when you start taking from the far reaches of the Empire."

As he walked away, Frankie picked up the soggy, unlit cigarette from the wet ground. "Jesus, we're training to fight in a war, not have tea with the goddamn king."

"That may be true, Private, but we're training to go to war with the king's men. We have to do things their way."

Daniel couldn't recall Winter ever addressing any of them as Private.

Winter made sure Ashdown was out of earshot before looking at them all, his eyes serious. "It might be best if you addressed me as Second Lieutenant Winter from now on." He hesitated, his eyes wandering again. "It's not me. You know I don't care." He pointed to a group of British officers in the distance. "But they do. And the last thing any of you need is to be targeted as insubordinate."

Left up to Harry, there'd be no formality, but it wasn't up to Harry. What was going on around them all now was very much out of their hands. Winter turned to leave, and stopped. He lifted the pack of cigarettes out of his pocket and tossed them at Frankie.

"You know, those fellers from St. John's aren't all bad," Daniel said.

Frankie grunted and carried on with a list of complaints as the rest of them laughed.

༄

"How are ya, Bern?" Daniel asked.

Bern was slumped on a rock wall just outside the barracks. "I'm going to be a father, Daniel." He shoved a letter toward him.

Daniel took the paper. "The young girl from Fort George?" he asked.

Bern nodded. "Fiona."

"Pretty little thing."

"We only did it once or twice."

Daniel grinned at him. "You're good."

Bern snickered. "Mother's going to kill me." He reached in his pocket for his cigarettes.

"For making her a grandmother?" Daniel laughed. "I'm sure she'll get over it."

"No, but she expects I'll be sending me cheque home to take care of her and me sister, Kathleen." He cupped the match, shielding it from the wind to light his cigarette, and puffed. "Now I got to get married." He blew a column of smoke straight up into the air.

"Do you love her?"

"Fiona?"

Daniel nodded.

He shook his head. "No."

They sat in silence, a sad injustice shrouding them like a blanket. In a few days, Bern would marry a girl he didn't love to do the right thing.

Daniel would never marry the girl he loved.

༄

May 1915
Harwich, England

The Regiment was shipped back to England for more training, and a second contingent of Newfoundland recruits arrived. Training was still intense, but Daniel had to admit even he was getting bored with the same old humdrum practice. It had been seven months now, and they were itching for some action, or anything to keep them busy, with less time to dwell on how much they disliked the British officers.

As their section left the rifle range, Second Lieutenant Winter was waiting for them.

"Lads," said Winter.

Daniel wondered time and again how Winter was going to get through this. Unlike most of the officers Daniel had encountered, Winter did not appear to enjoy his status.

"Company's forming up at fourteen hundred on the parade ground. There's been a train accident involving a Scottish regiment. We've been called up. Looks like we're shipping out."

"Where to?" Daniel asked.

"Gallipoli."

"Where the hell is that?" Bern asked.

"Turkey," said Winter.

"Never heard of it," Frankie said.

"Well, lucky for us, you won't be sailing the boat." Phonse slapped him on the back, knocking the cigarette out of his mouth.

twelve

August 1915
Near Alexandria, Egypt

DANIEL STARED OVER THE RAILING OF THE *MEGANTIC* INTO THE light blue water. Colourful fish of all shapes and sizes swam around the boat, as if coaxing it toward the shore. Purple, blue, red, and orange—the colours reminded him of his grandmother's quilt on his bed at home. Apart from cod, the scattered dogfish, and sculpin, there wasn't much to see in the murky green-black water around Middle Tickle. He shifted under the midday sun and wiped the sweat off his forehead for the hundredth time.

It never got this hot in Newfoundland, but when it was warm, Daniel and Frankie had spent more than one afternoon moored off in the bay outside Middle Tickle. On the rare occasion when the sun beat down and the water was calm, there was still always a chill in the air. Sometimes they would lie on the bench between the gunwales, shirts off, listening to the peaceful lop on the water and birds flying overhead. The only interruption in peacefulness was a whale breaching the surface with a low groan, like the creak of an old boat, and the swoosh of water blowing from its spout before it slipped back beneath the inky blackness.

A red-faced Frankie appeared, sweat pouring down both sides of his face. "By Jesus, Danny, I'm nearly rendered. Where in the name of God's creation are we?"

A finger of land loomed in the distance, though he'd spied it for some time without feeling like they were getting any closer.

"Egypt, I suppose."

Frankie huffed and wiped at his face again. "I'll never make it."

"You'll be all right, Frankie. You're getting to see the world." Daniel placed a hand on his oldest friend's shoulder. "Did you ever imagine you'd get to Egypt?"

"Don't suppose so, no," Frankie said. "It's still better than hauling the line, though, isn't it?"

Daniel ignored Frankie's question. Fishing wasn't so bad. "Think of the stories you'll tell your grandkids. They got camels here, and sand as far as the eye can see."

"Camels?"

"Yeah, camels, you know, them big animals with the humps on them? And they don't need no water. They ride them like we ride horses."

Frankie shook his head before grabbing Daniel's water bottle. "They mightn't need water, but I do."

He guzzled what Daniel had left. "Never mind camels, Danny." Frankie grinned. "I bet there's some fine-looking women in Egypt."

Daniel laughed. "You won't know much about it where we're going."

"What do you mean?"

"We're going to a training camp in the desert to get used to this heat. I don't imagine there'll be many women there."

"There's no gettin' used to this heat, my son. I'd like to strip off now and jump right over the side of this boat. I knows that wouldn't be nice."

Daniel rested his head on his forearms and looked down at the crystal clear water again, the aquatic escorts still moving with them toward this exotic place. He wished Emma could see this. She probably knew all their names. The thought struck him out of nowhere, and he frowned. Even when he didn't think he was thinking about her, he was thinking about her.

As they edged closer to shore, more and more men nudged and pushed their way toward the railing of the *Megantic*, and soon the ship docked in the busy port of Alexandria. The skyline was packed with rows of old stone structures and circular-roofed buildings trimmed in bronze. Middle Tickle had white saltbox houses, all alike apart from Mr. Mick's place. He had painted his house a bright yellow two years ago, but everyone thought he was losing his mind.

Frankie pointed toward the waterfront. "What the dear Jesus are they wearing?"

Daniel followed Frankie's finger. They appeared to be men, but they were wearing long shirts, like dresses, with scooped collarless necks and wide sleeves. Some of the garments were all white, others were tan, and some more were bold striped fabrics.

Phonse scratched his head. "Pyjamas?"

"Maybe because it's so hot, you know, they can't wear real clothes," Bern said.

Frankie rubbed his hands together. "Does that mean we can expect the women to be walking around in their small clothes?"

The boys broke into laughter. "Frankie, you're not fit."

Just beyond the pier was a hub of activity. Grey donkeys carried carts full of goods through the streets, stopping here and there to unload. Rugs and scarves of all colours hung from wooden structures intermingled with stalls of fresh fruit and vegetables.

"They havin' a garden party?" asked Bern.

Figures cloaked from head to toe organized goods on tables and in baskets. Daniel took a closer look and realized they were women. The lower halves of their faces were covered by white veils, and black scarves covered their heads and hair. They were draped in loose-fitting black garments, like blankets, which hid any hint of their shape.

Daniel leaned in close to Frankie. "You'll have to imagine the women in their small clothes, Frankie, because that's about as close as you're going to get to seeing them," he said.

"What do you mean?"

Daniel pointed at the men on the pier dressed in the white tunics. "Well, if that's what the men are wearing, who do you think is wrapped up from head to toe over there?" His finger drifted to the cloaked figures at the market stalls.

"Gentle Jesus, why would anyone want to cover themselves up, especially in this heat?" Phonse asked, wiping the sweat from his forehead.

"Want has nothing to do with it," Second Lieutenant Winter called out amidst the loud chatter around them. "Weren't you paying attention when the colonel explained there were many cultural differences between where we came from and where we're going?"

"No, not really," Frankie said.

Winter pushed his way to where the boys stood and frowned at Frankie. "Well, you should have. They're not like us in any way, and you'd do well to remember that when you're set loose among them."

Frankie shrugged.

In the distance, Daniel spied Major Ashdown making his way over. Winter glanced back and spoke up. "That's Second Lieutenant Winter, Private." He took a step back from the boys.

Ashdown nodded at Winter and kept moving.

"Those British officers are rubbing off on you," Frankie muttered.

September 19, 1915
Gallipoli, Turkey

It was twilight when Daniel's section left the safety of the *Prince Abbas*, moored in Suvla Bay. The low rumble of a Turkish shell thundered in the distance. Otherwise it was quiet as the Regiment came to shore in several *beetles*, flat-bottomed lighter craft. The full moon lit up the bay and the opening to the narrow Kangaroo Beach straight ahead.

"We're landing here?" asked Bern. "Sure, this is no bigger than Bait Cove, and I can swim across that in three strokes."

"Jesus H. Christ." Frankie leaned forward. "You see them cliffs?"

Daniel had been sizing them up for some time, wondering just how many Turkish snipers were tucked away, waiting for an opportunity to take out a Tommy or two, which meant them now.

Frankie's eyes were wide. "How in the name of God are we getting up over them?"

"Private Drover," Captain Ashdown said from behind them. "You can climb, right?"

Frankie rolled his eyes before looking back at Ashdown. "Yes, sir. I can climb with the best of them, but they're awfully steep, wouldn't you say?"

Ashdown placed his foot up on the bench. "Can you run, Private?"

"Yes, sir. I can run," Frankie said.

"Good thing, Private, because in about two minutes you're going to be running for your life. Worry about that first."

The *beetle* crunched against the sand and stone of the beach, and despite all their training, all the hours of drills, the result was chaos. The officers resisted yelling, but only because they wanted to land without drawing attention. They still delivered a few swift kicks in the arse in an effort to keep the men moving forward to clear the beach. Bern was right. The beach area was so small it would take the entire night to disembark all their men and supplies.

Men bumped into Daniel as they scrambled over the *beetle*'s side. He followed, falling into knee-deep water. Frankie fell on top of him, driving him under. He gulped a mouthful before Frankie pulled him up. Daniel's pulse raced as adrenaline flooded his system. He looked up at the cliffs again, the salt water stinging his eyes. The Regiment's plan was to land quietly, but the Turks were nestled high above the beach in those cliffs with a perfect vantage point. Daniel's boots were weighted down with water, and with a hundred pounds of kit on his back, he wasn't moving with much stealth.

"Come on." Frankie pushed him forward.

If anyone was watching, it must have been an impressive sight. A thousand soldiers disembarked overnight, moving fast and quiet, onto Kangaroo Beach, each one desperate to get under the hills. And without a single casualty.

Bern buttoned up the top of his wool uniform jacket. "For a place that's scorching during the day, it sure gets cold at night."

They were seven days into their ten-day rotation on the front lines.

"Any more water?" Phonse asked.

"No, b'y, I've got none left. Haven't for hours," Frankie replied.

Fresh drinking water was a real problem, since most wells were contaminated. Water was brought in by ship and stored in large containers on the beach, but there were delays in shipments and longer delays before it got to the front lines. Daniel stepped back into the trench and pulled the water bottle from around his neck, handing it to Phonse.

"Thanks, Danny." Phonse guzzled it, leaving some of the precious fluid for his friend.

Daniel blinked a few times, his eyes adjusting to the blanket of darkness creeping across no man's land. It was dark, but he knew what was out there. Mud, craters, and bodies strewn between the front lines. Dark clouds of flies buzzed and hovered until they got their fill. He'd rather the flies stay out there feasting than swarm the trenches when the Aunt Sallys came with rations.

He'd been crouched for hours in the same position, forearms leaning on the banquette, his rifle positioned up over the parapet, ready to fire. The officers had been paying attention to him at shooting practice. His father had taught Daniel and his brother Richard to shoot when they were young boys. They took great sport in shooting turrs and other seabirds from the boat, and it was always a competition to see who could get the most. Learning to shoot birds in flight from a rocking boat had made him an excellent marksman.

A few months before Richard died, they had raced from the wharf to the house, and Richard had waltzed across the kitchen floor with his haul held high in his hand. He kissed their mother on the cheek and grinned, holding up the birds like a prize. "Get out the big pot, Mother. I got enough for a week!" Her eyes lit up as she took them. She would never admit to having a favourite among the nine, but since Richard's death the light had faded from her eyes.

Bern stood up and swayed from side to side, stretching his back as the evening's first shot echoed overhead. He spun around and dived against the trench wall, muttering, "Goddamned Johnnies."

Daniel dug out his pocket watch, a sentimental reminder of home. It belonged to his grandfather and had sat on the bureau in his parents' bedroom for as long as he could remember. The day he left Middle Tickle, his mother had slipped it in his pocket. It was a rare thing for an infantry soldier to have; usually only officers had pocket watches. The watch read five past seven. "They're late this evening."

He sat down next to Bern and pulled up his pant leg. The fabric was almost worn through from his constant scratching. "You have to admire their persistence."

"Suppose so. But I can't understand why we haven't done something about it. I mean, they set up in the same spot every night. We know where they are. We can all but see them, for God's sake," Bern said.

Daniel scratched the skin around his calf, which was raw and bleeding. "You really want to go out there?"

"It's got to be better than this. Waiting for the same thing every night." Bern leaned back and closed his eyes.

Even when they were in the rear lines, the shelling was constant. The distance between the front and back lines wasn't far, so the danger was very real no matter where they were. So far they'd been holding their position, but they'd gained little ground. They were itching for some action.

"How are ya today, Frankie?" Daniel looked over at his friend slumped against the dirt wall, his face grey and gaunt. He looked marginally better than yesterday.

They'd all lost weight in their two months at Gallipoli, but Frankie was skin and bone. Hundreds had been sent to military hospitals in Mudros, on the Greek island of Lemnos, about sixty miles west of the Dardanelles. Those left behind suffered crippling dysentery and dehydration.

Frankie winked. "Never better."

With a sliver of twilight left, and when he was sure no one was looking, Daniel opened his uniform pocket and took out the photo of Emma. A world away from Middle Tickle, he lay beneath a blanket of stars, wondering if she thought of him.

thirteen

June 1981
Plymouth, England

"MRS. PURCELL, YOU MUST HAVE BEEN SO FURIOUS WITH your father," Sarah said, before taking a bite from the sandwich a servant had laid out hours ago. She sat cross-legged in the wingback chair with her notebook sprawled on the floor in front of her, all attempts at taking notes abandoned as she listened to every word of the woman's story.

Emma smiled over the rim of her teacup. "Sarah, I've just spent the last three hours telling you something I haven't told another living soul in half a century or more. Don't you think it's time you started calling me Emma? And, yes, I was furious. Finding out he was the cause of Daniel's departure was hard enough, but the rest of it." She lowered her eyes to the embroidered handkerchief folded in her lap. "Knowing the lengths the Beresfords had gone to pay their debts to my father, and they lost a son in doing so." She paused. "I had to plan my departure from Middle Tickle carefully." She looked up again. "Newfoundland's geography is a challenge, so leaving wasn't as easy as it sounds. The train often didn't run for one reason or another, with sections of the track needing repairs. The weather is erratic." She smiled again, looking past Sarah. "First I had to get out of Middle Tickle to St. John's, and then to England, neither of which was straightforward."

"Were you not frightened to be travelling across the world alone, especially with a war raging on the other side?"

"I was young and foolish, my dear. I could think of nothing else but finding Daniel, you see. At the time I was naive enough to think I could find him easily and persuade him to come home with me. And luckily for me, the Grey name still carried a lot of weight. Shall we continue?"

Sarah reached for the teapot and refilled their cups. "Absolutely," she said, stirring a lump of sugar into the white china cup and taking a long sip.

November 1915
St. John's, Newfoundland

Emma walked into the Water Street office of one of her grandfather's oldest friends. Edgar Bowring was a tall, thin man with wire-framed glasses. He wore a grey, pinstriped suit, and a gold timepiece dangled from his vest pocket. Several years had passed since she'd last seen him.

"Good afternoon, Mr. Bowring," Emma said, stepping inside the spacious office.

He stood behind the large mahogany desk and searched her face, a questioning look in his eyes.

"It's been a few years since we've seen each other. I'm Emma, Oliver's granddaughter."

"Emma! Forgive me. It's been too long." He stepped out around the desk and took her in a warm embrace much like her grandfather used to. "My heavens, you've grown into a beautiful young woman. Just like your mother."

Emma cast her eyes to the floor, hoping the similarities ended there.

His smiled faded. "I was sorry to hear of your grandfather's passing, my dear. He was a great man. We will surely miss him around these parts. I've lost a few friends lately. Makes one question his own mortality."

He looked around her toward the door. "Is your father joining us?"

Emma breathed in deep, letting it out slowly. "It's just me, sir. I'm hoping you can assist me."

"Of course. Please, sit." He pointed to a paisley wingback chair and sat across from her in an identical one. The gleaming silver from the pot of a small tea service on a table between the two chairs caught her eye.

"Join me?" He nodded toward the table.

"Yes, thank you," she replied.

He poured tea into a flawless gold-rimmed china cup, decorated with red roses, and laid it on a matching saucer next to a silver spoon and handed it to her. "I haven't heard much from your father this last year. I assume everything is all right?"

He handed her a cup and saucer and motioned to the sugar cubes. She waved a hand to decline.

Everything was most certainly not all right! Her father had lied to her, held a family's boat hostage, and driven away the only boy she'd ever loved. And now that boy was God knows where, fighting in a war, when he should be here with her.

"Father is incredibly busy, Mr. Bowring. As you know, the business side does not come easy to him like it did for my grandfather."

She lifted the cup to her lips.

He leaned back in his chair, crossed his long legs, and sipped from his cup. "Oliver confided in me on several occasions about his reservations where your father was concerned. How is business?"

If Mr. Bowring was as shrewd as her grandfather had always said he was, he might seize the opportunity to swoop in and take over if and when her father failed.

"Well, it's been a few difficult years."

"Mmm. For us all," he said, his eyes never leaving hers.

"But things will settle out. They always do."

She didn't believe that at all. She gave her father a year, at best, without her to balance the accounts. But it was no odds to her anymore. As far as she was concerned, he was on his own, and if he went belly up and Mr. Bowring moved in, so be it. Her only priority was getting out of St. John's before her father found her.

"So, what can I help you with, my dear?"

She sipped the strong tea. "I was hoping you could help me arrange passage to England. I'd like to go see my mother."

He raised his eyebrows over his cup. "I certainly can, yes, but wouldn't your father be best equipped to do so?"

Several seconds ticked by, and she took another sip. It was bitter without sugar. She had been using molasses in her tea since Daniel's mother had introduced it, but she wouldn't go so far as to ask Mr. Bowring for molasses. After all, it was a sentimental act.

"Several families have just arrived back from the Labrador with fish, and he's busy. I told him not to worry himself. I knew I could speak directly with you when I arrived here in St. John's. I assured him you would be only more than happy to help, since you and grandfather were so close." She was padding it on thick now, but she would do anything to get to England.

"Of course, Emma. In fact, you can travel on one of my vessels. When would you like to go?"

"Immediately."

He sat up straight. "So soon? All right, well, the *Rosalind* is leaving tomorrow. I can arrange a comfortable cabin for you."

Her heart beat wildly. She didn't care if she had to cross the North Atlantic in a dory.

The cup clinked against the saucer as she laid them on the table. "I am most appreciative, Mr. Bowring." She opened her small clutch purse and pulled out several colourful cash notes. She had no idea how much a crossing to England cost, but it had to be far more than what she paid to get to St. John's.

He laid down his cup, spilling the remainder of its contents into the saucer. He left it. "Emma. Put that away. Your money is no good here. Your grandfather would have done the same for one of mine."

She stood, and he wrapped his arms around her, rubbing her back for a few seconds before he stopped.

"Thank you, sir," she said.

He stepped back and eyed her. "Been some time since you've seen your mother."

Her mother be damned.

She nodded and pulled in a deep breath. She had done well until now and was close to getting what she needed. She must keep it together a little while longer.

He placed a light hand on her shoulder as he led her toward the door. "All right, let's see what we can do to change that."

In St. John's harbour, nestled beneath the snow-crusted South Side Hills, Emma made her way to the busy waterfront to board the *Rosalind*. According to Mr. Bowring, it was about a ten-day passage to Devon, though as always it was entirely weather-dependent.

She spied the boat, just one of many in Bowring's Red Cross Steamship Line, and made her way toward the long, navy blue and white vessel. Black smoke billowed from the stack, and men came from every direction carrying cargo aboard. Mr. Bowring had explained the *Rosalind* usually did the Halifax–New York run, but most of his vessels were being used by the government now for official war-related business. The *Rosalind* was on her way to England for just such use, and this was her last trip carrying regular passengers and cargo.

A young man, maybe a few years older than she, stood next to the gangway and spied her with anxious eyes, his hands fidgeting by his side.

"Miss Tavenor?"

"Yes."

"Please, come aboard here." He gestured toward the gangway and reached for her case. "My name is John Pearce. I'll take your things."

Emma smiled. "You have a Devon accent." It had been a while, but it was reminiscent of her grandfather's servants.

He smiled. "Plymouth."

"What a coincidence. I'm going to Plymouth, too." She returned his smile as he took her arm and led her up the gangway to the *Rosalind*'s deck.

"Yes, I know. You're Mr. Grey's granddaughter." He opened the door and held it, ushering her inside.

She blinked, adjusting to the darkness inside. The smell of polished wood filled her nostrils. She turned to him. "You knew my grandfather?"

"No, not personally, but everybody in Plymouth knew who Mr. Grey was."

"Yes, of course." Her grandfather had employed half of Plymouth at one time or another. She felt a pang of sadness. It was beginning to sink in; he would not be in Plymouth when she arrived. She avoided thinking about what would be there. Her mother.

"This way, Miss Tavenor." He turned left. "Follow me."

She lifted the hem of her skirt as they went down several flights of stairs until they entered a hallway with dark wainscotting. He swung open a door and stepped aside for her to enter.

It was a spacious room with a double bed covered in a crimson spread and two square pillows. A painting of St. John's harbour hung on the wall over the bed. Underneath the round porthole were two chairs and a small table with ornate woodwork on their legs. Cream-coloured stationery and a fountain pen lay on a wooden desk that was fastened to the floor. She recalled travelling to England in a similar cabin with her mother several years ago.

She walked around the room. "Oh, this is quite lovely."

John stood in the doorway with her bags in his hands. "May I come inside?"

Emma swung around. "Of course, yes."

John's shy smile reminded her of Daniel, especially when he cast his eyes to the ground. Daniel always looked down, as if he wasn't sure if he should be looking at her at all.

He crossed the room, laid her dark blue travel cases next to the bed, and returned to the doorway. He took his hat off and held it in his hands.

She watched him a moment longer.

"Is everything all right, Miss Tavenor?"

"Hmm? Yes." She shook her head. "Sorry, you just remind me of someone."

"I will leave you to settle in. The captain has invited you to be his guest at dinner this evening. He dines promptly at eight. I will be back at quarter to the hour to accompany you."

Emma looked around the room again. "That's quite all right. I'm sure I will find my way. You need not fuss over me."

John looked at her like she had ten heads. "Oh, no. You can't be left wandering the ship on your own, Miss Tavenor. The captain wouldn't be happy about that. In the meantime, if you need anything, just send for me. I'll be taking care of you on the voyage."

"Taking care of me?"

"Mr. Bowring insisted on it, and the captain has given me strict orders, and I take my job very seriously."

"And what would happen if you didn't?"

His eyes widened. "Oh, dear, well, I wouldn't want to find out."

She laughed. "Thank you. Please, give my thanks to the captain."

"Yes, Miss Tavenor. If there's nothing else, I'll be on my way."

He put on his hat and backed out through the door, closing it behind him.

Emma crossed the room and looked in the mirror at her pale reflection. What was she doing? She hadn't given much thought as to how she would find Daniel when she got to England. She couldn't just waltz into a training camp with thousands of men and start asking for him. And how would he even react to seeing her? He'd left because of what her father had done to his family. He may want nothing to do with her again. She blinked a few times and walked over to her brown valise.

She pulled out a bulky leather-bound book bulging with letters. She untied the straps, and the letters flowed onto the bed. They were all addressed to Daniel. She would never embarrass him in front of the others, so she had never sent them. She wrote them for herself, mostly, but hoped one day maybe they would read them together. She lay back on the pillows, opened one, and started reading.

fourteen

November 1915
Gallipoli, Turkey

DANIEL BLEW INTO THE TRIGGER MECHANISM OF HIS RIFLE. Another layer of dust had already settled there, even though it had been cleaned a few hours ago. He caught movement out of the corner of his eye and turned. Captain Donnelly walked toward them, bent forward so his head was lower than the edge of the trench. Their eyes met.

"Heads up, fellas," Daniel said, his eyes flicking to the side.

Frankie, Phonse, and Bern straightened up, careful not to let the cleaned rifle pieces tumble from their laps. Saluting an officer in the field was forbidden.

"Afternoon, sir," Bern said.

Donnelly crouched next to Frankie. "You lads belong to Second Lieutenant Winter?"

"Yes, Captain, that's us," Daniel said.

"Up for a bit of recon work?" he asked.

Daniel swatted at the swarm of flies clouding his face. The flies were thicker than anything he had experienced on the wharf after cleaning and gutting ten barrels of fish. His eyes moved between his three friends.

"Yes, sir," Daniel said. He wanted to add they'd do anything to break the monotonous routine they'd adopted since landing in the bay two months earlier. Daniel wasn't sure which was worse: standing the long watches, or digging endless lines of trenches, all under the constant harassment of snipers and artillery.

Captain Donnelly laid a hand-drawn map on top of a barrel and pointed to a section of terrain about a mile from their current location.

"We're going in as far as this ridge to see if we can do something about those Johnnies up here." His finger traced along the map. "On the path from the dugouts to the trenches, we're losing too many men to those sniping bastards in the evening hours. If they won't do us the courtesy of giving us a few hours' peace, we'll have to take it, won't we?"

Phonse piped up. "'Bout time I says."

Donnelly looked at Phonse. "Well, the CO shares your sentiments, Private. Are you up to it?"

"Looks like pretty rough terrain," Bern said.

"It is. You'll need your full kit and a day's rations. And as much ammo as you can carry."

The boys raised their eyebrows.

"I expect they'll be there as they have been every night. Only question is how many."

The boys looked at each other without speaking.

Donnelly slapped his hand on the map. "But we'll be there first, won't we?"

"Yes, sir, we will," Phonse replied.

"Good. We'll leave at fifteen thirty to give us enough time to get there and get set up well before dark." He picked up the map. "I've been told you lot are good shots, especially you." He pointed at Daniel. "So let's see what all the fuss is about, shall we?"

"Yes, sir!" they all replied at once.

Donnelly stowed the map and disappeared around the corner.

"He's got some thought of himself," Frankie muttered as he assembled his rifle.

Phonse pointed his thumb in the direction Donnelly had just gone. "He came looking for us. He can't be all that bad."

"Smarmy bugger," Frankie said with a mock British accent, sly eyes, and a grin.

Daniel leaned back against the trench wall and pulled his cap down over his eyes. Since his arrival at Gallipoli, he'd had no problem doing his fair share of firing from the refuge of the mud pits, but this was going to be different.

Daniel, Frankie, Phonse, Bern, and four other men followed Donnelly from the trenches and through the brush. The waning sun was at their backs as they moved toward the knoll where the snipers set up shop every evening. Donnelly assured them the route was outside the Turks' field of vision.

Daniel fell in next to Phonse. "What do you think?"

Phonse hesitated. "Not so sure about this, Danny."

"Why? You thought it was a good idea this afternoon."

"Don't think we should be leaving while it's light out."

"The whole point is to get there before they do, Phonse. Besides, even if they could see us, the sun is in their eyes now."

"I know, I know, but it's still dangerous."

Donnelly and the others were well ahead.

Daniel laughed. "You just figured that out?"

Phonse chuckled. "Don't get me wrong. I'm happy to take my chances back there like all of us. But this?" He hesitated. "It's like inviting trouble."

"The way I see it, we have the advantage," Daniel said.

"How?"

"We know where they're going."

"So?"

"They don't know we're coming."

"Hmm."

Daniel placed a hand on his friend's back as they hiked through the dense brush and rocky terrain, knowing the Turks would soon be en route from the other direction. He'd never imagined a whole lot for his life. He figured most of it would be spent in a boat. Along came Emma, and his world took on a whole new realm of imaginings. But of all the things he'd imagined, he'd never thought he'd be climbing over fallen trees and up steep slopes thousands of miles from Newfoundland with an army of men a few yards away trained to kill him. Then again, he'd never imagined a world without Richard in it. And he still didn't know how to live in a world without her.

This was the farthest they had been from the beach. With the chill in the air, he could almost believe they were wandering the big hills behind Middle Tickle. It took less than an hour to reach their destination.

"This is it." Donnelly climbed to the top of the knoll and got on his knees, looking down at the British front lines below. The boys followed and crouched beside him. The vantage point showed several places where their men were exposed as they passed through their own trenches.

"Probably how McWhirter got it that day," Daniel muttered, thinking of a fellow they'd become acquainted with at Fort George in Scotland. He'd come over with the second wave of recruits from the west coast of Newfoundland and had been shot within days of landing at Suvla Bay.

"Well, no more, lads," Donnelly whispered. "Not after tonight."

Captain Donnelly moved to his right and motioned for the men to join him. They were at the top of the ridge, now, in an area obscured by thick brush. Empty ammo boxes littered the sniper posts along the ridge line, and—judging by the smell—a makeshift latrine was nearby. A well-beaten path looked like it led away from the ridge toward the Turk lines.

"Find a spot to hunker down where you can stay concealed. Wait until they're close enough and there's nowhere for them to go. Don't move or fire until I give the order. Understood?"

"Yes, sir," they replied in hushed voices.

Laughter erupted to their right. Captain Donnelly held his hand up.

Daniel's stomach did a loop.

"Go. Wait for my signal," Donnelly said, raising a finger to his lips.

Frankie was on his heels as he crawled to a spot where a dying tree was intertwined with several others into one large trunk. The trees must have been hundreds of years old. Daniel settled in against the roots and pulled a tumbleweed in front of him. He had a clear view of the ridge-line and could just make out Donnelly settling down on the path's right side.

He glanced back to see Frankie settling on the tree's opposite side. "We're supposed to spread out, Frankie."

Frankie arranged the branches so they covered him, his rifle cocked and ready. "I'm not going nowhere by myself."

Daniel held a finger up to silence Frankie and looked away. The shadows grew longer as the sun dipped toward the horizon. Voices drifted on the cooling air. Boots crunched rocks, and twigs snapped.

Something poked Daniel in his side. He waved Frankie away without looking back.

The stick dug deeper into his side.

Daniel spun his head around, ready to snarl at Frankie. Instead, Frankie's mouth was hanging open, his eyes wide. He pointed up. Daniel followed the direction his finger indicated and came face to face with a snake hanging so low it almost touched his head. Wound around a large branch, its body was thick and black with a light-coloured zigzag pattern going down its back. They'd been warned about snakes in Turkey, but nobody said they were this big. Daniel was locked in place, out of awe more than anything else.

The voices grew. Daniel stared into the snake's black eyes. It hissed, as if saying it didn't appreciate the trespassing, its tongue darting out in a quick flash. Daniel gulped. He had never seen a snake before.

The voices were only yards away. He tightened the grip on his rifle and held his breath. The snake's head shifted to the left, its gaze still locked on Daniel.

Captain Donnelly shouted. The snake shifted again. Voices screamed words Daniel didn't understand.

"Fire!"

Without thinking, Daniel rolled away from the snake as fast as he could manage with a rifle against his chest. Once. Twice. Rifles fired, all Lee-Enfields. He stopped and glimpsed the snake, hanging in the branch as though nothing had happened. Daniel crawled forward and began firing his rifle just as the shooting stopped.

He looked from side to side. Two Turks lay motionless near some wooden boxes. A canteen dripped water. A third man sprinted along the path.

"Beresford! Whelan! Stay here. I'll get him," Captain Donnelly shouted.

Daniel brought up his rifle and aimed at the fleeing soldier, but he didn't shoot, as Captain Donnelly dropped into view.

"Where's he going?" Frankie asked.

They waited. Bern crouched to check the dead Turks. Daniel looked for Phonse. He stood a few yards away, his back to Daniel, but he wasn't watching for Donnelly. He was looking down.

A rifle fired down the path. Lee-Enfield again.

Daniel stood and joined Phonse. "Think he got him?" he asked.

Captain Donnelly emerged holding his rifle tight to the enemy's back. "Hold your fire!"

"What's he doing?" Frankie whispered to Daniel.

"Christ, he got a prisoner," Bern said as they lowered their weapons.

"Any more around?" Phonse called out.

"Not that I could see, but you can bet this little exchange has been heard. There'll be more coming," Captain Donnelly said, motioning to Bern. "Tie his hands."

He pushed the Turk toward Bern. Between rapid breaths, the soldier pleaded, babbling in his own language while Bern worked, tying his hands behind his back. Occasionally they heard the word "please."

"Beresford and Whelan, you two head back to the lines for reinforcements," Donnelly said.

"What are you going to do with him?" Bern asked when he finished tying the Turk's hands.

The Turk looked at Daniel with eyes not a day older than his own. He fell in a heap at their feet and slouched over, repeating some kind of chant.

Donnelly grinned. "I'm not going to do anything with him. You're going to take him with you."

"What?" Frankie glanced at Daniel. "Seriously?"

Captain Donnelly got in Frankie's face. "You have a problem, Private?"

"No, sir. I just—"

Daniel chimed in. "What do you want us to do with him once we get there?"

Captain Donnelly looked at Daniel. "The CO will decide. Tell him we need more men. If we intend to keep this ridge, we'll need a dozen or so."

"Yes, sir," Daniel replied, and looked at Frankie. "Get him up. Let's go."

Daniel and Frankie set out for their own lines with the prisoner walking between them. The young Turk had stopped pleading or praying, or whatever it was he'd been doing, and seemed to be accepting his fate. Anyone watching could have mistaken them for three buddies rambling through the woods, except for Daniel's rifle in the boy's back. They picked their way through the thick brush and rocky ground, using the dying glow of sunset to lead them toward their own trench.

"You know these guys were coming here tonight in the hopes of picking us off?" Frankie said.

"I know."

"So, why are we taking him back alive?"

"I don't know, Frankie. Maybe they want to question him."

"What if they hand him back? He might eventually shoot one of us."

Daniel stopped. "What are you saying? That we should shoot him?"

"No. I don't know." Frankie let out a long, audible sigh. "I don't know what I'm saying."

Voices erupted in the darkness. Daniel spun around, straining to hear the language.

"Johnny Turk?" Frankie asked.

"I don't know."

Their prisoner shouted.

"Jesus!" Daniel collared the young Turk, pushing him down on the ground and slapping his hand over the prisoner's mouth. The Turk bit down on his hand, and Daniel cursed a string of profanity as he recoiled. Something struck his head, and he rolled over, his ears ringing. He blinked, trying to clear his vision. The stars above were spinning.

"Danny!"

Daniel pulled in a full breath and tried to sit up. Nausea drove him back down.

"Danny! His arms are free. Danny!"

The voice sounded like Richard's. Men grunted a few feet away. The stars got brighter and spun faster.

"Danny, get over here! He's got a knife."

Daniel struggled to sit and felt around for his rifle. Instead, he found rocks and thorns. He reached around and pulled his bayonet from its scabbard and looked up. Red blurred his vision. He wiped it away and staggered toward the two forms.

"On top, Danny! He's on top of me!"

His vision cleared, and the figures came into view. The Turk straddled Frankie, and both had their hands on a knife hovering just inches above Frankie's head. Daniel held the bayonet with both hands and scrambled toward the pair. He hauled the Turk off Frankie and collapsed on top of him, driving the bayonet into the Turk's belly.

The boy gasped, his brown eyes so wide Daniel could see them in the dark. The Turk gurgled, and his chest heaved in rapid spurts as he struggled for air. He held Daniel's shirt and tried to speak, but choked on blood instead. His breathing slowed, and he released Daniel. A tear formed in the corner of his eye and dropped. A moment later, the boy was dead.

"Jesus. Jesus. Jesus."

fifteen

November 1915
Somewhere in the North Atlantic

EMMA LEANED AGAINST THE *ROSALIND*'S RAIL AND STARED AT the endless smooth sea. She had convinced John to go outside on the way to the captain's dining room. She adjusted her coat and scarf against the crisp November wind. The moon was bright and shone like a beam clear across the North Atlantic.

"It's beautiful out here," she said.

"'Tis so," John replied. "Enjoy it while it lasts. We'll encounter some heavy seas before we get across."

She turned to face him. "John, can I ask you a personal question?"

"Certainly, Miss Tavenor. Though I can't imagine what you might want to know about me."

"Why have you not enlisted with the British Army?"

An afternoon of reading the letters she'd written to Daniel had made her curious. Their eyes met for a split second before he averted his gaze toward the ship's deck.

"I'm afraid I cannot, miss."

"You mean you cannot bring yourself to enlist?"

She understood Daniel's reasoning now for wanting to get away, though she still believed joining the army was a bit severe. He could have just gone to St. John's, but men were signing up for the Newfoundland Regiment and the naval reserve in hordes and droves at home. Here was a proper Englishman, and he hadn't signed up.

"No, it's nothing of the sort. I would go if I could, if they would take me, but they won't." His head drooped. "My three brothers have all enlisted."

She placed a hand on his arm.

"My mother is broken-hearted." He took off his hat and twisted it in his hands. "She worries something will happen to them and she'll be left all alone. My father died years ago."

"You being home is a good thing, then."

"There's nothing good about it. Most of my friends are gone, too, but I . . . it's my lungs, you see. They're good enough to work, but not for the rigours of army training. The boys are off on a big adventure. Is there a more noble cause than to fight for your country?"

"Someone needs to take care of your mother." She patted his hand, and he stopped twisting his hat. "And that's a noble thing to do."

He placed his arm at the small of her back. "Come, Miss Tavenor. The captain will be wondering where you've got to."

John rapped twice on the door and opened it, motioning for her to step inside the spacious dining room. A sixteen-seat table was set for three, with bone-white china and a silver service setting. Those in the Bowrings' employ were spared no details in comfort, even when they were at sea.

Captain Winslow stood as she entered and extended an arm. "Ah, Miss Tavenor, thank you for joining me this evening."

He was a tall, burly man with a thick, grey beard and kind eyes that reminded her of her grandfather's.

She held out her hand, and he accepted. "Thank you for having me, Captain. It's lovely to meet you."

"We're just waiting on one more."

As if on cue, the door opened, and a slender woman at least five years her senior appeared.

"Miss Cluett," Captain Winslow said. "Do come in."

Emma smiled at the woman, whose dark brown hair was pinned high on her head.

"That will be all, John," Captain Winslow said, as he pulled out their chairs and seated them both. "What a lucky man I am to dine with two beautiful ladies this evening."

Miss Cluett shifted, her cheeks reddening. Emma didn't thrive on compliments, by any means, but was aware her appearance was appealing. She was guessing from the woman's deep blush that Miss Cluett was not.

"Miss Tavenor—" Captain Winslow started.

"Call me Emma, please."

"Very well, Emma, allow me to introduce Miss Frances Cluett from Belleoram."

She smiled. "Call me Fanny."

"Hello, Fanny, it's nice to make your acquaintance."

Fanny's wide-set chocolate brown eyes matched her brown hair. She wasn't a stunning beauty, but she was tall, and her plain brown dress accentuated her slender form. She had a soft demeanour and an overall pleasantness about her.

"And you."

A quick knock sounded at the door. Two men entered with platters and served the threesome.

"I detect a trace of an accent. You going home, Emma?" Fanny asked.

She supposed in many ways England was home, but since her grand-father's death, she no longer felt a deep connection to the place anymore. She felt even more disconnected because her mother had been hiding there for several years, without returning or even sending for her.

"My mother is English, and I did most of my schooling there."

Her grandfather had insisted she be schooled in England, so she had spent only the summers in St. John's, but when he got sick, her mother sent her to live in Middle Tickle with her father. While there, she'd grown to love the small outport and its inhabitants, one in particular.

"My father is from Newfoundland, and I've lived there for some years now. So, Newfoundland is my home." Emma tried a spoonful of fish soup that had been laid in front of her. "Are you visiting family in England?"

Before Fanny had a chance to answer, Captain Winslow chimed in. "Would you believe Fanny's off to join the war?"

Emma's spoon clanked in the china bowl and splashed liquid onto the tablecloth. "What on earth are you going to do?"

"That was almost the same reaction my father had when I told him," Fanny said. "I'm going to train and work with the Voluntary Aid Detachment."

"As what?"

"They call us VADs."

"She's going to be a nurse," Captain Winslow said.

Fanny shook her head. "A nurse's helper, really. I will assist nurses and carry out some housekeeping duties." She picked up her spoon and tried the soup. "This is delicious, Captain. You have a fine cook on board."

"It makes the journey more bearable." He lifted his glass to them. "That and the brandy."

Emma's mind raced as she tried to process Fanny's words. She had a ton of questions but didn't know where to start. "Where will you train?"

"At the Royal Victoria in South London, but there are training hos-pitals all over England now."

"Will you go to France?" Emma asked.

Fanny laid down her spoon and looked thoughtful. "I'll go wherever they send me, I suppose."

"But why would you want to do such a thing? Surely you'd rather stay home?"

Fanny shrugged. "Why should our boys be the only ones partaking in the adventure? Besides, there's a real need for VADs. I feel like I would be doing my part, you know?"

Emma didn't know. She'd wasted several pages of foolscap trying to get her thoughts straight so she could convince Daniel to give up this business of fighting in the war.

"Surely it's not going to last long enough to warrant female enlistment, will it?" Emma looked back and forth between Captain Winslow and Fanny.

"It's already gone on much longer than any of us thought it would," Captain Winslow said.

Fanny nodded, sipping the Merlot in her glass. "Yes, and this business in the Dardanelles is not going well. Since our boys are there now, I feel more strongly than ever that I should be doing my bit, considering what they're going through."

"You're a brave girl, Miss Cluett. I commend you." Captain Winslow raised his glass to her.

Emma thought back to her geography courses.

"The Dardanelles," Emma said, the words catching in her parched throat. She swallowed hard. "That's in Turkey, but our boys are in a training camp in England, are they not?"

Fanny shook her head. "No, the Regiment has been in Gallipoli since September, about two months now. My cousin, William, wrote to us just before he shipped out. Apparently a Scottish Regiment was en route but got involved in a terrible train wreck, and the Newfoundland Regiment was called up."

Emma's heart threatened to stop. All this time she had believed Daniel was safe in England.

"Terrible business," Fanny said. "William says they're all quite sick and the terrain is difficult to navigate."

Fanny continued with details of her cousin's letter, describing the general war conditions in Turkey, but Emma heard nothing else. She had to get back to her cabin before she broke down. She stood, holding the table to keep her balance. Her breathing was shallow.

Captain Winslow placed a hand on her arm. "Are you all right, Emma?"

"I'm sorry. Will you please excuse me? I must lie down."

Fanny jumped to her feet and placed an arm around Emma. "Of course. Please, let me help you."

"I'll be fine. It's just a bit of seasickness."

"John!" Captain Winslow called.

The door opened, and John appeared.

"Miss Tavenor is feeling ill. Would you please see her to her room?"

John's eyes widened, and he stepped forward and took her arm, leading her to the door. "Yes, Captain."

Remembering her manners, she turned around and gave a half-hearted smile. "Captain Winslow, thank you for the lovely meal. Good night, Fanny."

"Good night, Emma. I will check in on you before I turn in for the night," she said with a slight smile. "Get some rest."

Emma was thankful for the silence as John guided her back to her cabin. It gave her time to think. Daniel was in Turkey, and the conditions were poor. Was he sick? Had he been wounded, or worse? Her knees went weak.

John tightened his arm around her waist. "Come on, Miss Tavenor, we're almost there."

Her heart thudded in her ears.

He guided her to the bed and helped her sit back against the soft cushions. "Are you all right, Miss Tavenor? Would you like me to get you anything?"

"I will be, John. I just received some unexpected news." Her lip quivered, and she covered her mouth with her hand.

"I will fetch you some brandy."

She drew her legs up to her chest and wrapped her arms around them. Her mind raced while she waited for John to return. Because of her, Daniel was in some godforsaken country fighting a war that had nothing to do with him.

John appeared before her with a tumbler of amber liquid. "Here. Drink this."

In her entire life, Emma hadn't had more than a few sips of wine, but she snatched the tumbler of brandy and emptied it. She handed him back the glass.

John raised his eyebrows. "Shall I get you another?"

The brandy burned on the way down, but her racing thoughts slowed enough so she could think straight.

She shook her head. "No, I'm fine, John, thank you. It's just what I needed."

"Do you need anything else?

"No." She smiled. "Thank you for your help. I'll be fine now."

"Good night, Miss Tavenor."

"Good night, John." The door clicked behind him.

She stayed there, her body swaying from side to side as the ship rocked over the waves. A few short months ago she felt safe and loved, and now her life was spiralling out of control. Daniel had slipped beyond her grasp and was fighting in some foreign land. She had to carry through with her plans. She would find him no matter the cost. A soft knock broke through her thoughts, and she crossed the room.

Fanny's big brown eyes stared at her. "Emma. How are you feeling now?"

She opened the door wide and smiled. "Better, Fanny, thank you. Can you come in for a few minutes?"

Fanny stepped inside.

Emma closed the door and turned to face her new friend. She gestured to the chair at the table. "Please, sit." Fanny sat, and Emma sat across from her. She folded her hands and placed them on the table. "I need your help."

"Anything."

"How does one become a VAD?"

sixteen

November 1915
Plymouth, England

EMMA STOOD ON THE DOORSTEP OF HER GRANDFATHER'S sprawling estate in Plymouth. The last time she'd been here she was twelve years old. She stepped into the large wooded atrium, and her eyes scanned the grand staircase carpeted in a deep crimson. Fresh flowers adorned the shiny surface of the foyer's round table, its intricately carved legs a piece of art in its own right. To the right, a set of double doors led to the library where she'd spent many hours reading in the comfortable window seat. Everything about the place looked the same. The only thing different was her.

"Excuse me!" a sharp voice called. "What do you think you're playing at?"

A young housemaid hurried toward her. Emma laid down her bag and pushed back the bonnet of her blue velvet cloak. It had been raining when she'd left the train station.

"Hallo. I'm—"

The girl wagged her finger and leaned in so close Emma could smell tea on the girl's breath. "I don't give a toss who you are. The servants' entrance is at the back. If you want the job bad enough, you'd better go quickly before anyone else sees you. Now go. 'Round the back."

The girl grabbed Emma by the shoulders, trying to turn her around, but she resisted, turning herself back around. "No, you don't understand."

"I understand perfectly well. Mrs. Evans will have your head, not to mention what Mrs. Grey will do. She'll go off on one of her tirades, and believe me, none of us needs that. It's bad enough as it is."

Even though her mother had married her father, she had never taken his name. And what did she mean by one of her tirades?

"Mrs. Evans is still here?" Mrs. Evans was an Irishwoman who'd been employed by Emma's grandfather since long before her grandmother died. She ran the household and had practically raised Emma after she was born.

"Of course she's still here." The girl stepped back, sizing Emma up. "Has she recommended you for the job, then?"

Emma leaned forward, lowering her voice. "How much does the job pay?"

Mrs. Evans appeared in the library's doorway. "What in the name of all that's holy is going on out here, Betsy?"

After all these years living away from Ireland, the lyrical lilt of her brogue was still intact. Emma smiled as the click of the woman's shoes got closer.

The maid threw her hands up in the air. "Oh, you've done it now. I warned you."

She took a step back from Emma, as if to show Mrs. Evans she had nothing to do with the stranger's grave error. The maid wheeled around to face the woman as she strode into the foyer.

"I'm sorry, Mrs. Evans. I told her to go to the servants' entrance, but it seems madam here has a thought of herself."

Mrs. Evans gasped. "Emma!"

Emma's eyes widened, and she smiled. "You are a welcome sight, Mrs. Evans. I didn't think you'd still be here."

"Where else would I go?"

Emma laughed. "You recognize me."

Mrs. Evans pulled her into a fierce hug. "I'd know you anywhere, my child." She kissed Emma on the forehead, her hands cradling her face. She looked into her eyes. "Beautiful, beautiful girl. I would never forget those eyes."

"What's going on? Who is this?" Betsy asked.

Mrs. Evans wiped at her eyes and put an arm around Emma's shoulder, ushering her past the library and into the drawing room, ignoring Betsy's questions.

"Right. Let's get you settled." She leaned in close. "I take it she's not expecting you?"

Emma shook her head. "I left suddenly. There wasn't much time to write." That wasn't entirely true.

Mrs. Evans looked her up and down. "Are you hurt?"

She put her hand on her chest and stifled a cry. "Just in here."

Mrs. Evans embraced Emma and led her to a red settee. "Betsy, she's not here for a job. This is Emma Tavenor, Mrs. Grey's daughter."

Betsy's eyes widened. "Really? But . . ."

"But what, dear girl?"

"She seems so nice."

Emma and Mrs. Evans laughed so hard, they fell against each other.

"Please, Betsy, can you get us some tea?"

Betsy took a moment before tearing her eyes from Emma. "Yes, Mrs. Evans."

Mrs. Evans put her arms around Emma and offered a smile. "My dear girl, I've missed you. But you're home now. Tell me what has you so upset, dear. Whatever it is, we can sort it out. It can't be that bad."

Emma sighed. "It is, Mrs. Evans," she said, dabbing her eyes with a handkerchief. "It's terrible, and it's all my fault."

She began the long tale of what had happened in Middle Tickle, her father's part in driving Daniel away, as well as her guilt at his enlistment in the Newfoundland Regiment. All of this was compounded by new fears now that he was fighting in Turkey. Mrs. Evans listened to every detail, and neither bothered to look up when Betsy arrived with tea and biscuits.

Emma straightened her skirt. "I just need to find him."

"Emma, dear, the boy has joined the war. I'm afraid it isn't as simple as just finding him. He's committed to serve his country. He'll have to go wherever they send him."

Emma nodded. "Yes, but he's done it for the wrong reasons. I need to stop him before something happens."

Mrs. Evans stroked Emma's long hair. "You can't stop him, dear girl. It's impossible."

"It isn't. I just need to know where he is."

"How are you going to learn this?"

Emma pulled away and blinked the moisture from her eyes. She straightened the hem of her skirt. "Well, not by crying. I need information, that's what I need. Information on the Newfoundland Regiment and where they're going next."

The woman patted her hand. "Right. Well, first things first. Let's get you some lunch, shall we?"

Mrs. Evans could always comfort her, even when she was a small child. A pang of guilt jabbed in her stomach. She'd been pouring her heart out, and not once had she so much as asked about her mother. Emma heaved a long, tired sigh and stood, looking toward the door and back to Mrs. Evans.

"I am hungry," she said in a hushed voice. "But before I can even think about eating, Mrs. Evans, I have to ask. How bad is it?"

Mrs. Evans shook her head. "It's not good, I'm afraid. Not good at all."

～

Emma wandered through the library, sliding her hand across the neatly shelved books. Her grandfather's sturdy walnut writing desk still faced the window with the estate's lush gardens as a backdrop. She sat and leaned back in his chair. There were so many memories in this room. She closed her eyes, recalling how she would start out hiding from Mrs. Evans and wind up in here. Her grandfather was most always working at this desk, and she would leap into his lap, begging him to read her a story. No matter how busy he was, he would always oblige, and within a few minutes she had forgotten her game of hide and seek and was enthralled with the words coming out of his mouth.

She opened up the drawer to see if *The Blue Fairy Book* by Andrew Lang was still there. After all these years, someone had probably removed it by now. The drawer groaned and hesitated a little as she pulled it out. Tucked tight against the drawer's side wall, she recognized its cover and removed it, opening it carefully. The cursive loops on the inside page read, "To My Darling Emma, With Love, Grandfather Ollie." After flipping through a few pages, she closed it, hugging it tight against her chest.

The house was empty without him, and from what Mrs. Evans had told her, the staff were nearly at their wit's end with her mother's late-night drinking binges and violent outbursts. She suggested maybe Emma's arrival was just the thing to bring her out of this cycle. She'd been bad before, but this was the worst in years, and she showed no signs of coming around.

When her grandfather was alive, he was able to manage her mother's erratic behaviour. Saying he could control her wasn't quite accurate, but she did listen to him from time to time. Oliver Grey was a kind man, and over the years he did everything he could to keep his daughter happy. Sadly, she didn't deserve him, for if she feared anything, it was the loss of the financial security he provided. He was no fool, but he loved her despite her shortcomings. Her grandfather had always told Emma he hoped she would change, but like Emma, and her father, he'd always known it was unlikely.

Emma was old enough to understand her mother now and realized Rose Grey lived her life in a series of whims, moving from one to the next, giving very little thought to her actions and how they impacted those around her. Her father had been one of those whims, and though it pained her to admit it, Emma knew she was the result of that particular whim.

Taking up with the handsome Edward Tavenor, a man of no means, while visiting her father in Newfoundland one summer was bad enough, but becoming pregnant with his child was a scandalous ordeal for the entire family. Her mother had no intention of marrying Tavenor, but after careful consideration, her father insisted. Tavenor might be a good-for-nothing, but Oliver Grey would not see his only grandchild born into the world as a bastard.

She heard Mrs. Evans's voice in the hall. "Good afternoon, Mrs. Grey. How did you sleep?"

"Is there any mail today?" a curt voice replied, ignoring Mrs. Evans's pleasantries.

"Yes, ma'am. There are a few things, and lunch is set in the dining room." Mrs. Evans hesitated. "And there's a surprise visitor waiting for you."

"I'm not taking visitors today."

"I expect you'll be wanting to see this one."

Her mother sighed with expressed irritation. "I am not a child, Mrs. Evans. I hate surprises. Well, come on, let's get it over with."

Emma's hands shook. She took a deep breath and opened a seldom-used door between the library and the drawing room. When her mother entered, Emma was standing near the fireplace.

"Yes, well, Mrs. Evans, this had better be good."

Her mother's eyes widened, and she stopped just inside the door. She still had an affinity for the finer things, Emma noted, taking in the purple chiffon dress and the handsome pearls strung around her neck. Emma's eyes shifted to the protruding collarbone. Her once bright skin was sallow, and her eyes were lifeless.

Emma fidgeted with her hands. "Hallo, Mother."

When she'd shown up, Mrs. Evans had embraced her immediately. Her mother stared at her as if she were some random maid who had come for the job. Emma had never felt as close to her mother as she did her father, but she hadn't expected this degree of coldness.

Her mother was fixed in one spot and hadn't so much as blinked. Her eyes held questions, and she opened and closed her mouth several times before she finally spoke. "Emma. What are you doing here?"

"How are you, Mother?" she asked.

Her mother's eyes darted around the room. "Is your father here?" It was as if she expected him to hop out from behind a piece of furniture.

Emma shook her head. Mother and daughter stood on either side of the room. The few feet of floor separating them felt as wide as the ocean she'd just crossed to get here. Mrs. Evans strode across the room and clutched Emma's hand, guiding her toward her mother.

"Well, isn't she a sight for sore eyes, Mrs. Grey? So beautiful, and all grown up." She coaxed Emma forward. The closer she got to her mother, the wispier the woman appeared. She'd seen healthier-looking corpses.

Her mother blinked a few times, as if still trying to process Emma's sudden appearance. She smiled, as if a switch had flipped, and welcomed Emma into her arms.

"Darling, it is so good to see you." She kissed her on the forehead.

As they embraced, Emma felt bones poking in every direction. She pulled away, feeling overcome with an uncomfortable strangeness.

"It's been a long time, Mother."

She touched her daughter's face. "Too long."

"Why haven't you sent for me?" She hadn't planned to launch right into the questions, but they bubbled so close to the surface.

Her mother moved to the settee Emma had shared with Mrs. Evans earlier and patted the spot next to her. "Come, sit. Mrs. Evans, some tea, please."

"Of course, Mrs. Grey."

Mrs. Evans gave Emma an encouraging smile and winked before leaving the room.

"It's been tough, Emma. Father's death was . . ." She sighed, trailing off.

"Nearly four years ago."

"Yes, well, you wouldn't understand."

"I miss him, too, terribly. But you just left me with Father and never came back," Emma choked out, and turned away. She promised herself she wouldn't break down. In many ways, she was far better off in Middle Tickle than she would have been here with her mother, judging by the state of her.

Her mother's eyes narrowed. "Has something happened? Has your father hurt you?"

Interesting question. Of course he hadn't hurt her in the physical sense. He never would. But, yes, he had hurt her. He'd hurt her very much. But she wasn't ready to share that part of her life with her mother. Not yet.

"No."

"Why didn't he wire to tell me to expect you?"

Emma smiled. "That's a bit of a long story."

A quizzical look crossed her mother's face, and she gave a curious smile. "Emma, does your father know you are here?"

It was likely he knew now. He would have made his way into St. John's, and she hadn't covered her tracks that well. If he asked enough questions, he'd eventually find out Edgar Bowring had helped her get to England. She winced at deceiving her grandfather's dear friend. Someday she would apologize to him and explain herself.

"Let's just say Father and I had a difference of opinion."

Her mother reached for Emma's hand. "I truly am happy to see you." She brought her daughter's hand to her mouth and kissed it, rubbing her cheek against it much like a cat would rub against its master's leg. "And of course you are welcome here. This will always be your home."

Uncomfortable with the sudden show of affection, Emma withdrew her hand. "Thank you, Mother."

Her mother stood. "It'll be nice to have another face in this house." She looked away. "It's been lonely here."

Emma pushed the anger down. "All you had to do was send for me. I could have visited." She shrugged. "Or you could have come home."

A scowl settled over her mother's face. "Newfoundland is not my home, and it's not yours, either."

She didn't entirely agree with her mother's statement. Middle Tickle had been a good home. The people had been kind to her, and if she hadn't gone to live with her father, she would never have met Daniel. But there was nothing left there for her now.

Everyone she cared for eventually abandoned her. First her mother, then Daniel, and as far as her father was concerned, well, he drove her away. She hoped Daniel was safe and would remain so until she found him again. Her mother's shrill voice brought her back.

"Darling, seeing as you're here, you'll need to be fitted for some nice gowns." Her mother looked her up and down. "In fact, we should do it soon, I'm having a dinner party next month."

Leave it to her mother to be more concerned with the frivolities of life.

"That's not necessary. I brought most of my clothes from home."

"Yes, well, I'm quite sure whatever flour-sack attire passes in New-foundland these days is not suitable for my party." A pinched look crossed her face, as though she were in pain. "I'll speak to Mrs. Evans about taking care of it."

Emma stared at her mother. The gall of this woman. "If you feel I will be an embarrassment, I can take my meal with Mrs. Evans and the other servants."

Servants. That would take some getting used to again. She frowned. And she shouldn't have said that. She never thought of Mrs. Evans as a servant.

Her mother smiled. "Don't be a child, Emma. I have certain obligations as head of this household you couldn't possibly understand."

Nor would she want to. It appeared as though her mother had become more of an egotistical chit than before.

"Cousin Helen will be here. You haven't seen her for many years."

Emma was surprised. Her mother had never liked Helen. She was a little younger and was an absolute stunner. She was smart and had married a very handsome man from a good family, according to her grandfather.

"Oh, yes, Helen. She's a wonderful person, a nice bit of fun. And very pretty, if I recall. I would very much like to see her." A snide look crossed her mother's face, and Emma continued. "Grandfather said she married a lovely man. A businessman, was it?"

She had no idea who cousin Helen had married, but she had stuck the knife in and was enjoying watching her mother squirm a little. Maybe she was more like her grandfather than she'd realized. He loved to bait her mother and sit back and watch as she unravelled. To invite Helen and her husband to dinner meant she needed something from them. It was more probable she needed something from him, if he had business interests.

Her mother wandered to a side table in the drawing room, which held an array of liquors, and poured amber liquid from a crystal decanter. It couldn't have been later than two o'clock in the afternoon. She sipped the drink before she answered.

"He's an army man, darling. They all are now."

Emma's face fell. She felt sorry for cousin Helen. Like Daniel, he was probably gone off to war, and Helen must be going out of her mind. She felt guilty for picking at her mother now and using Helen and her husband to do so.

"Oh, that's terrible. Well, I mean, not terrible. It's quite noble, I suppose." She didn't believe that. "But I feel for Helen, not knowing where he is from day to day."

Emma trailed off, lost in her own thoughts of Daniel and what he must be going through.

Her mother tossed back the glass's contents and laughed. "Oh, hold your pity, Emma. He's not in the trenches. He's actually running the war."

Emma was startled. "What do you mean? I thought you said he was in the army."

"Yes, I did. But before you start pinning a badge of honour on him, he's not in France or anywhere else. He's in London, in the War Office."

Emma raised her eyebrows. "What's he doing there?"

"He's a major or a general or something up here." Her mother raised her hand up to indicate a high ranking. "From what Helen says, he practically runs the British Army."

Emma sat still for a few minutes while her mother poured another drink.

"Well, Mother, perhaps we should go shopping for that dress."

A slow smile spread across Rose Grey's face.

seventeen

November 28, 1915
Gallipoli, Turkey

"DANNY! GET UP, COME ON, WE'VE GOT TO MOVE!" PHONSE'S voice broke through his fitful sleep. He was cold and wet. Phonse pulled on his arm, and when he opened his eyes, there was water everywhere. His head dipped under, and he coughed and gagged. Water rushed through the trench with much the same force as a raging waterfall, like the one he'd seen the year they fished in Labrador. His head dipped under again as the muffled sound of chaos above the surface gurgled in his ears. He bobbed above the water again, trying to find his legs to stand upright. All around them, men called for help.

Daniel seized something solid and found his feet. "What the hell is going on, Phonse?" he asked, spitting mud and water.

He glimpsed Phonse struggling to hold his balance. His mouth screamed words, inaudible against the powerful surge of water in the trenches. Daniel lost his footing again and hooked on to Phonse's shoulders, pulling him along. The current carried them a few feet, and they bumped into floating bodies and other debris. Daniel lost his grasp on Phonse, who caught on to Daniel's belt. Daniel clawed at the trench wall. The wire tore at his hand as the weight of Phonse holding on to his belt yanked him forward. Daniel held, gritting his teeth against the pain. His free hand swept behind him, looking for Phonse. He found fabric and pulled. He reeled Phonse in, and his friend climbed along Daniel's body until he found another piece of wire to grab on to.

He gripped the barbed wire for dear life, bending over to catch his breath. Blankets and books and rifles rushed by. Phonse leaned back against the wall and huffed.

"We're right underneath those hills," he shouted, pointing up. "Water is coming down by the barrel. The trench walls have given way on each side. The front lines are washed out, and so is the firing line!"

The chaos of howling winds and rushing water drowned him out, but Daniel got the gist of it.

"Where's Frankie and Bern?"

He pointed up the trench. "Back there!"

"Come on, let's make our way back." Daniel patted Phonse's shoulder, and the two plodded along in water well past their knees.

Thick, sticky mud settled on the trench floor, and they fought to move their heavy, waterlogged boots. Each step was physically draining.

"These Christly boots!"

Daniel looked around. Bern stood, his legs sprawled apart, and Frankie was bent over, hauling at one of Bern's legs.

"Daniel, Phonse!" Frankie shouted. "Get over here. He's stuck!"

The cold wind drove the rain into their faces. The drops stung like nails on the skin, a different kind of crucifixion.

Daniel and Phonse took hold of Bern's left leg and pulled, using all their strength to free his boot from the mud. It didn't budge an inch. Daniel grunted and pulled until his eyes bulged in their sockets.

He shook his head. "That boot's going nowhere."

Bern gripped Daniel's arm. His lips trembled. "Danny, don't leave me here to die like this."

Daniel caught Bern by the shoulders and looked him in the eye. "Don't be so foolish, Bern. You're coming with us. You just won't have no boots. Phonse, pull up on his leg."

Phonse was strong as an ox and as broad as one, too. Daniel kept Bern in place so he wouldn't fall over as Phonse pulled one of Bern's legs free. It came clear out of the boot, and Bern teetered, but Daniel held on tight. Frankie held Bern's newly freed leg, keeping them all balanced as water rushed through the trench. Phonse pulled the other leg out, and they let Bern down slowly.

"Now, come on!" Daniel called out. "Head for the support lines!"

"Over here, boys!" Lieutenant Donnelly called out as they rounded a corner.

Men with shovels and picks were furiously digging outlets in the trench walls to divert the rushing water.

"Beresford! You lot take these and go back where you came from, and do the same thing down there. We've got to give this water a place to go, or in another hour we'll all be floating in Suvla Bay!"

It took them half an hour to reach the trench's other side, wading through freezing, waist-high water.

"Bern, you okay?" He remembered his friend had no boots.

"Sure, Danny, I'm okay."

The water level hadn't gotten any higher over the last hour, so whatever Donnelly and the boys were doing to divert water on the left flank was working. More soldiers followed them to the trench's outer edge and started digging. Within two hours, the water receded and was no more than ankle deep in spots. Every muscle in Daniel's body ached as he stopped digging. Frankie, who was in some kind of trance, was still digging like a madman.

Daniel laid a hand on his friend's shoulder. "Frankie."

Frankie dug the spade into the mud and grunted as he tossed it overhead.

"Hey, Frankie. It's okay, b'y, you can stop now."

Frankie kept digging, aimlessly driving the shovel into pockets of mud.

"Frankie. If you don't stop, we're going to come through over on the Turks' side."

Frankie kept digging. The others stopped and leaned on their shovels.

Daniel yanked Frankie's shovel away. Frankie let go, wheeled around, and scrambled for his rifle. He took aim at Daniel, his eyes staring through him like he was the enemy.

Daniel stepped back with his hands in the air. Phonse leaped forward and pushed Frankie against the trench wall, hauling the rifle out of his hands.

"Frankie, what are you doing?" Phonse asked, as Frankie struggled against him.

Phonse pinned Frankie's arms down, and after writhing a few seconds, he collapsed against the muddy wall.

"I—" Frankie looked from face to face and dropped his head into his hands.

Phonse stepped back and threw Frankie's rifle on the ground.

"I'm sorry, Danny, I'm sorry. I don't know what I was thinking."

Daniel crouched next to him. "It's okay, Frankie." He looked around at the others. "I don't know if any of us know what to think anymore. Come on, get up. Let's get back to the support trenches and see what's going on."

He lifted Frankie up, and the boys said nothing as his sobs filled the night sky. Bern was limping, and Phonse took his arm to help him along. An eerie quiet fell over them. There had been no exchange of gunfire in several hours. Perhaps the Turks wanted a break as much as they did. It was still wet, it was still cold, and, after all, they were still human.

They were worse for the wear when they made their way through what was left of their trench near the front line. The communications trenches were gone altogether, and several dugouts had caved in. Daniel wondered if anyone had been inside and if they'd made it out. Apart from small pockets of soldiers huddled here and there, the battalion had congregated as far back as the artillery lines.

Second Lieutenant Winter stood with a group of soldiers and waved them over. Frankie moved forward like a zombie, the others following, as they made their way over to a makeshift camp where hot tea was being rationed out. They helped Bern down against some sandbags, and Daniel took a moment to look around. Dusk was fast approaching, and hundreds of soldiers filled the area. He didn't doubt the overflow spilled almost back to Kangaroo Beach, where they had landed a little over two months ago.

The Regiment tried to salvage what they could from the flood to begin the tedious job of rebuilding. Clad in their Mediterranean-issued outfit, they weren't prepared for the ice storm that ravaged the peninsula two days after the flood. Daniel stood in line and got a cup of tea for Bern. He brought it over and knelt down in front of him. "Let's have a look at them feet." He passed him the tin cup. Bern's shaky hand spilled the hot liquid as he brought it to his lips.

"I'm all right, Danny. Can't even feel 'em." Bern gave a half smile and sipped the tea.

Daniel looked down. A layer of caked-on mud was frozen over the thin, once navy-coloured socks. The cast of mud reminded Daniel of the mummies from the Egyptian tombs. Somehow he didn't think Bern's feet were as well-preserved as the mummies had been. Bern slipped into an exhausted slumber, and Daniel took out his pocket knife and cut away at the frozen socks.

Second Lieutenant Winter crouched beside him. "Jesus."

He was gone in a flash, and when he returned, he had an armful of supplies. Daniel and Winter said nothing as they worked. Winter laid out some straw and two empty sandbags and removed a small container from his pocket. Bern's toes were swollen to almost twice their normal size and were a deep purple colour. The top of his foot was red with large, pus-filled blisters. Daniel touched a blister in an effort to drain it, but it too was frozen. He put his hands around his friend's feet in an effort to warm them, and shuddered. Bern's feet were as hard as two junks of ice.

Winter opened a tin of whale oil and slathered it on Bern's feet before coating each foot with straw. Daniel placed each of Bern's feet inside a sandbag, arranged more straw as padding, and tied the bag around the man's calf with twine.

Daniel stood up and nodded at Winter. "Thanks for your help."

"It doesn't look good," Winter said, gripping Daniel's shoulder, a worried look creasing his forehead. "Keep an eye on him."

"I will," Daniel replied, as Winter walked away.

His body felt like lead, and he collapsed next to Phonse, who handed him a cup and a piece of hard biscuit. Daniel examined his right hand. A shallow wound ran the length of his palm, but the cold and mud had worked to stop the bleeding like a bandage. He watched Frankie and Bern, who had fallen asleep leaning against each other. Bern's wounds were terrible, but they were easy to see, unlike Frankie's.

It had taken months of hard labour to put their trenches in place, and in a matter of a few hours they had been destroyed. Supplies were required before they could even think about rebuilding, but the weather had been bad for days and showed no signs of letting up, so no ships were getting in. A few days later, it went from bad to worse as the temperature dropped.

"I can't believe I ever complained about the heat in this place," Phonse said through clattering teeth. "Seems like it was a dream."

Thank God there was still no action from the Turks. Maybe their guns were frozen. God knew it was cold enough. Daniel had seen some dirty northeasterlies blowing over the rugged shores of Middle Tickle, but he'd never seen anything like this. The rain turned to sleet, and ice pelted at them, driven forward by the unforgiving winds. Everywhere, men sat huddled in groups, trying to stay warm. They were usually a rowdy lot, laughing and carrying on despite what they'd been sent here to do, but not now. They'd been here two months, and three quarters of them were sick with one ailment or another. Hundreds were shipped out weekly to the hospital in Mudros. Now they'd just had the piss beaten out of them.

Mother Nature was relentless. The wind howled. Daniel had nothing left to give. He couldn't feel his fingers. He thought about Richard and what it must have felt like to freeze to death. The moisture gathering in his eyes froze to his eyelashes and stung. Maybe this was it. He would die here with his friends on the beach in Suvla Bay, thousands of miles from home. He faded in and out of sleep or unconsciousness, he couldn't tell which.

A lone voice broke through the howling wind.

"When sun rays crown thy pine-clad hills . . ."

eighteen

January 1916
Plymouth, England

"MY DARLING EMMA! WHAT A BEAUTIFUL YOUNG woman you've grown into." Cousin Helen embraced her, kissing both cheeks. "Lovely to see you. Are you back for long?"

Emma followed the woman's lead since her upper-class manners were lacking these days. She wasn't expected to hug or kiss anyone in Middle Tickle, besides Daniel, and their affection for each other went far beyond a little peck on the cheek. She blushed just thinking about the last time he'd kissed her.

She smiled. "Nice to see you, too, cousin Helen. I'm not sure how long I'm staying. I'm undecided."

Helen reached behind for her husband's hand. "George, this is Emma. Uncle Ollie's granddaughter."

She found it odd Helen referenced her dead grandfather as opposed to her living mother, who still hadn't joined them.

George reached for Emma's hand and kissed it. "George Whitby.

Pleased to make your acquaintance, Emma. You're even more beautiful than your grandfather described."

Her cheeks grew hot. "Thank you, Mr. Whitby."

"Nonsense. We're family. Call me George."

Emma's mother swooped into the room wearing an emerald-green gown with her hair pinned high on her head. Emma's eyes landed on her grandmother's ivory cameo choker, which was fastened around her mother's neck. "So sorry to have kept you all waiting," she said. "Helen, darling, it's been too long."

She half-heartedly embraced the woman before pushing her away and rushing toward George. She pawed at him.

"George, you handsome devil." George coughed and, after a moment, wriggled free from the embrace.

Emma cast a sideways glance at Helen, who wore a tight smile.

Her mother had taken special pains with her appearance this evening, and she looked exquisite. She was happy and animated, too, in a way Emma remembered but hadn't seen since her arrival in Plymouth. Emma sipped her sherry and looked at her mother over the rim of her glass, wondering what was up.

Only a few minutes into dinner, her mother's glass was empty again, and when a footman came forward to refill it, Emma glared at him, using her hand to indicate *no more*. The young man raised his eyebrows in a look that said he would be hanged if he stayed back. She dismissed him with a flick of her head. She would deal with whatever the repercussions were.

"So, Emma," George said, laying his glass aside. "Your mother tells me you've made overtures to St. Augustine's about joining the Voluntary Aid Detachment."

She looked at her mother, wondering when she had divulged that information. Truth be told, she had ignored Emma and Helen the entire evening. Instead she focused all her attention on George, leaning as close to him as possible. Her behaviour was appalling, and Emma held back from voicing her disgust more than once. She felt sorry for cousin Helen, but every time she tried to make eye contact with the woman, she just looked away.

"I have, yes. An acquaintance of mine from Newfoundland was kind enough to put in a word for me with the matron in London. I start training next week."

"This war is a terrible business." Helen raised her glass and smiled. "How very noble of you, Emma. I commend you for getting involved."

"I think it's utter nonsense," her mother said in a voice that couldn't be ignored.

All three of them stared at her.

"Seriously, Emma. Why not leave it for the women who need to work?"

"I'm sure she's not doing it for the money," Helen said.

Her mother's brow furrowed, and she narrowed her eyes at Helen. "Why would one volunteer to empty bedpans and change bandages if one didn't have to?"

George put his hand up as if to mediate the situation.

"I'm not saying I agree with your mother's assessment, Emma, but she has a point. Nursing can be hard work, and some men are damaged so severely they are unrecognizable. They suffer from horrific wounds inside and out." He shook his head. "All I'm saying is, it can be difficult work for the body and the mind."

Emma shuddered at George's description and said a silent prayer for Daniel. If only she could find out where he was and if he was safe.

Her mother laughed and reached for her empty glass. "Enough about my daughter's desire to be the next Florence Nightingale." She batted her eyes at George. "How is the war treating you, darling?" Before he had a chance to answer, she rubbed his hand like a mother comforting a small child. "You poor dear, you must be exhausted."

Emma cut into the tender duck on her plate with much more force than was required. How dare her mother belittle her in front of everyone! It was embarrassing, and Emma had had enough. She rolled her eyes. The only thing George should be tired of was being fawned over all night. She was tired of watching it. Why was Helen putting up with it?

"Well, Mother, he's hardly digging in the trenches, now, is he?"

"Emma! What an unkind thing to say. George should be commended for what he is doing for this country."

George reached for his glass, but stopped. Instead, he leaned back in his chair, looking first at his wife, and then at Emma.

"No, Rose, she's right. Compared to what our men just went through in Gallipoli, and what others are facing on the Western Front, my hours in the London office are not comparable."

Her mother scowled in her direction before flashing George a wide smile.

"Be that as it may," she said, "someone has to stay behind to make those decisions, and it isn't easy."

George opened his mouth to reply, but Emma cut him off.

"And why can't you make those decisions from over there, Mr. Whitby?"

Her mother shot daggers at her now, but Emma ignored her.

"Wouldn't you make sounder decisions if you were on the ground, seeing things for yourself?"

"A fair point, Miss Tavenor. But I don't lead troops. I am with the tactical planning division." He sipped his wine. "And like any good soldier, I'm just following orders."

Her mother patted his arm again. "Never mind my surly daughter, George. She knows nothing about the war or what kind of man it takes to fight one." She looked at Helen, ignoring Emma. "It will take our most educated young men to put Germany back in its rightful place in the world. I have every faith in Britain's best and brightest, like George here."

Emma's fork clattered on the plate, startling her mother and Helen.

"You have no idea what I know, Mother. You haven't been a part of my life for years! And it will take all kinds of men to win this war." She looked at George. "Not just highly educated British tactical planners."

"I'm sorry. I must excuse myself." Helen leaped from her seat with her hand covering her mouth and ran from the room.

George pushed his seat back and stood.

"I'll go," Rose said. She pointed a finger in Emma's face. "You should be ashamed of yourself for insulting Mr. Whitby and upsetting cousin Helen. You owe him an apology for your insolent outburst."

She called for Mrs. Evans and rushed after Helen.

"Have I upset her, truly?" Emma asked.

"No, my dear. Not at all." A smile crossed his face. "You see, she's with child."

"Oh!" she replied, hesitating for a moment to sort her thoughts. "Oh. Well, thank God. You must be very happy."

"I am, yes."

She tilted her head and looked him in the eye. "Mother is right. I do owe you an apology. Whatever is going on between us, it has nothing to do with you. I am sincerely sorry for my flippant comments."

He studied her from across the table. "How long's he been gone?"

Startled, Emma laid down her glass. "Who?"

"The man who has captured your heart."

Her cheeks felt hot. "Don't be silly. Nobody's captured my heart."

He leaned forward. "In my experience, Miss Tavenor, nobody gets this worked up unless the stakes are high."

Daniel was a soldier, fighting in a war that her father pushed him into, and all to keep him away from her. The stakes couldn't be higher. Maybe he could help.

"Please, call me Emma."

"I assume your mother has no idea."

"My mother has no idea about a lot of things, Mr. Whitby."

"Please, call me George."

She folded her hands in her lap. "All right, George." She smiled back. "Do you know where the men are? I mean, do you know where they are fighting?"

"Of course," he said with a chuckle. "I wouldn't be much good at my job if I didn't know where the troops were." He sipped his wine.

"But do you know where everyone is?"

"Within a certain degree of reason, yes."

Her stomach fluttered. "Can you tell me, George?"

"Tell you what?" he asked reluctantly.

"Where someone is? If he is wounded, or—" She stopped and cleared her throat before taking a deep breath. "It's very important to me."

He laid down his glass. "Possibly."

A tear slipped down her cheek. "It would mean so much to me."

He nodded. "Now, before you get too excited, Emma, I can make some inquiries, but I don't know what, if anything, I'll be able to find."

"His name is Daniel Beresford, and he's from Middle Tickle. He's serving with the Newfoundland Regiment."

And it's my fault he's there.

"All right, I'll see what I can find out about him. You know I can't tell you exact locations, Emma. I'd be shot if anyone ever found out. Literally."

She nodded. "I understand."

"Not that it matters." He chuckled. "It's not as if you'll be going to France on a holiday any time soon."

She smiled through glassy eyes.

No, not on a holiday.

nineteen

February 1916
Suez, Egypt

"WHEN'S BERN COMING BACK?" FRANKIE ASKED, TOSSING A cigarette behind him. Daniel and Phonse exchanged a look as they removed ammunition from a large crate. They were tasked with organizing some kit that had been retrieved from Gallipoli. Despite the bone-chilling cold and the number of men lost to sickness, the Regiment had remained there until the British Expeditionary Forces finally pulled out in January. Those who were left had sailed back to Alexandria and made camp outside Suez, where they had been for about six weeks.

"I don't think Bern will be back, Frankie," Daniel said.

Within a few days of the torrential flood and ice storm that destroyed their trenches in Gallipoli, Bern was shipped to Mudros. His feet had suffered severe frostbite. Yesterday, Second Lieutenant Winter told Daniel both Bern's feet had been amputated when he arrived back in England. Frankie seemed not to comprehend this. He was still not himself in any way.

Daniel had hung his head and said a silent prayer for his old friend. At least he was still alive, even if he would never be the same again.

Would any of them?

"It's the Middle Tickle boys." Captain Donnelly walked toward them, with Second Lieutenant Winter in tow.

They hadn't seen much of Donnelly since their skirmish on the ridge in Gallipoli, a ridge they had named Caribou Hill in honour of the Regiment's symbol and their successful capture from the Turks. Winter had later told them Donnelly said they were a good, reliable bunch of men.

"Afternoon, Captain," Daniel said. "Second Lieutenant Winter." Daniel nodded in Winter's direction.

"I hope you've been enjoying your rest here in the desert. Won't last much longer."

Daniel replaced the cover on the crate he'd been unpacking. The rumour mill was rampant about where they would go next. Some thought they were going as far east as Salonika, in northern Greece, to join the Serbian Army. Others said it made more sense to go to Mesopotamia to push the Ottomans back to Constantinople.

"Are we finally getting out of here?" Phonse piped up.

Donnelly laughed. "I wouldn't be so eager, lads. It won't be quite as cushy."

"I don't care where we go, but it's got to be better than here," Frankie said. He had not adapted to the heat in the desert, and his face was red and blistered from too much sun. It was just one more thing to add to his list of complaints.

"You think so?" Donnelly picked up a box of ammunition from Daniel's pile and placed it on the crate. "Let's just say, where we're going, there'll be a lot more to do than babysit ammunition."

Their curiosity was well raised now. The boys listened as Donnelly confirmed their next stop was at the very heart of the conflict, the Western Front.

~

The Regiment arrived in France in March and were billeted on a farm in Louvencourt, less than ten miles from the front line. Despite this, they had escaped front line duty and were busy laying light rail near Levalliers.

"This is bloody hard work." A young fellow named Dundas leaned on his shovel and breathed heavily, lighting up a cigarette. "I don't see what we got to fix their railway for. It's bad enough we've got to fight for them. What have these Frenchmen ever done for us?".

Daniel wiped the sweat from his forehead and leaned on his shovel, also, looking at the young boy. "We're not fixing their lines for them. You see the state of them roads? Nothing's getting through there, my son."

The roads and rail lines in the Somme Valley between Arras and Amiens had been all but destroyed after two years of bombing and shelling.

"So?"

"So, if you were at the front, wouldn't you want some grub getting through to ya?" Phonse asked.

Dundas shrugged. "I suppose so, yes."

"Well, you'd be wanting your fags, that's for sure." Phonse plucked the cigarette out of Dundas's mouth and puffed on it. On a slow exhale, he said, "They've got decent wine."

Daniel looked at him. "Who?"

"The French. He asked what the French have done for us. They make good wine."

Dundas spat on the ground. "That cheap plonk? There's better than that in England. And that's saying something."

Phonse snorted, and the boys all laughed. "The English don't make wine, ya gommel. What you get there comes from France!"

Dundas laughed and took a long draw on his cigarette. "Well, they've got beautiful women."

Phonse smiled. "That they do, my son, that they do."

Dundas had befriended Daniel and the boys not long after they joined "C" Company in early April. They were still getting used to Bern's absence, but Dundas continued tagging along after them, until they emerged into a new foursome without even realizing it. He hailed from the slums of East London near Bethnal Green and once described it as a desperate place where eight to ten family members lived in cramped, one-room flats and spent most of their days dirty and hungry. When the war broke out, he was only thirteen. He waited two years before enlisting. He said the promise of a bed and three square meals a day was enough, and they threw a wage on top. What more could a man ask for?

Dundas's tale put Daniel's own life in perspective, as he thought of his comfortable house nestled in the cove in Middle Tickle. They weren't well off by any means, but he was beginning to see poverty was relative.

"What do you say, Frankie?" Daniel asked his friend.

"Hmm," Frankie muttered, and pulled his water can from over his shoulder, chugging a nice bit.

Daniel and Phonse looked at each other. Ever since Gallipoli, it was hard to drag a word out of Frankie, not one that made much sense, anyway, but he continued to work like a dog. It had taken him a while to recover from the trench fever, and he'd even put a bit of weight back on, but he continued to retreat further into his own mind. The happy-go-lucky boy who had danced a jig on the train as it steamed away from the rock cuts surrounding Middle Tickle had disappeared.

Daniel wondered if he'd ever see him again.

Phonse picked up his shovel again. "A drop of stuff wouldn't go astray tonight, would it?"

"No, b'y. That's what it wouldn't," Daniel replied.

"Crowd of nurses landed today. Some new ones." Dundas grinned, cigarette hanging out the side of his mouth.

Phonse laughed. "Old or new, not much odds. They wouldn't be caught out with the likes of us."

Dundas took a puff. "Depends."

"On what?"

"How convincing we are." He laughed. "And as long as we bring him." He pointed at Daniel.

Daniel looked at the young lad. "Me?"

"Jesus, the French women love him. Haven't you seen the way they look at him?"

Phonse sniffed and lit a Woodbine. "Can't say as I've noticed."

"It's true," Dundas said. "Right, Danny?"

Daniel ignored him and drove his spade back into the dirt.

Dundas elbowed Phonse in the ribs. "He's had some girls since he's been here, haven't he? And I bet he don't pay for none, neither. I don't care how much he gets, as long as he shares it around, hey, boys!"

Dundas and Phonse laughed.

Frankie smirked and whispered something under his breath. Daniel was sure he'd heard the words "pining" and "old Tavenor's daughter" in there.

Maybe there wasn't as much wrong with Frankie as he'd thought. He kept digging.

Despite the hard work of railroad detail, it was a holiday compared to the front lines. None of them knew how much longer before they were pulled into trench rotation and this bit of freedom they'd been enjoying would end.

Later that evening, the four of them cleaned up and made their way into Levalliers to the local *estaminet*. The last time a woman had leered at him, Daniel had been ten years old. He'd chased Frankie into Mrs. Clooney's garden, and they ran right through her clothesline. Frankie ran full speed with Mrs. Clooney's drawers wrapped around his head as she yelled and shook her fist at them from the bridge. By the time Daniel made his way home, his mother knew all about it, and so did the whole harbour, a hazard of outport life. She made him apologize and return the underwear.

After giving him a drop of orange drink and a biscuit, which he took to be polite, the old woman wanted to know what his fascination was with her underpants. He tried explaining it had been an accident and neither he nor Frankie wanted them. They were the biggest ones he'd ever seen, at that, but then she asked him if what he really wanted was to see what was underneath them. Before she got her navy blue dress hiked up any higher, he skinned out of there as fast as he could. Every Sunday, the old woman winked at him in church.

They got their real introduction to whorehouses in Alexandria. The Newfoundlanders had found kindred spirits in the Aussies and the Kiwis, who dared them to follow into paradise, as they called it. More than a few of them had gotten syphilis, their balls swollen to the size of bull birds, and couldn't go to Gallipoli. They were lectured by the CO and had to drop their pants while the doctor examined the entire Regiment's cocks before they were cleared to ship out.

Phonse stood next to Daniel during the ordeal and, after they were cleared, said, "I guess we got lucky, eh, b'y?"

"You call this lucky?" Daniel buttoned up his pants.

Phonse chuckled. "Well, we didn't catch anything."

Daniel nodded. He shouldn't have been surprised Phonse was partaking in the local offerings. Daniel was probably the only one who wasn't.

In France, it seemed like the women were just waiting for you. He couldn't understand it. Their country was being torn apart by war, heaps of rubble all around, their homes and cities destroyed, but they were willing and able any time and almost anywhere. Madame Tessier's small *estaminet* in Levalliers was no exception. The moment they walked in, all eyes turned their way.

"You see that, Phonse?" Dundas rubbed his hands together. "It's because we got dream boy here with us."

"Nah, b'y, it's the smell." Daniel shrugged off the comment and walked to a table in the corner, laying his hat on it.

The boys laughed and followed him. Before they'd even had a chance to sit, a barmaid, wearing a dress cut so low her breasts almost spilled out, leaned down and placed a decanter of wine and four small glasses in front of him.

"What I wouldn't give for a drop of shine now," Frankie said as he reached for a glass and poured up the wine.

Daniel and Phonse stared at him. It was the most like himself he'd sounded in a long time.

"Yes, b'y, me too," Daniel said, making eye contact with Phonse and winking. Maybe he'd come back to them after all.

Phonse took a swig and shook his head back and forth, making an ungodly noise.

Daniel grinned at him. "Thought the French made good wine."

"This must be the English stuff, hey, Dundas?" Phonse pulled the young fellow into a wrestling hold.

"Happy to amuse you," Dundas said from underneath Phonse's arm. "Phew! You're right about the smell, Danny!"

The boys all laughed.

"*Toi.*"

Daniel swallowed his wine and looked up just as a young French girl draped her arms around his shoulders.

She tugged on his arm. "*Viens avec moi.*"

He shook his head and turned away. She pouted, pulling the cleavage of her dress down a little farther.

"*S'il te plaît,*" she said.

"No." He twisted his arm from her grasp and stared down at his wine.

"I'll silver plate her!" Dundas stood up and made eyes at the young girl, vying for her attention. He pointed both thumbs at his own chest to show he was more than willing.

"Jesus, Danny, b'y, ya can't turn her down, surely." Phonse elbowed him.

She looked at Dundas with raised eyebrows and placed a hand on her bony hip. She threw her arms around Daniel.

"*M'aimes-tu*?" She dragged out the word and licked her lips, touching his face. He ignored her, staring straight ahead, his face growing warm.

Phonse said in his ear, "Go on, Danny. A man has needs. Even in the middle of this hellhole."

"I've got needs," Dundas whimpered like a five-year-old and sat down.

She brushed her hand on Daniel's thigh, and he caught her by the arm. "No!"

He locked eyes with her for the briefest of seconds, blinking in surprise at the cool, grey eyes staring back. They weren't as kind or as beautiful as Emma's, but they reminded him of her. Emma would never throw herself at a man like this. His stomach roiled.

Even if they would never be together again, he couldn't dishonour his feelings for her with a quick romp in a farmer's barn with some French whore who meant nothing to him. Unconsciously, he reached up and rubbed his pocket where he kept her photograph. Most days he just went about the business of getting on with it, carrying out his orders, but she was always there with him.

Frankie smirked while Phonse consoled Dundas.

She shrugged. "*Tant pis pour toi.*" She rounded the table and poked Dundas in the shoulder. "*Tois, alors?*"

All the syrupy sweetness was gone from her voice. He looked up at her eagerly.

She held her hand out and in perfect English said, "Money first."

The French women knew more English than they let on. They believed it was part of their mystique if you thought they didn't understand you. Dundas jumped up so fast his chair fell back, and he chased after her like a bumbling puppy.

Phonse looked at Daniel. "Merciful God. How could you pass that up?"

"Too young for me." He tipped his glass up, gulped back its contents, and stood.

Phonse stood up, following behind. "We're in the middle of a war here, Danny, b'y. Beggars can't be choosers."

"He's got high standards, is all," Frankie muttered, following them out.

The next morning at six o'clock sharp, they were awakened and ordered to form up in the large training field.

"What's happening?" Dundas asked.

"We're being called up, I figure." Phonse yawned and stretched his body from side to side. "Good thing you got your bit last night. Might be the last you'll see for a while."

Dundas's eyes were wide. "Do you think so, Danny?"

"I'd say so, yeah."

"Why, now?" Dundas asked, his lip quivering.

Frankie lit a Woodbine and spat on the ground. "Jesus, we're here to fight a war, not picnic by the river eating cheese and drinking wine. We're lucky we've escaped the front this long."

There was a quietness about the morning, despite the hundreds of soldiers milling about at the crack of dawn, all waiting to be told what was next.

"You hear that?" Daniel asked.

Dundas jumped. "What?"

"Nothing."

The constant thud of shelling in the distance had become the norm. The silence somehow seemed louder. It was so quiet he might have heard a scattered bird chirp, if there was one left around. But even they had moved on to more civilized destinations.

"You think it's over?" Dundas asked.

"No, but I'd like to think they're enjoying the quiet as much as we are."

Frankie douted his cigarette and looked at them all. "Graveyard shift ain't over yet, is all. Give it fifteen minutes and they'll be back at it again, make no mistake."

The new Frankie had a contrariness about him that wasn't present before.

"Graveyard shift? What does he mean?" Dundas looked at each of them, waiting for an explanation.

No one said anything.

"I know you boys were at Gallipoli, and you've already seen some horrible things," Dundas said. "But me, I just got here a few weeks ago. Laying rail is all I know about the war."

Phonse grinned at him. "That's okay, Dundas," he said, and winked at Daniel. "Stick with us. We've gotten this far, we'll get through it together."

A pit formed in Daniel's stomach. They'd been enlisted for two years now, in a war everyone thought would be over by Christmas in 1914. The Germans were dug in deep throughout France and Belgium. There was no way of knowing when it would be over or how much worse it would get. Phonse was right about one thing—two years in and they hadn't been served too badly yet, but Daniel had a funny feeling that was going to change.

Recent rumours from the front weren't encouraging. There was no way to break through and push the Germans back, no matter how many men the British sent out there. The losses were rising. Phonse shouldn't be making anyone any promises.

"Have you killed anyone?" Dundas asked.

His question hung in the air like Mrs. Clooney's drawers had before Frankie tore them down.

Phonse laughed. "I've fired enough ammunition. I sure as hell hope I hit some of them bastards. Hey, b'ys?"

"No, I mean have you had to look them in the eye—" He hesitated. "—and kill them? Because I know it's what we're supposed to do, but I think when it comes down to it, it would be an awful hard thing to do."

"Dundas, my son, it's kill or be killed out there," Phonse said. "The sooner you make your peace with it, the better. Don't overthink it. Don't think about it at all."

Daniel avoided Frankie's stare. They'd never discussed what happened on their way back to their lines in Gallipoli that day.

Dundas sighed and kicked at some loose gravel, making his way over to Daniel. "Danny. I don't know if I'm cut out for this."

Daniel patted Dundas on the back. They were just two boys, a few years apart in age, one looking for reassurance, the other wondering if they would make it out alive. He looked into Dundas's young, brown eyes and flashed back to another set of young, brown eyes he looked into a few months ago.

Kill or be killed.

A single shot sounded, and he jumped.

"Jesus, Danny, you gettin' soft or what?" Even Phonse had taken to calling him Danny these days.

He smiled. "Nah, b'y. Just got used to the silence is all."

Frankie took one last draw on his cigarette and hopped off an old barrel. "Graveyard shift's over."

"Will somebody tell me what he means?" Dundas asked, throwing his hands up in the air.

Frankie stepped on the butt and walked toward a large group of soldiers who had assembled for their morning orders. Daniel locked eyes with him for a minute. His old friend nodded and flashed a brief smile. Frankie was damaged, but he was still in there somewhere.

The officers yelled and ordered them to form ranks. The CO marched to the front and faced the Regiment. He ordered them to stand easy. They fell together and formed into lines as a loud voice boomed. "Soldiers of the Newfoundland Regiment, are you ready to serve your country?"

twenty

May 1916
Compton, England

THE ENGLISH COUNTRYSIDE FLASHED BY AS THE TRAIN RACED toward Compton, a farming village on the outskirts of Plymouth. The spring magnolias were in full bloom, and even the cherry trees had blossomed.

"I'm so glad you decided to come home with me for the weekend," said Mabel Purcell. "I've told mother all about you. She's chuffed you're coming along."

Mabel had befriended her on their first day at St. Augustine's, and with her wide, caramel-coloured eyes and a smile as wide as the Thames, it didn't take long for Emma to realize she was a genuine friend. Emma still kept much about her personal life to herself, but Mabel had eventually won her over.

She had begged Emma to bring her home for a visit several weeks ago, a thought which petrified Emma to no end. When she refused to agree, Mabel suggested Emma come home with her instead. It hadn't taken too much coaxing, since Emma's mother had been on a drunken binge for over a month. Mrs. Evans had assured her the time away would be good.

Emma wondered how long her soft-hearted friend would stick it out working as a VAD, but Mabel had surprised her. The training wasn't that hard, but taking care of the men was. They were in pieces and would never be whole again, physically or mentally, sometimes both. She felt their pain deeply, because all she thought about was Daniel. Her desperation to know if he was alive or dead always bubbled close to the surface. Whenever a new shipment of patients arrived, she volunteered for a double shift since they were always short-handed. On those days, the feeling of dread was so heavy she felt the weight of all the dead bodies she had cleaned and prepared, as if she had carried them on her back to their burying ground.

On those days, the ritual was the same. She wandered the wards, scanning faces, checking tags. Every face was etched in her mind. She was always relieved when she didn't find him, among the dead or wounded, but prayed to God daily for some sign that he was still alive. She conjured all sorts of images based on the things she'd seen and heard. These days were hard on the mind, but harder on the heart. She looked after each of them as if they were her own, as if they were him. Her empathy had naturally made her a favourite among the men.

Emma had one goal—be the best VAD possible and get to France. It didn't take long for her fierce work ethic to earn her a reputation for being fearless. She jumped into any situation regardless of its complexity or gruesomeness, and cheering her from the sidelines was Mabel, her biggest fan. But the one topic they had never discussed was Daniel.

"Did I mention my brother Thomas will be here?"

Emma gazed out at the green fields as the train wound its way through lush farmland.

"That's nice," she murmured.

Her mind was miles away, across the English Channel. It was hard to fathom England remaining so beautiful and calm while a short distance away there was such fierce fighting going on.

"Mother wrote last week to say Thomas had been granted one week's furlough. He should have arrived at home yesterday," Mabel said, hesitating to pull in a breath. "I'm so excited. I can't wait for you to meet him."

At the word "furlough," Emma snapped out of her trance. "He's serving?"

Mabel nodded. "Oh, yes. Mother was devastated when he first enlisted, but Father said it was the right thing to do. He'd be gone himself if he could."

"How long has he been in France?" Her interest was more than piqued now, and she wondered if Mabel's brother might have any information about the Newfoundland Regiment's whereabouts. Her heart raced.

"He's been there for about a year now. He's with the sanitation section."

Emma's hopes fell. They weren't usually on the front lines, so he probably knew very little, unlike Daniel, who probably knew too much. What an awful thought. She almost covered her mouth. She had no business comparing Daniel to Thomas. It was true that, as an uneducated boy from Newfoundland, Daniel was doing grunt work and fighting at the front in the worst conditions mankind had ever seen. She heard about it daily from the soldiers she cared for. She certainly saw the effects of it every day, too, but she had no right to compare them. The fact that Thomas Purcell enlisted at all made him no different than Daniel.

Emma patted Mabel's hand. "Your parents must be proud of him."

Mabel's eyes wandered. "Well, Mother is happy enough. She thinks he's sitting in a tent somewhere teaching men all about cleanliness and how following some simple sanitary precautions could save their lives." She sighed. "And of course he was, but they're always short-handed, and he's been working as a medic, wandering around no man's land, helping people for months now. If she knew he was in such serious danger every day, I think she'd take to her bed and not get up until he came home." She looked out the window. "But yes, of course, we are proud of him. He's learned so much about medicine doing this job. Father wants him to become a doctor when it's all over."

Emma listened as Mabel waxed on about Thomas, but all she could think about was Daniel. What would he do after the war was over? Would there be an after?

A grin grew on Mabel's face as she looked sideways at Emma. "And Thomas looks so handsome in his uniform. I'm sure he'll have a wife before the war is over."

It was a grim thought, but the truth was that, at the rate the British were losing men and boys, Thomas would have his pick of women when the war was over.

"I don't know how he does it, really," Mabel said. "I wouldn't be caught there."

"You wouldn't go to France if the opportunity arose?" asked Emma.

Mabel's mouth dropped. "Not for all the tea in China. The front's no place for ladies like us, Emma." She clasped her hands together "Though I do hope to get a husband out of this. I can picture it perfectly. A handsome young soldier will wander into my ward, and I will nurse him back to health. He'll fall madly in love with me, beg me to be his wife, and we'll have lots of children and live happily ever after." She fell back against her seat and sighed, looking up at Emma through dreamy eyes. "Don't you wish for the same thing?"

"I guess I do, yes."

❧

Emma sipped red wine from a wide-mouthed crystal goblet. The smell of roast pheasant stuffed with apples and chestnuts, beets with butter, and Potatoes O'Brien wafted up to meet her. Mabel's father raised a glass to his mouth and finished the last drop of wine in his glass.

"If I may ask, Tavenor is not a Plymouth name, correct?"

Emma set her glass down. "No, it isn't. You know the family history of the area well, Mr. Purcell." She smiled at Mabel's father, unable to ignore the fact that Mabel's brother, Thomas, hadn't taken his eyes off her from the moment she'd walked in the room.

"My father is from Newfoundland," she said.

He refilled his glass. "Ah. The land of fish," he said, raising the glass to her.

"But I thought England was your home," Mabel's mother said, looking crossways at her daughter, as if she'd caught her in some masterful lie.

Emma shifted. This was why she had no desire to make friends or get too close to anybody while she was here. They'd all want to know about her and where she came from, and it wouldn't be long before they would find out who she was. Her grandfather had owned three quarters of Plymouth when he died. She shivered at the thought of all of that money belonging to her mother now. How much of it had she squandered away on booze? Her cheeks reddened as she wondered how many people knew of her mother's philandering ways.

"My mother's family is from Plymouth, and my grandfather had a home there. He still does, actually. I spent a lot of time there as a child. It is my home, in many ways."

She hoped they didn't prod much further.

"Do you enjoy your work as a VAD, Emma?" asked Thomas.

She looked up, thankful for the change in topic, and found his gaze burning into hers. "I do, very much, yes."

"Emma's very good at this work. She should be a doctor." Mabel turned to her brother. "Like you, Thomas. You and Emma have much in common."

Subtlety was not Mabel's strong suit, and Emma realized within a few hours of arriving at the Purcells' that Mabel saw this as an opportunity to play matchmaker. She had laughed it off, figuring it was the meddling of a younger sister. What she hadn't counted on was Thomas being keen on it.

Thomas cleared his throat. "I have no desire to be a doctor, Mabel, as you well know." He shot a look in his father's direction. "I should think I would like to become a lawyer when the war is over."

Father and son shared a look.

"What about you, Emma? What will you do with your life when the war is over?" Thomas asked, turning to her.

Emma didn't know what life held in store when the war was over, but she hoped she and Daniel would figure it out together. She lifted her eyes. His stare was so intense it was unnerving.

"I don't know, Thomas," she said, her voice wavering. "I don't even know what kind of world this will be when this godforsaken war is over."

Quiet settled over the table, but Mabel was determined. "One of the instructors showed us how to sew stitches in case we needed to," she said, rolling her eyes. "Which I'm sure we won't."

Sometimes Mabel seemed so out of tune with the realities of their work that Emma wondered why the girl had joined the VAD in the first place. *Obviously, to find a husband.*

"The instructors said Emma would make a good surgeon," Mabel said. "She's quite good with her hands."

"Now, dear," Mabel's mother said, patting her daughter's hand. "Rolling up bandages and cleaning bedpans hardly constitutes a doctor's duties."

Mabel's mouth gaped, but it was Thomas who responded on their behalf.

"Mother, I'll have you know VADs offer an essential service in the field hospitals and on the front lines. But I also understand you couldn't possibly know this, as you haven't volunteered to do anything since the war began."

Mrs. Purcell's cheeks reddened, and she touched her face as if recovering from an invisible slap.

"Thomas, don't speak to your mother in that tone."

"Well, Father, someone has to," he said, pointing at Mabel and Emma. "The VADs in France, young women like Mabel and Emma, work under extreme circumstances in the most dangerous conditions. They don't deserve to be likened to silly housemaids. They're heroes."

Mrs. Purcell's eyes bulged, and her hand fanned over her chest. "I'm sorry, Miss Tavenor, excuse me." She pushed her chair back and rushed from the room.

"Yes, Thomas, I think you've made your point." His father pushed his chair back. "If you'll excuse me, Miss Tavenor, I think I'll retire for the evening."

Emma stared down at her plate, not knowing what to do, until she heard Mabel giggle.

"You can never leave well enough alone where Mother is concerned, Thomas, can you?"

"Well, honestly, Mabel. What she said was insulting."

Mabel shrugged. "It was, but you know it's how she sees the world."

"I'm sorry if my mother offended you, Emma," said Thomas.

Emma laid down her glass and grinned. "Quite the contrary. I think she offended you much more than she did me."

Thomas opened his mouth to speak, but stopped. Mabel glanced at Emma, and the three broke into a fit of laughter.

After Mabel turned in, Emma retrieved a shawl from her room and stepped outside to take in some air. She stared up at the stars as she did every night, thinking only of Daniel. Cousin Helen's husband, George, had come through with the information as he had promised, and she knew Daniel was in France. As far as George could tell, Daniel wasn't at the front yet, but there was constant rotation in and out, and he warned it could be any day.

That information was at least two weeks old now. Was he still safe? Every time the same terrible what-ifs set in, she stopped herself. She had never lost faith he was still alive, and somewhere deep down she believed she would know if he were dead.

A hand touched the small of her back, and she closed her eyes, wishing, hoping, but she couldn't pretend. It was there for the briefest of seconds, and when she opened her eyes, Thomas was in front of her. She looked up into his face. Mabel was right; he was lovely, and very handsome in his uniform. She could only imagine how handsome Daniel looked in his uniform. The look in her eyes must have told Thomas everything he needed to know.

"You belong to another."

She closed her eyes and nodded.

He brushed his thumb across her cheek. "Mabel never said."

She opened her eyes and stared into his green ones. "She doesn't know."

"He's in France?"

"Yes," she whispered.

"Have you heard from him lately?"

"I've not heard from him at all."

He waited a few seconds. "Oh, well, that doesn't sound encouraging, I'm afraid."

She pulled the shawl tighter as the wind curled around her. "It's kind of a long story."

He put his arm around her. "Would you like me to listen?"

"No."

He looked wounded, and drew back.

"But I would like your help."

"Anything."

"Help me get to France."

His eyes widened. "Emma. You don't know what you're asking." He shook his head. "I can't. It's . . . it's . . ."

"Hell," she said.

"Yes. It's hell. How can you ask me to do that to you?"

"I need to find him."

"Emma, it's not that easy. He could be anywhere."

"Just help me get there," she said, her voice trembling. "Please."

He shook his head. "Emma, please don't ask me to do this."

"Thomas, my life has been hell for two years. It can't possibly get any worse."

He cupped her face in his hands. "Yes, it can, Emma." His voice broke. "France is a terrible place right now."

She rested her forehead against his, knowing full well she was using his attraction to her to her advantage. She would do anything. "Help me get wherever you're stationed. I'll take care of the rest."

"You're not going to give up on this, are you?"

"No."

"Are you as good as Mabel says you are?"

"Better." She smiled.

He sighed. She took it as his compliance and kissed him full on the lips, hugging him tight. "Thank you," she whispered in his ear.

He held her for a minute. "He's a lucky man, whoever he is."

twenty-one

June 1916
Somewhere in France

"JESUS H. CHRIST!" DANIEL DROPPED THE WIRE CUTTERS AND wheeled around. Blood spurted, covering his face and the front of his uniform. A piece of wire about six inches long protruded from Frankie's arm. Gunfire sounded overhead, and Daniel jumped, pushing Frankie to the ground.

Frankie struggled to stand, grabbing at his injured arm. "What the hell, Danny?" He scrambled away, but Daniel caught him again and pulled him down.

"Sorry, Frankie, but a bit of wire in the arm is nothing compared to a bullet in the head." He pulled him closer to examine Frankie's arm. "What happened?"

"I got me arm caught in the goddamn stuff! Pull it out."

He'd seen much worse in the way of wounds in the last few years, but it still needed to be treated so Frankie didn't become a casualty to infection like many others. He reached in his haversack for some rope to tie above the arm to slow the bleeding.

A rumbling like thunder filled his ears, and the earth shook as a shell exploded a few feet away. Dirt and debris fell like rain from the sky, and Daniel covered his head with his arms. His ears buzzed with an intense ringing. He stayed down for a few minutes before easing from his protective position. Frankie cursed as he sat up and tucked himself in tight against a wall, favouring his arm. He started to speak, but Daniel put his hand up to stop him. They waited a few more minutes. All morning they had been laying a section of thick barbed wire and had moved a nice way from their own lines.

"Just pull it out." Frankie closed his eyes, breathing heavily.

"I need something to staunch it with, Frankie. I can't just pull it out."

Daniel reached into his sack for a field dressing and rummaged around for something to tie around Frankie's arm. He pulled out a pair of grey socks, which had come in a Red Cross package from home. Thousands of women from across the island had come together to knit socks for the Newfoundland soldiers. They came in packages with cigarettes, biscuits and letters of encouragement, along with bandages and other supplies. You could barter a fair bit with the British soldiers for a pair of grey socks from Newfoundland when the weather got cold. He looked at the dark grey wool, soft against his fingers. For all he knew, Emma could have knitted them.

Frankie winced. "Danny. You doin' something with them, or you gonna look at them all day?"

Daniel tied a sock around Frankie's arm, above the piece of protruding barbed wire. "Sorry, Frankie." In one quick motion he pulled the wire out, tossing it to one side.

"Ahh! Jesus, Mary, and Joseph!"

Daniel took the other sock and stuffed it into the wound the wire had made in Frankie's arm. "That should do it until we get you to a field hospital."

"I ain't goin' to no hospital." Frankie grunted and pulled his arm back, cradling it like a baby.

Phonse and Dundas approached from behind. "Come on, b'ys, we've got to move back out of here. There's some heavy firing going on. We've already lost a few—" Phonse stopped when he noticed Frankie's arm. "What happened?"

"Frankie's got himself in a bit of a state."

Dundas paled. What would the poor boy do when he saw a real wound?

"No. Let's just get back to base. There'll be a medic around some-where," Frankie protested.

"Medics have more important things to be doing than stitching you up." Daniel rolled his eyes at Phonse. "Get him over to Field Hospital C. It's not far. A nurse can clean it right and stitch it up."

Frankie grumbled and cursed but went on with Phonse and Dundas. As his three buddies moved away, Daniel retreated in the opposite direction to check out what was happening farther down the lines. The firing was unusually heavy this morning, and as he rounded a bend in the trench, bodies were strewn throughout. His heart pounded, and he waited a few minutes until he thought it was safe. He pushed up against the outer wall and worked his way along, scanning the bodies. No one he recognized at first glance.

Daniel crouched next to a soldier with a bullet through his fore-head. One slow trickle of blood flowed from the wound down his tem-ple, matting his hair. He lay lopsided with his hand still on the trigger. Daniel removed the rifle from the boy's hand and straightened him out, folding his arms across his chest. He reached for the twine around the boy's neck. Locating the small disc, he looked at the name. It took him several minutes to process the letters and sound out the words as Emma had taught him to do. Private Cyril McCarthy. Daniel pushed the tag underneath the collar and closed the boy's eyes.

Laughter sounded from above, and Daniel strained to hear the muffled voices. German. He held his breath and scurried to the nearest wall, flattening himself against it. Some tunnelling work had been done here not so long ago, and there was an opening close by. Bullets ricocheted off the trench wall as he scrambled into the tunnel. His chest throbbed as adrenaline coursed through him. Shots followed by more laughter. He positioned his rifle and waited a few more minutes before peeping down the muddy corridor. Dead rats. They were shooting at rats. He let out his breath and slid down the wall, sighing with relief.

Field Hospital C

"Do you have a name, sweetheart?"

Emma wrung the washcloth in the stainless steel pan of warm water. "Of course I have a name. It's Miss Tavenor."

She met the soldier's eyes for a second before giving him a small smile. She ran the cloth down his arm, cleaning his wounds without putting too much pressure on the deeper ones.

His green eyes danced, and he touched her hand with his free arm. "Come on. Tell me your first name. Miss Tavenor is too formal for someone who has washed all my bits and bobs."

The boys laughed, and Emma held back a smile. She'd seen a lot in her time as a VAD. The least of which bothered her now were the bits and bobs.

"Come on. I might not have long left for this world, and I can't possibly meet my maker without knowing the name matching that beautiful face."

Emma applied a bit of pressure to one of his many wounds, and he winced, withdrawing the wandering arm, but leaving the injured one in her care.

"Sorry, Lieutenant. Hazard of the job." She grinned and continued working. "And you have lots of time left. These wounds are purely superficial."

"I'll be dead within the hour if you keep digging at them like that!"

True to his word, Mabel's brother Thomas had called in a few favours and had convinced Major Bingley, the hospital's head, to take some of the VADs who had trained at St. Augustine's. Thomas vouched for her personally. Only two other VADs from her class had volunteered for service at the front. Augusta Browne realized her mistake the first week and went home, and an older woman, by the name of Kitty Spencer, kept her head down and didn't speak to anybody. Mabel thought Emma was mad for even entertaining this idea and told her so, several times, before she left and in subsequent letters.

She had been in France less than a month, but it was easy to see how so many of her nursing sisters had taken up with soldiers, despite orders forbidding it. There were a few charmers kicking around, like this one. She admired the ones who could still flirt, who were still full of harmless fun after all they'd seen and done. It was a distraction from those maimed beyond repair, and the others with their haunted eyes and catatonic stares. There was nothing to be done for them.

The matron reminded them daily they were caretakers, letter-writers, readers, and comforters, but nothing more. Some needed more reminding than others, but not her. She had never crossed the line with a patient. She paid them all equal attention. Lord knew she analyzed their every feature, but she searched for one.

Since arriving at Field Hospital C, about ten miles behind the front lines, she had gone about her work much the same as she had in England. She checked the tags on every unrecognizable corpse, thanking God as she read each name it wasn't him. Out of respect, she said a little prayer for the poor soul who would never see home again. Of course, she knew between the time George Whitby confirmed Daniel's approximate location and her arrival, he could have been killed or even be missing in action. And even if he was wounded, he might not be taken here. But somehow she believed in her heart he was still alive. Believing he was still out there kept her going.

"Okay, I'll have to call you Nurse."

"Well, that would be wrong. I'm not a nurse, Lieutenant."

"You're doing nursing things." He reached for her arm again.

She pulled away and kept working. "Some, yes, but I'm not really a nurse. I'm a VAD." She wrung out the cloth and started again.

"What's that stand for?"

A young soldier in the next bed, who'd come in with a bullet in the leg, leaned over. "Ah, that's easy. Very Adorable Darlings."

The patients in the next four beds laughed, and pretty soon they broke into a roaring rendition of "If You Were the Only Girl in the World." The young lieutenant led the charge with his head tilted in her direction and his good hand positioned over his heart.

She listened to the lyrics, thinking of Daniel, and wishing they were true. Maybe if she was the only girl in the world and he were the only boy, maybe then they could have been together with no one to interfere or pass judgment. And if that wasn't bad enough, then there was this bloody war.

She tried to imagine Daniel joining in chorus with these boys, singing at the top of his lungs, but he was much too quiet. If he were here, his mouth would curl in a playful grin, his shy eyes sparkling at their mischief. That was Daniel. She hoped the war hadn't changed him too much. It had changed some worse than others.

"What the blue blazes is going on here?" Matron Strong, a stern-faced older woman who'd well earned her reputation for contrariness, particularly with the young VADs, stormed down the centre aisle. "This is a hospital ward, not a performance hall, I'll have you know," she said.

"All right, boys, fun's over. Here comes the head of the starch brigade," said a young corporal two beds down.

"Corporal, have some respect," Emma said, before turning to face the fast-approaching Hilda. The singing died out. "Good evening, Matron."

"Miss Tavenor, have you such little control over your charges? Perhaps we shall have a chat with Major Bingley. Maybe he was too hasty in giving so much responsibility to one with so little training."

Emma felt from the beginning the matron had suspicions about how she got to France. Nothing specific had been said, but she was definitely under her watchful eye. Any time Thomas sought her out, the matron hovered and eyed them, as if waiting for an opportunity to catch them doing something to get Emma sent home.

"Ease up, Matron, Miss Tavenor here didn't do anything wrong," the lieutenant said.

The matron wheeled around and faced the lieutenant, who sat up on the bed with his feet on the floor, looking much more serious than he had a moment ago. "This is none of your concern, soldier. Back in bed. Now!"

"That's Lieutenant to you, ma'am, and unless you've just been promoted to captain in the British Army, I don't believe I answer to you."

The matron stopped and turned to face him, her eyes blazing. "Make no mistake, soldier, you're in my hospital, on my ward, and you will do as you are told."

She pointed at Emma. "You. Since I've been told time and again about your superior stitching abilities, when you're finished here, you're needed in triage. There's a soldier with a wound that needs to be bipped and stitched." She marched off the ward with better form than most soldiers.

❧

Emma pushed aside the tent's flap and stepped inside. It was a warm June day, and under the tent it was stifling. Soldiers who hadn't had a proper wash in weeks lay on stretchers and cots. Between the sweat and grime, and other bodily fluids, combined with the stench of gangrenous gases oozing from their wounds, the smell could knock you over.

She swallowed hard and moved inside. She'd come a long way since holding her nose on the wharf in Middle Tickle. The smell was wretched but, after a while, could be forgotten. What would never be forgotten were the sounds the dying made as they openly wept for their mothers.

She took a package of supplies she had put together when she'd come on shift that morning at six o'clock. It held all the usual suspects: gauze, bandages, a small brown bottle of carbolic lotion, and a stitching kit. As she weaved her way through the maze of bodies, she spotted a soldier sitting on the end of a cot, cradling his arm.

She laid her supply package on the bed and reached for his arm. "Hello, Private, let's get you fixed up."

He lifted his head, and they locked eyes. She gasped. "Frankie."

His blank eyes flickered for a second before he smiled. "Well, aren't you a sight for sore eyes."

She grasped him in a fierce hug.

"Hey, now, watch the arm," he said, only half-joking.

She stepped back, her smile fading. "Daniel. Where's Daniel?"

"Same place I left him, I suppose."

Relief washed over her. "You mean he's okay?"

He nodded. The blank look in his eyes returned, and when he refocused, he furrowed his brow. "What are you doing here?"

She smiled and wiped her face with the back of her hand, unsure if she should tell him the truth or not, but she didn't have to.

"He doesn't know you're here."

She shook her head.

He grinned. "I knew young Billy was right. I owes him a full pack of cigarettes when I gets home," he said under his breath.

She hadn't the foggiest what he was on about, but she had more pressing questions. "Has he been wounded? How long have you been here? Is Daniel okay?"

The pain returned to his eyes, and all of a sudden she remembered the poor fellow was a patient and was here because he was hurt.

"Frankie, I'm sorry about all the questions. Your arm. Let me see it." She untied the blood-soaked wool sock and examined the wound.

Frankie winced and nodded toward the sock. "That's yer man's handiwork there, luh."

"Daniel did this?"

He nodded.

It seemed like just yesterday they were kids roaming through the woods behind Middle Tickle, kids who didn't know or care about anything. Now they were a world away. She was a VAD and Daniel was a soldier on the Western Front, and they were both trapped in a global conflict on a scale the world had never seen.

As she examined his arm, he took her hand and pulled her close, a look of sheer wildness in his eyes. "Give me something for the pain."

"Frankie, I know it hurts, but it's nothing compared to these fellows." She waved an arm around her.

The men's cries filled the tent and echoed off the canvas. It was enough to break even the sanest, but you couldn't give in to it. Emma was so used to it now, sometimes she wondered if she had become cold and unfeeling because of her ability to tune it out. For anyone new to the scene, it was more than unsettling. She didn't think she would ever enjoy a peaceful silence again, for every time there was quiet, her ears filled with the phantom cries.

"Please, give me something. Anything." His eyes filled. "Just give me something to make me forget. Just for a little while."

Emma closed her eyes as he leaned forward and hugged her waist, rocking them both back and forth.

"I just need to forget. Please. Make me forget," he whispered. She tightened her hold around his bony frame as his shoulders shrunk and curled over his chest.

A small sob escaped her lips. He might not have been in the same physical agony as those around him, but who was she to say his mental agony wasn't as bad?

"Sit tight, Frankie. Let me see what I can do." She stepped back and squeezed his hand. She took one look at his face and turned away. She helped him lie down on the cot. "I'll be right back."

She looked around for the nearest supply cabinet. In all her time as a VAD, she had never broken the rules, but now she was about to break a serious one. Morphine was for those in extreme need, and it was always in short supply. She wandered around the tent, heading for the back to locate a supply chest. On the way she came upon a young nurse in near hysterics.

"What's happened?" Emma kneeled down beside her.

"I was supposed to be helping him," she said.

Emma looked down at the young man on the stretcher. His chest was blown wide open, and the side of his face was missing. He was a mangled mess of tissue and blood. Her stomach lurched, and she held a hand over her nose for a second. The poor boy was beyond any help and already gone. Emma put her arm around the girl's shoulder as she wept.

"Sometimes there's naught to be done but hold their hand and wait."

The nurse's crying grew louder. "But I promised him I would make him better. I told him to hang on."

Emma rubbed the girl's arm. "He is better now, my dear. His pain is gone. He's in a better place than here."

Emma took the girl's hand in hers, leaned across the young soldier, and closed his eyes. "Sleep well, Private. Sleep well."

She held the nurse's hand, and together they recited the Our Father. When they finished, Emma wiped the girl's face. "What's your name?"

"Sally." She searched Emma's eyes. "Are you going to report me to the matron?"

"There's nothing to report, Sally. It's a difficult job. Sometimes we break down. The important thing is we do the best we can and help each other through the tough bits." She hugged the girl. "You need to collect yourself now and move on to the next soldier who needs helping."

Sally sniffled and nodded her head. She wiped her eyes in her apron and stood up. "Thank you."

Emma smiled as Sally headed off in another direction. She looked down and saw the girl's triage kit. She called after her, but amidst the chaos, she was gone. Emma opened it and lifted a large piece of gauze from the top. Underneath was a needle full of clear liquid. She looked back to where Frankie lay slumped on the cot. She knew she shouldn't. She bit her lip and looked around.

Soldiers covered the tent floor, and dozens more poured in through the tent flaps. Medical staff ran from body to body, organizing them in order of priority between those who could be helped and those who could not. She couldn't help them all, but she could help one.

She took the needle and ran back to Frankie. Without warning, she grabbed his arm and plunged the needle in deep. He blinked and started to protest, when it registered what she was doing. His eyes fluttered, and he fell back on the bed. He gripped her hand. "Thank you," he whispered, as his grasp slipped and he let go.

She sank to her knees and rubbed her hand against his forehead. "Have a rest, Frankie. By the looks of things, you deserve it." She took a deep breath and cleaned the wound in his arm with carbolic lotion before stitching him up. He never so much as stirred.

twenty-two

June 1916
Somewhere in France

DANIEL ARRIVED BACK AT HIS OWN LINES JUST BEFORE nightfall. Dundas ran toward him. "He's back!" He slapped Daniel on the back. "You had us worried there, Danny."

Phonse grinned and handed him a tin plate of bully beef and a hard biscuit. "You all right?"

"Hiding from a few Alleymen, is all."

Phonse's grin faded. "I knew we shouldn't have left you there."

"It was nothing. Where's Frankie?"

Dundas pointed at the motionless figure asleep between two wooden crates, his head resting on a sandbag.

"He's soggin' off some nap," Phonse said in between forkfuls.

"Good for him. They must have given him something strong," Daniel said.

Phonse nodded, shovelling the bully beef in his mouth and washing it down with tea. "We should go back and thank them for shutting him up for a while."

Daniel sat next to Phonse and ate what was on his plate. He'd given up torturing himself with memories of his mother's cooking. Just the thought of boiled cabbage, salt meat, and potatoes made his mouth water. And what he wouldn't give for a feed of stewed fish. There were times in his life he couldn't care if he never saw another fish. Not today, though.

They played a few games of cards as Frankie slept between them all. Later on, as they settled in for some rest, Frankie turned over and moaned. "Daniel, you there?"

Daniel sat up and slid over to his buddy. "I'm here, Frankie. How's the arm?"

He opened one glassy eye and shifted so he was lying flat on his back. "She's here."

"Who's here?"

"Your girl." He closed his eyes again.

"They must have given you some strong stuff, Frankie Drover. What are you on about?"

Frankie smiled, his eyes still closed. "Nothing wrong with me, Daniel. I'm just fine. But I'm telling you, she's here."

"Who?"

"The one whose picture you're looking at every night when you think we're all asleep."

The hair on the back of Daniel's neck prickled as he stared at Frankie.

"Tavenor's daughter is here. She stitched me up." Frankie yawned and turned toward the trench wall.

Daniel stared at Frankie's back for what seemed like an eternity.

Emma? Here? No, that couldn't be right. She was safe at home in Newfoundland. Panic flooded through him like ice water rushing through the trench in Gallipoli. He stood and tripped over someone's leg. He couldn't even pace, for Christ's sake. The trench was full of men propped up against one another trying to get a few hours' sleep. A feeling of helplessness smothered him, and he just wanted to break out of this maze of misery and run until he couldn't run any more. This was it—he was finally losing it. Every man had his breaking point.

Daniel had to get to the field hospital and see her for himself. His heart thudded so loud it was deafening. He ran his hands through his hair and clasped them together, trying to stop them from shaking. He scanned the trench, looking for his best way out. If he could get back to the reserve lines, then maybe . . . He caught the sentry guard's eye. The guard held his rifle in position, and the two locked eyes for the briefest of moments. Maybe he could plead that Frankie needed more medical attention. He looked down at his friend, who looked more peaceful tonight than he had in months.

The steady roar of gunfire rumbled in the distance. He took a step back and slid into the dirt wall, settling next to Frankie and counting the seconds until the next one. Our side, their side, a useless competition of death. Another shell exploded, and the trench walls shook. He waited for the next one and the next one. The counting was almost therapeutic. Every second he counted meant another second he was still alive. Dirt and rocks fell from above, and the earth protested with a groan like their old boat when she heaved from side to side in a heavy sea.

He was used to it. It had become commonplace. Normal, even, but every now and again it still didn't feel real. Tonight was one of those nights. Whenever he sat down and thought about what they were doing here, there were more reasons to stop than to go on. Both sides had carved out their side of right with their men burrowed deep into the ground with the rats, spending long days trying to find better ways to kill each other. Between them lay no man's land, once a fertile piece of land that sustained new life; it now collected their dead and served as a daily reminder of the horrors they committed against each other.

Daniel unbuttoned the breast pocket of his uniform and took out her picture. His eyes watered as he traced the lines of her face. Why would she be here? Almost two years had passed since they'd seen each other. She had never talked about becoming a nurse. Maybe she was married. Surely no man would let a woman he cared for come here. If he'd still had any say in her life, he would never have let her come here. But he hadn't. He gave up any right to that when he left her. A single thought wriggled its way through his mind. Could she have come here because of him? His stomach fluttered with hope, but he pushed it away.

He looked up at the clear night sky. The haze had settled, and the stars were brighter than he'd seen in months. So many nights like this one he'd spent thinking of her, wondering if she saw the same stars from her window in Middle Tickle. Now she was here, less than ten miles away, and yet she might as well have been ten thousand. Sadness filled every crevice in his broken heart. If they were anyplace else but here, he might allow himself to wonder about the what-ifs, but this was a hellish place for man and beast, and it was no place for the promise of a new life.

It was no place for his beautiful Emma.

Frankie laid his last card on a makeshift table, which was really a stack of supply crates. "And that's game, b'ys."

Phonse shook his head and laughed. "How many times have I told ya? You can't lay a queen after he's already laid the ace, Dundas."

"Can you explain the rules to me again?" Dundas asked.

Private Morris Kelly from St. John's pointed his finger at Frankie. "He's a keener. He won again and only had a dummy partner."

"Now, now, there's no need to talk about Dundas like that," Phonse said.

"Gentle Jesus, Dundas, we could teach the Hun over there faster than we can teach you, and they don't even understand the king's good English," Frankie said.

Dundas screwed up his face. "Neither do you."

Daniel looked on as the boys laughed and packed up their cards. Frankie and Phonse had been trying to teach Dundas how to play one hundred and twenties for months, but the poor bugger just couldn't grasp it. Daniel had declined to play. He hadn't been able to focus on anything since Frankie had told him Emma had stitched him up at the field hospital.

"You going back to Middle Tickle?" Phonse asked Frankie.

"What, tonight?" Frankie lit a cigarette and stretched his legs out in front of him.

"No, ya gommel. When this is all over," Phonse said.

"Well, I sure as hell ain't staying in St. John's with that uppity crowd." Frankie looked at Kelly sideways and took a long puff on the cigarette. Kelly whacked him in the arm.

"I think I'll go visit Bern and his family in Scotland before I makes me way home. Might have a few more stops, too. I'm over here now, might as well see the world."

After his amputations, Bern had gone to Scotland, married Fiona, and settled into his new home near Fort George with his wife and daughter.

"I've seen enough of this world now. I'm going home. And I'm getting as far away from these British bastards as I can. Good riddance," Frankie said.

"What was that, Drover?" Dundas hooked Frankie around the neck.

Frankie's distaste for Dundas's fellow countrymen was widely known. Lucky for him, most did not take offence. His hostility was directed more at the officers than those of his own rank.

"I didn't mean you, Dundas. You're all right."

"What about you, Daniel?" Phonse asked.

A moment passed.

"I might stay in England for a while. I liked it there."

Truth was, he didn't know what he wanted to do. As much as he tried not to, he couldn't help wondering where Emma would go after the war, especially now.

"What are you asking him for? He'll have to wait and see what the missus says. Won't ya, Danny?" Frankie asked.

Daniel shot Frankie a look.

"What's he talking about?" Phonse asked.

"I'm talking about his missus, Emma Tavenor," Frankie said, drawing hard on the cigarette. "She's here."

Phonse looked back and forth between them. "Tavenor's daughter? What's she got to do with anything?"

"Who's Tavenor?" Dundas asked.

Daniel reached for his water can and glanced at his friend. He got a chilly look in return. Phonse's eyes widened. "Emma's here? Did you know?"

Daniel took a swig from the can. Wiping his mouth with the back of his hand, he shook his head. "No. Frankie told me. She stitched him up last week."

Phonse raised his eyebrows. "She's a nurse?"

"Looks like it," said Daniel.

"Well, I'll be." Phonse shook his head, a smile curling at the corner of his mouth.

Daniel cast a look at Frankie. Smoke snaked its way up from a cigarette that hung from the corner of his mouth, and his eyes were far away, to that place he retreated to more frequently than ever. The differences in Frankie over the last two years were subtle for someone who didn't know him well, but for Daniel they were obvious. This wasn't a discussion he wanted to have with anyone right now, and Frankie knew it.

Daniel wished Emma was nowhere near this place. It was all he could think about, which wouldn't do him any good, because out here he needed to keep his head clear. If he could just get near her and talk some sense into to her. Even if she just went back to England. Her mother was still there, or so he thought.

"Fellas." Corporal Skinner hovered over them. "The CSM is looking for volunteers to move supplies with the medical section tonight. Preparation for the big push. I just need one more to ride with me. Any takers?"

Frankie groaned and held his arm up. "I got a chit, Skinner. Me arm's still bothering me, and I can't be lifting anything heavy right now."

Phonse rolled his eyes, and Dundas smirked. Daniel stood up. He'd go if it meant getting closer to Emma. "Where are you going for supplies?" he asked.

Skinner looked down at his clipboard. "I'm afraid there's not much left in any of the casualty clearing stations, so we're headed to Field Hospital C. It's not too far, but the road's pretty beat up from the shelling, so it'll take a few hours going and coming."

Daniel's heart raced. "We better get going."

Skinner pulled his clipboard to his chest. "Oh, well, that was easier than I thought. Right, then. Evening, lads." He nodded at Frankie, Phonse, and Dundas.

Daniel followed him without so much as a glance back, even though he felt the weight of his friends' stares. It took about fifteen minutes to weave a path through the lines. They had to go through the communications trenches, the reserve lines, and back through the artillery lines, until they finally emerged a few miles back from the front. Daniel followed Skinner to a convoy of trucks pointed toward Arras. The back of the truck was a box-like structure with a wooden frame covered in green canvas with red crosses painted on each side. Daniel had seen these vehicles in the distance, but so far had never been inside one.

"That's her," Skinner said, hustling to the front of the convoy and jumping in the first truck. Daniel hiked his boot up on the running board and hoisted himself inside the truck as the engine roared to life. Twenty minutes later, he could still hear the heavy rumble of guns and shelling behind them.

"How fast can this thing go?"

"About forty miles open full, but you can't get anywhere close to that on these roads."

Skinner wasn't kidding. The roads were almost impassable. With skill, he manoeuvred the truck around huge craters in their path. Daniel watched in awe as he hauled on the wheel, almost standing up straight to gear down in order to avoid the debris and the mountainous mud mounds.

"You drive this thing all day?"

Skinner caressed the dashboard like he might a woman's thigh. "Now, before you say anything unkind about her, she's my old Betsy. She's saved many lives, even my own a time or two."

"It just seems so dangerous," Daniel said.

He looked over at Daniel for a second, his eyes wide. "Says the man I just plucked from the front lines. You are joking?"

"This is different. At the front there's lots of us. This seems like it would be lonely."

"Oh, I'm rarely alone. There's enough room on the floor for three stretchers, and at least five men can fit on both benches. My partner usually rides with me, but he's on leave. Sometimes we squeeze another in the middle. We try not to leave anyone behind if we can help it. With the state of the roads, you don't know when you'll get back."

Daniel bounced around the seat as the truck drove through a large mud crater, and he felt nauseous. He couldn't remember the last time he'd eaten. Sometime that morning. In the distance, a faint glow of lights appeared. "Is that it?"

"Yes. It'll take another ten minutes or so to get there. The road is pretty rough on this next stretch.

"This close to the hospital?"

Skinner nodded. "We've been hit a time or two. No one knows if it's intentional or an accident, but what does it matter? We're not as far from the front as we tell ourselves. There's bound to be misfires."

Daniel stared out the window, unable to respond. Since learning Emma was here, he was comforted that she wasn't in harm's way at the field hospital, but Skinner was right. None of them were safe.

Skinner pulled to a stop just outside the entrance to the hospital's grounds and was saying something, but Daniel was no longer interested. He had very little time to find Emma. He opened the door and jumped out, wandering away from the convoy into the bustle of activity.

Skinner caught up to him with his clipboard in his hand. "I'll need to fetch the quartermaster and see about securing the supplies for the whole line, so I'll be a while. There's a mess tent in there. You can't miss it. Food's decent. There's probably a hot cup of tea going. Meet me back at the truck in two hours."

Skinner hurried away with a few other medical corps drivers, and Daniel watched people rushing by, each one looking like they were on an important mission. The irony was not lost on him: he was trained to take lives, and they were trained to save them.

He wandered for a few minutes out of curiosity and pulled aside a tent flap, stepping inside. Dimly lit lanterns hung from wooden beams, supporting the tent's frame. Shelves ran the full length of each wall, filled with brown bottles of every shape and size, various labelled tins, and grey boxes, along with rows of prepackaged bandages and gauze. A large chest of wooden drawers at the tent's rear had stainless steel bowls stacked high. Other supplies hung from hooks along a wooden beam running crossways along the tent's ceiling.

He backed out and lowered the flap, stepping onto a duckboard path that led in different directions. As he rounded a small copse of trees, dozens of green and white tents came into view. His pace slowed as he walked past a canopied tent with no side coverings. Cots ran the tent's perimeter with a back-to-back row running through the middle. He wondered why they were all wearing white, until he got close enough. White bandages. Some men looked as if their whole bodies were covered in one big bandage, like the mummies he'd seen in Egypt.

He didn't have to dig deep to imagine what the wounds underneath looked like. Men standing right next to him had been blown to kingdom come, their body parts left to rot where they landed. Ashes to ashes, dust to dust. Sometimes those thoughts crept into his mind, but at the front you don't have time to think about it. Thinking about it would get you killed. No, you had to get on with the daily slog to keep alive. People think you're most vulnerable out in the open air, fighting, but that wasn't true at all. A soldier was his most vulnerable in the early morning when there were a few hours of quiet. He could run from the enemy; he couldn't run from the creeping images of death.

There were dozens of tents and hundreds of men in various states. Here they dealt with the brutal effects of war every day. There was no escape from it. How could Emma handle it? She was so gentle and soft in spirit. She would be a comfort to those fortunate enough to be assigned to her. But, oh, the things she must have seen. He longed to take her in his arms. He closed his eyes for a minute and breathed deep. Someone brushed past him, and he opened his eyes.

"Are you lost, soldier?"

He opened his eyes, and women in Red Cross uniforms spilled through tent doors, hurrying past him. He looked at every face, hoping for even a glimpse of her.

"Are you lost?" the voice asked again, and he looked down at the woman standing in front of him.

She did not have a British accent as he expected. In fact, she sounded very much like she was from Newfoundland. "No. I'm looking for someone. Emma Tavenor. Do you know her?"

Her eyes flickered. "What's she to you?"

The question caught him off guard. "She's . . . well . . . she's . . ."

"Emma's busy, and you don't look hurt. Are you hurt?"

They always assumed the wounds were on the outside. "No."

"Well, I've got lots who are, and so does she. I've no time to play Cupid, soldier. Carry on." She turned around and grinned. "But I'm not altogether heartless. Can I tell her who's asking after her?"

"Tell her Daniel is here."

"All right, soldier, off you go. We only tend to the sick here." She started off down the duckboard path.

"Hey!" he called after her. "What's your name?"

She turned around. "Maisie. Maisie Parsons from St. John's." She grinned. "Don't worry. I'll tell Emma handsome Daniel was here."

A familiar hand squeezed Emma's shoulder, and she looked up into Maisie's smiling face. They'd met on Emma's second day in France, and she was so relieved to find someone from home there.

Maisie looked down at Emma's latest charge, a young soldier who was bandaged from head to toe. "How's he doing?"

"If he makes it through the night, he might have a fighting chance, according to Captain Morris," Emma said, trying to stifle a yawn.

A shell had exploded in front of him. Blew his legs right off, and one of his arms. It also ripped his chest open wide. The surgeons had done what they could. They made him comfortable, and the rest would run its course. Emma had spent most of the evening here as he drifted in and out of consciousness. Michael was his name, and he was a young boy from Liverpool. Even though his papers said he was nineteen years old, she put him at fifteen, at best. She held his hand and reassured him he'd be up and around in no time. Sometimes she felt guilty about lying to them, but what else could she do?

"Let's get you a cup of tea. You've been here all night."

Emma hesitated. "I should stay. Just in case." She swallowed hard. "I've lost six patients in the last two days, Maisie. I can't bear to lose another tonight."

Maisie rubbed her hand. "Emma, darling, you've done more than your fair share for this boy. It's in God's hands now. Come." She tugged on Emma's arm, pulling her to her feet.

Her whole body ached. It had been a week of non-stop work. Just when the last man was taken from triage, the trucks showed up and filled the tent again. Bodies were piled behind the resuss tent as far as the eye could see. Senseless, tragic deaths. There were times when she wondered if there would be any men left when this was over.

She stifled a yawn. She'd been up since five and hadn't had more than three hours' sleep before that. If you could call it sleep. It was more like an exhausted coma.

"When did you eat last?"

"This morning."

"There must be something warm left from supper. Let's go." The two linked arms, and Maisie led her outside. The air was warm, and a gentle breeze ruffled her hair as they headed toward the mess tent.

"Oh, by the way, you had a visitor earlier," Maisie said.

Emma tilted her head to the side. "Really? Who was it?"

"Don't sound so innocent, Emma Tavenor. I'm jealous of the company you keep. That's one handsome man asking after you." Maisie jabbed her with her elbow. "My question is, how'd you meet him, anyway? He looks too healthy to have been a patient, and you never leave this place."

Emma stopped mid-stride to stare at her friend. "Meet who?"

"Handsome Daniel. I think he blushed when I called him that." Maisie giggled.

Her heart skipped a beat. "Daniel's here?" The blood rushed to her face.

"I ran into him when I was leaving the surgery tent earlier. Quiet. Very mysterious. How come you haven't told me about him?"

Panic set in fast, and her hands began to shake. "Is he a patient? Is he hurt?"

Maisie shook her head. "No, he definitely did not look hurt to me. He said he was looking for you."

Emma scanned the area around her, but it was dark, and there were still lots of uniformed men milling about. He wouldn't easily stick out in the crowd.

"Emma, sweetheart, what's wrong? You look petrified." Maisie's big blue eyes held concern. "Has he done something to you? He has, hasn't he?"

She shook her head, trying to find the words to explain. She opened her mouth, but it was all too much. Ever since Daniel had left her two years ago, her life had become one enormous pit of loss. She'd lost her father, even though it was his own doing, and her mother was lost to the drink. Since arriving in France, she'd seen more loss of life than she could have ever imagined possible. Before she came here, she was naive enough to think she could make Daniel see sense and leave the war. She knew now that could never happen. There was only one way out.

Frankie must have told him she was here. For two years she had orchestrated a way to get here to find him. Now he had come looking for her, and she didn't know what to say to him. She felt empty inside. She was aware she was still moving, but everything was a blur. Eventually, they were seated at a table inside the mess tent. Maisie placed a cup of lukewarm tea in front of her and a bowl of soup.

"Now, tell me. What has this fellow done to you?"

"It's not what he's done to me, Maisie. It's what I've done to him. My father destroyed his family. It's the reason he's here at all." Her breath hitched. "Don't you see? If something happens to him here, it will be my fault."

"Let me get this straight," Maisie said. "You knew him when you lived in Newfoundland?"

Emma nodded. "Yes."

"Who is this Daniel?"

"He's the love of my life," she answered, smiling. "But my father destroyed his family and brought them to the brink of financial ruin." She told Maisie the whole story, starting with Richard's death in the spring of 1914.

When she was finished, she looked at a wide-eyed Maisie and swallowed hard. "The war broke out, and he just left. I haven't seen or heard from him since. I came to England and joined the Voluntary Aid Detachment, and at the first opportunity I transferred to the front. I always wanted to find him and tell him I was sorry. He chose his family, and I don't blame him. How could he stay with me after what my father did to him? To all of them? Deep down he must hate me for everything that has happened. He's lost so much." She wiped her eyes with her sleeve. "And now he's here and could lose his own life, and I drove him to it." She placed her hand over her mouth and leaned her elbow on the table, unable to go on.

A tear rolled down Maisie's face, and she wiped it away. She took Emma's free hand. "Emma, darling, that's the saddest story I've ever heard."

The two sat for a few minutes, neither knowing what to say to the other.

Maisie's face brightened. "You have to talk to him. He's here. He came to find you. He must want to see you." She stood up. "Let's go find him."

twenty-three

June 1916
Field Hospital C

DANIEL'S HEART SANK. SHE COULD BE ANYWHERE, AND HIS time was up. Damn it! He should have been more insistent with that nurse. It was foolish to think he'd be able to find her among hundreds of people, and he'd let the one person go who could help him.

In the distance, a tent with rows of steam flowing from the top caught his attention. It reminded him of the chimneys blowing full blast around Middle Tickle harbour. He walked toward it. He might be going back to the front, disappointed at not seeing her, but he wouldn't be going back hungry.

He approached the mess line. A young girl poured him a cup of tea so black it looked like it had been boiling all day. She handed him a plate of whatever was on offer for the evening meal. He slumped down on a bench at the end of an empty table and looked down. Half a cup of warm dishwater and skilligalee mocked him from the tray, but it was better than he had most evenings.

Skinner came toward him, looking flustered. "Beresford. There you are."

Daniel pushed his tray aside and stood, but Skinner waved him down. "Sit down and eat. We're going nowhere tonight."

"What? But I have to get back to the front. I'll be—"

"There's a shell hole the size of Amiens blocking the road, and there's no way around. Just went off behind one of our convoys coming in. Goddamn Bosch bastards. A section will be sent out first thing in the morning to fill it."

"But they'll think I'm AWOL."

"I gave your name to HQ. They know you're with me." He placed his hand on Daniel's shoulder and laid his clipboard on the table. "Listen, you're getting a night away from the front. Be happy. We'll even find a bed for you, and if you play your cards right, you might even get a proper wash." Skinner looked down at Daniel's plate and turned up his nose. "I might have been wrong about the food, though." He picked up his clipboard. "See you at zero six hundred. Get some rest," he said, before leaving the mess tent.

Daniel rubbed his face and sighed, realizing just how tired he was. He couldn't remember the last night he'd spent in a bed. Even if it was a cot, it was better than a dirt floor, wedged between four smelly men. He picked up his cup and was about to sip the now cold tea when a group of nurses entered. Among them was the young Parsons girl from St. John's he'd spoken to about Emma earlier. By God, he wasn't going to let this happen a second time.

He laid down the cup and walked over to the group of girls. "Miss Parsons."

She turned around, her mouth set in a grim line until she met his eyes. Her mouth widened. "Handsome Daniel! You're still here." She threw herself into his arms, and he stood stiff as a corpse, surprised by her reaction. She pulled him to the table he'd just left.

"I'm so sorry about earlier. You must come with me. I'll take you to Emma. She needs to know you're still here."

He was relieved, but wondered why the change of heart. "Why have you changed your mind?"

She threw her hands up in the air, and her eyes filled. "Because we're here in this terrible place, and tomorrow we might not be. Tomorrow we might be dead." She wiped her face. "And because she can't go on like this. She's wearing herself out trying to save every man who walks through these doors. And now I understand why."

"I'm not sure I do."

"She feels guilty, Daniel. She's trying to save them all because she's trying to save you. She feels responsible for you being here. She told me everything. About what her father did to your family." Her eyes held pity as she looked into his. "She told me how your brother died."

He couldn't talk about Richard here like this with a stranger. He had to find Emma. Grief swirled around him, creeping into his body. "Where is she?"

"She was just here, but she's gone back to one of her patients. She's been with him all day." She looked down. "He's not going to make it, but she wants to be there with him when he goes. She stays with them all." She cast her eyes down.

"Take me to her."

She nodded, and Daniel followed, leaving his plate of food for the flies to feast on. A lump formed in his throat. In his absence, Emma must have realized her father's role in the near ruination of his family. In all reality, Richard's death wasn't his fault, but when you hated someone so much, it was easy to lay blame. But none of this was *her* fault. He could never hold her responsible for her father's actions.

Guilt clung to him so heavily it was like climbing a hill with one hundred pounds of kit on his back. If something happened to her here—he couldn't let his mind go there, even if they were never together again. She was here not because she wanted to be. She was here for him, but for all the wrong reasons.

Maisie pulled open the door and stopped, looking back at him. "This is the resuss tent. You might, ah . . . you might want to prepare yourself."

"For what?"

"It's where we send the patients who are in bad shape. Most are dying and just need to be made comfortable until, well, until it happens."

He watched her kind eyes for a few seconds, trying to find a tactful way to reply. "Do you think there's anything in there that can shock me any more than what I've seen out there?" He pointed back toward the front lines. As if on cue, a shell rumbled in the distance, like a thunderstorm working its way toward them.

She squeezed his hand and gave a half smile. "No, I suppose not."

The tent was dim, but peaceful compared to the hustle and bustle of the hospital grounds. This one was laid out a bit different. There was more space between the cots, and a series of stations was set up around the tent.

The ward clerk greeted them. "Good evening, Miss Parsons."

"Good evening, Tommy. I'm looking for Miss Tavenor," she said, smiling at the young man.

Daniel scanned the rows of beds filled with dying men. He should feel something when he looked at them, but he didn't. He was numb. He turned his head to the left, and stopped. He would know her anywhere. Her dark hair, her slim frame, her gentle movement. She was leaning over a patient, caressing his forehead, his hand tucked into hers. Daniel walked past the ward clerk, despite his protests. Maisie touched the clerk's arm and held him back. Emma leaned close to the soldier's ear and whispered something. A look of contentment crossed the boy's face, for that was all he was.

It was a moving gesture, and his heart filled with emotion. Everything he had ever loved about Emma flooded his mind and his senses. She lowered the soldier's lids and crossed his arms over his chest, a painful sob escaping her lips. His heart ached. She shouldn't be here to see this pain and suffering. She covered her face with her hands, and he couldn't help himself any longer. He reached down and touched her shoulder. At first she didn't react, but within seconds she straightened, her hands falling away from her face. It took another moment before she looked up, but when she did, the look on her face said she knew it would be him standing there.

"Daniel," she whispered, standing to face him. She reached out to touch him, as if not believing he was real.

His heart thrust near out of his chest as he absorbed everything about her. She looked different than he remembered, and nothing like the photograph. Her once pale skin was darkened from so much time in the elements, but she was even more beautiful. His hand rose, and in an unconscious movement, his thumb brushed a tear from her cheek. He searched her face until he locked on the one thing that had always drawn him to her. Her eyes. The young girl he'd left in Middle Tickle two years before had eyes full of fire and hope. Now they held sadness and pain, and it killed him for his part in that.

"Are you all right?" she asked, her eyes widening.

He nodded, swallowing hard as he fought to keep his emotions in check.

"Good, because I—" She looked at the dead boy beside her and around at the lifeless bodies on the ward before looking back at him, her eyes filling. "I don't know what I'd do if something happened to you, too."

She stumbled, and he caught her before she fell. He scooped her up in his arms and held her tight, looking at Maisie. "Where can we take her?"

"Follow me," she said.

The familiar smell of lavender from her hair filled his head. She draped her arms around him, and her breath, faint on his neck, stirred something deep within. He followed Maisie past the gaping-mouthed ward clerk and down the path toward the entrance to the hospital's grounds. Within a few minutes they were back at the supply tent he had first peeked inside when he arrived.

Maisie held the door flap for him, and he bent to step inside, his arms still wrapped tight around Emma. Her breathing had slowed, and she had drifted off to sleep.

Maisie retrieved a lantern from a shelf at the rear of the tent and lit it, motioning for him to follow. "There's a room back here where some of us steal a couple of hours' sleep when we can. You won't be disturbed here."

It could have easily been mistaken for another cabinet, but it was little better than a makeshift closet scrapped together with some old wood. There was hardly enough space for one person in there, never mind two. A cot had been wedged in against the wall, and a wooden stool sat across from the bed. A small stand with a wash basin decorated the other corner.

Daniel laid a now sleeping Emma on the bed and looked at Maisie. "Thank you for your help, Maisie." She handed him the lantern, and he laid it on a shelf next to the washstand. He offered her a rare smile. "Emma's lucky to have a friend like you."

"Take care of her, will you? She's always taking care of everyone else. Nobody takes care of her." Maisie leaned down and kissed her friend on the forehead.

"I'll try," he said. "If she'll let me."

Maisie closed the door, and Daniel sat on the stool, taking in the full sight of her. He brushed a stray wisp of hair off Emma's face, his hand lingering, caressing her soft skin. He had so much to say, but for now he was content to watch her sleep.

As she slept, he removed his uniform and hung it over the chair. He peeled off his inside clothes, which stuck to him like old wallpaper, and began the arduous task of washing up with a bar of Sunlight soap he'd found in a supply box under the washstand. He even found a small shaving kit there. It took him the best part of an hour to scrub the mud and dirt from underneath his fingernails and from every crevice of his body. It was never easy to shake the rancid smell of death. It clung to his uniform, his hair, and skin, and it usually took hours before his mind even registered the sweet-smelling aroma of soap.

He was quiet when he lay down beside her in nothing but a white undershirt and pants he'd found while rummaging in a trunk. He slid an arm underneath her neck and wrapped the other around her small waist, his hand coming to rest at the small of her back. His face found a home next to the soft bed of her dark hair as he closed his eyes and listened to the distant rumble of shells smacking into the ground. It was the most content he'd felt in two years.

Hours must have passed, as the overwhelming sense of exhaustion had left him, but something willed him to open his eyes, and when he did, he found her grey eyes piercing his. He touched her cheek, and she squeezed her eyes shut, tilting her head to let his hand fully cup her face. His beautiful Emma. How many nights had he dreamed of this? Her eyes were wet, and he brushed the moisture away. He placed a finger under her chin and raised it until their eyes met. He searched hers, wondering what she wanted from him, if anything. They'd never been intimate with each other in Middle Tickle, apart from kissing and some touching through their clothes, but they were just kids then.

With a single finger she traced the outline of his lips before wandering down his jawline toward the natural incline of his neck. His skin felt hot where her fingers touched him, and his pulse quickened. He was surprised when she reached for the hem of his shirt, and he shifted to let her pull it over his head. Her hands slid down his chest and across his stomach before coming to rest on his hip. Her cool, grey eyes remained fixed on his without so much as blinking.

His fingers slid into her hair, picking out the pins that still held some of it in place, and it cascaded around him like a curtain as he kissed her neck just under her ear. His other hand followed the curve of her breast. Her breath caught, and she whimpered. His stomach tightened. He didn't deserve anything from her now, least of all this. He had left her with no explanation, no goodbye.

Her fingers came around his neck and ruffled his hair before coming to rest on either side of his face. She stared at him until her eyes flared with need. She pulled him closer, until their lips were one breath apart.

"Emma."

"Can you ever love me again?" she whispered.

Her look was pleading. It asked for what he'd never given to another living soul.

"I never stopped," he breathed. He wanted her fully, completely.

She licked her lips, and he was tantalized beyond reason. He leaned forward and caught her bottom lip with his own, and with the gentlest of movements he pulled her forward. Their mouths mingled, and her velvet tongue pushed its way inside. His parted to let her in, and she kissed him with an urgency he'd never experienced with her before. Her hands left his face and wandered down his body to the waistline of his underpants. She gently tugged until they were around his thighs, and he lifted his legs until he worked them off. His erection was bared for her to see, and he worried she would turn away in embarrassment. Instead, she pulled him toward her as she sat up on her knees, their mouths still entangled.

"Behind my neck," she whispered into his mouth.

He reached under her hair, feeling the smooth metal clasps that held her VAD uniform in place. He pulled them apart, and the dress loosened. Her mouth still on his, she wriggled her arms out from the sleeves. Breathless, she pulled away and lifted the grey dress and white apron over her head, flinging it behind her onto the floor.

She knelt in front of him in nothing but a transparent white shift. His eyes roamed her body, and only then did she look away. Kneeling before her, he gently turned her face toward him. He pushed her shift's thin straps down over her silky shoulders, revealing her smooth, white breasts. Her skin glowed in the faint light.

"You're beautiful," he whispered.

Her eyes blazed, and she opened her mouth to speak, but stopped. Instead, her mouth crushed down hard on his. He guided them into a lying position, and she came to rest beside him. Their hands explored each other's bodies fully for the first time, skimming, caressing, loving. He closed his eyes, every nerve in his body tingling. His hand covered her breast, and he plucked her nipple. She shivered in response, and he broke their kiss to look at her. She opened her eyes, a raw look of want on her face. He felt himself harden to the point of pain. With a trembling hand she reached down and touched him.

He covered her hand. "Emma—you don't have to do this." He wouldn't be selfish, as much as he wanted her. What could he offer her? They were here in the middle of a war. He could die tomorrow.

She entwined her fingers with his. "I don't have to, but I want to."

"But you're trembling."

She kissed him, and her lips fluttered against his as she smiled. He would never forget the feeling.

"I don't know how to do this," she whispered.

"That makes two of us," he said, running his fingers through her silky hair and leaning in to kiss her again.

She sat up, her eyes wide with surprise. "You mean there's been no one else?"

He sat up next to her and shook his head. "It's always been you, Emma. Only you." His breath caught as her mouth covered his, and she kissed him with tender longing. Within seconds, the urgent need returned, and they broke away, breathless.

"I'm just happy to have found you, Emma. I'm happy enough to hold you in my arms tonight. We don't have to do anything more than that." He brushed her hair aside and caressed her cheek.

"I'm happy you found me, too, but tomorrow you go back to the front and I go back to tending the wounded and the dying." She cupped his face and kissed him tenderly. "And right now we're here together." She caressed his face. "We might never get this chance again. I won't waste it wondering about the what-ifs."

He looked deep into her eyes. "I love you, Emma. It's only ever been you."

She shifted one leg over to straddle him, her arms resting around his shoulders. "And I love you, Daniel Beresford. Always and forever." Their lips met again.

Somewhere in the distance, a shell sounded closer than the others had all night. He rolled her onto her back and knelt before her. As the next shell exploded, he slid inside her as her head swayed back, and she cried out.

Daniel never took much leave. Home leave was no good, as Newfoundland was too far away. He had no real reason to go to England, and if he was in France, he might as well stay with Frankie, Phonse, and Dundas. Many times Winter had encouraged him to take twenty-four hours and go to Amiens for the day, just to get away from it all. He rarely did. So, Daniel wasn't surprised by Winter's shocked face when he showed up one morning and asked for a twenty-four-hour leave ticket.

"Everything okay, Daniel?"

"Never better, Second Lieutenant, never better." His voice sounded almost happy.

He caught the train into Amiens and took a room at the Priory

Hotel on Winter's recommendation. Daniel had never seen a hotel before, let alone slept in one. He opened the door to the room and stepped inside, placing his kit at the foot of a high, four-poster bed with a dark blue embroidered cover. He removed his haversack from his shoulder and sat on the end of the bed, looking around the room. A table and two chairs were situated near a window, and he wandered over to look at the street below.

The square was full of soldiers. They milled about in small groups, while others walked arm in arm with females. Daniel's heart surged. He should have gone to the field hospital first and convinced Emma to come to Amiens with him, though in all seriousness he couldn't just walk in and expect her to leave. Besides, showing up like that could get her into real trouble with the matron. He knew there were strict rules in place about mixing with the soldiers.

But he wasn't just any soldier.

After a long bath and donning some clean clothes, Daniel emerged a new man. He smelled decent and he'd ironed the lice right out of his uniform, for now, anyway. He left the room and wandered into the street, looking in the shop windows and wishing very much Emma was by his side. One day when the war was over, they'd come to Amiens and get a room at the Priory Hotel and walk these streets together as husband and wife.

Daniel passed a shop, and a glint caught his eye in the late afternoon sun. He took a step back to consider it more closely. The bells on the door jingled as he stepped inside and made eye contact with a short, balding man with glasses and a thick moustache. Daniel beckoned him to the window and pointed. The man reached inside the display, took out two narrow gold bands, and laid them in Daniel's palm. He smiled and closed his hand around the rings, reaching into his pocket for some money.

twenty-four

June 28, 1916
Somewhere in France

DANIEL SHIVERED AND SHIFTED HIS POSITION IN THE TRENCH. He held the collar of his greatcoat closed and tipped his helmet forward, trying to keep the driving rain from running down his chest. His fingers tingled from the cold.

A match flared and cast an orange glow against the mud. Phonse inhaled smoke from a cigarette, the end glowing like a flare in the night sky. His face was black from the burned cork they'd used to darken their faces.

"Jesus, Phonse," Daniel said. "You trying to get your head shot off?"

Frankie slapped Phonse on the arm. The cigarette wavered. "Or worse. You'll get my head shot off."

"Relax, b'ys," Phonse said. "Old Fritz is scrambling to fix up their lines. They're not worried about the four of us sitting out here freezing our arses off in this godforsaken rain."

Daniel couldn't disagree as he tried to think back to the last time he was completely dry. One thing was certain. He'd never complain about the rain back home again.

"One of the arty guys said they've dropped a million shells on them," Frankie said. "I'd say the only scrambling they're doing is for cover."

Dundas shook his head. "I don't know, Frankie. They've been dug in a long time. If there is a big push coming, I don't think they're going to roll over and play dead."

Daniel pulled his coat tighter around his neck. The trenches were ripe with rumours, but Daniel didn't believe anything anymore. Not since they were told they'd be home for Christmas. Something was up, for sure. Ammunition was being stockpiled like he'd never seen before. Large numbers of reinforcements had arrived, and even the food had improved. The shelling was almost non-stop, and, deep down, they all expected to go over the top any day.

Several elite units had conducted a number of raids in the past few weeks, testing the German trenches for weakness, and as far as Daniel was concerned, nothing had changed except the number of craters.

"Well, it can't come fast enough," Frankie said. "The sooner we push Fritz back, the better."

"Better be," Dundas replied. "I'm chin-strapped, tired, and sore. And wet. This war stuff just ain't for me."

Phonse laughed while puffing out ringlets of smoke. "It's a good thing you told us, because we never would have guessed. What are you in such a rush to get home for, anyway? I thought it was poverty's arse and all in Bethnal Green."

"Oh, it is," Dundas said. "But at least no one's shootin' at me there."

"Amen to that," Daniel muttered to himself.

Footsteps sloshed in the soupy mud, and Frankie peered over the top, looking back toward their own lines. Second Lieutenant Winter slid into the trench and slapped the cigarette out of Phonse's hand.

"What are you doing? I can see you from the reserve trench." Four others joined them in the trench. "All right, boys," he said, "we're heading out. Same as before. Assess the lines and get back in one piece. Questions?"

They all shook their heads. They had completed special training and had conducted a half-dozen raids in the last three weeks. They knew the routine.

Winter raised his hand and signalled the advance. Frankie slid a trench knife out from underneath his pant leg. Phonse and Dundas held pistols, and Daniel grasped a bayonet, whose long handle had been cut down and driven into a piece of wood to make for a more manageable weapon.

The group moved slow and low, careful not to make any noise that could be heard over the incessant rain. They headed for a gap in the line they knew had been made during the shelling earlier in the day. Daniel stepped over shredded lumber and pieces of tangled wire and walked the perimeter of craters filled with water. Only the ground a few feet in front of him was visible, but the amount of wire and wood indicated they were close.

Something whooshed and exploded in front of him, and Daniel dropped to the ground as a flare streaked across the sky. He blinked away the stars. Night turned to day. The bright light exposed them in the open a few feet from the German trench. Voices shouted in a language he couldn't understand, and grenades flew up from inside the trench, arced over Daniel, and landed a few yards behind him.

Gunfire erupted. Grenades exploded. Men screamed. Daniel stowed the bayonet and yanked his rifle from his shoulder, firing toward the Germans. Frankie crawled next to Daniel, rolled to his side, and flicked a grenade into the trench. Daniel dropped his head as debris peppered his helmet.

"Take that, ya German bastards!" Frankie shouted.

Daniel raised his head and spotted movement in the trench. He thought about what his father had taught him. Focus on your target, then shoot. Daniel used the light from the flares to his advantage. One by one he chose his target and took his shot. As each man dropped, he moved on to the next.

Frankie lobbed another grenade. "I've got your back, Danny boy, keep 'em going."

Someone shrieked, and Daniel looked back to his right. One of his comrades had misjudged the gap and was hung up on the wire. A fellow soldier reached up to pull him back, but the man's animated struggle ceased with the crack of a rifle. The second man jerked sideways and disappeared. Daniel glimpsed the wounded form crawling through the mud toward their own lines.

"Eyes forward, Danny!" Frankie yelled, before tossing another grenade.

Daniel hesitated before turning back to the scene playing out before him. He spotted the silhouette of a Brodie helmet in the German trench. Private O'Neil emerged from the trench carrying a German helmet. He scrambled toward Daniel, but stopped short. A German grenade dropped between them, bounced, and rolled to O'Neil's feet.

"Look out, boys!" he called out. "I got it!"

He dropped his rifle and the helmet and scooped up the grenade. Seconds after it left his hands, it exploded, driving him back to Daniel's right.

Daniel looked back. O'Neil struggled to roll over, and for a moment Daniel thought he heard O'Neil laughing. The flare extinguished itself and shrouded the battlefield in black.

"Retreat!"

Daniel didn't need to hear Winter's order a second time. He dragged O'Neil to where the others were gathering, about twenty feet away. He moved as fast as he could before the Germans could light them up again.

He scanned the landscape of the lifeless battlefield where so many comrades lay. His eyes focused on the sagging tree a few feet away. He had never noticed it before. He blinked a few times and for the briefest of seconds imagined what this land had looked like before they made their mark here. In the not so distant past, this tree was tall and full of branches and bright green leaves, full of life itself. Now it was dead like everything else here.

Daniel didn't think anything could beat the horrors at Gallipoli. He'd never believed such a level of misery existed until they'd arrived at the Western Front. Hundreds died every day, and the obedient replacements were sent to take their place. Eventually the dead would fade from living memory, but what was happening here on this land couldn't easily be forgotten. One hundred years from now, the land would still bear the scars from the atrocities committed here, but would anyone remember the men who fought here?

Daniel dropped O'Neil next to the mangled tree.

"Winter," Captain Butler said. "What have we got?"

"Four dead, Captain." Winter stopped for breath. "Skinner's on the wire. We gotta get him down."

Soldiers limped toward the group, helped by their comrades. O'Neil's eyes fluttered as he looked up into their staring faces.

He sat up and rubbed his shoulder. "B'ys, was anyone hurt?"

After a few days' rest, the Regiment was ordered to the front. They'd been issued their ammunition, and rumours that the big push was on spread through the lines.

"I don't understand how there isn't more damage," Phonse said as he jogged between Daniel and Frankie. "Christ Almighty. We shot more daisy cutters and toffee apples on their side this week than the duration of the entire war."

"Must have fired more duds than we did live ones," Frankie said.

Dundas caught up to them as they shuffled into line. "Surely they wouldn't be planning anything big now until we take out more of their lines with artillery, would they?" he asked.

Daniel spotted Second Lieutenant Winter speaking to Major Ashdown. Ashdown pointed his finger in Winter's face. When he walked away, Winter looked at Daniel and started to go after Ashdown, but stopped, turned, and approached the boys instead.

"Good morning, sir," Phonse said.

"Morning, lads." He joined them and rubbed his chin. "It seems there are conflicting reports about the level of damage to the German front lines."

"Nothing conflicting about what I saw," Frankie said. "It's all still there. Skinner was hanging from it. Ain't that proof enough?"

"We heard they fired a million shells this week," Dundas said with wide eyes. "It must be tore up over there. I bet half of them have turned around and gone home!"

Winter looked at Daniel. "It seems like we might not have made as big an impact as was first reported."

"So, what's going on today?" Phonse asked. "Seems everyone is going forward."

Winter was quiet.

Dundas looked at Phonse, then Winter. "Second Lieutenant?"

"The big push you've been wondering about. It's on. Tomorrow."

"Jesus Christ," Frankie said.

The Regiment formed up in ranks and was given orders to march to the front. As the sun set, the townspeople lined the street. A boy ran out and hugged a soldier's leg.

"*No, monsieur. Restez ici, monsieur.*"

The boy's mother pulled him back and collapsed to the ground. Daniel scanned the crowd as they shouted in French what he assumed were words of support. He scanned their faces.

"Christ, they're crying," Dundas said. "They're all crying."

"Think they know something we don't?" Phonse asked.

Daniel said nothing. They knew what he knew.

The crowd dwindled as dusk settled, and someone struck off with "Keep the Home Fires Burning." They marched five miles to the community of Mailly-Maillet, where they stayed for nearly three hours. Just before two o'clock in the morning, the Regiment reached St. John's Road, a trench they had constructed two weeks earlier. The four friends settled in with orders to get what rest they could.

Daniel was in the middle of a glorious dream about lying in Emma's arms when soft crying woke him. He cocked his head, straining to pinpoint the direction of the faint sobs. Frankie and Phonse were turned in to the wall, fast asleep.

Daniel sat up and blinked a few times. "Dundas?" he said in a hushed voice.

"Yeah, Danny."

Daniel hoisted himself up and stepped outside. Dundas was propped with his legs up, chin on his knees and his arms wrapped tight around them, rocking back and forth.

"What are you doing out here, Dundas?"

"Nothing, Danny."

Daniel knelt in front of him. The boy's eyes were red and swollen, and his entire body shook.

"It'll be all right," Daniel said in an unconvincing voice. "Come on in and get some sleep."

"No, it won't, Danny." Dundas swallowed. "This will be the end of us." His dark-rimmed eyes, which once gleamed with youth, were now vacant and lifeless.

"Don't be so foolish. Of course it won't. We've been through worse than this."

"Our lives mean nothing. They'll just replace us until we're all gone. Until there's no men left."

"We're in good shape for tomorrow. They won't know what hit 'em."

Dundas shook his head back and forth and dropped his head in his hands. "I can't do it, Danny. It's madness. The whole thing is utter madness."

A rat the size of a tomcat scurried by them carrying something in its mouth. Dundas whimpered like a small child, and Daniel kneeled forward and put a hand on the boy's shoulder. A glint caught his eye, and he looked down. Dundas was holding a pistol in his hand.

"Come on, Dundas, you can't give up now. We've got a job to do. There's people counting on us."

Dundas grew still, and his face lost all expression. His thumb slid back and forth over the pistol.

"Dundas. No. Think about your mother. She needs you."

"I'm sorry, Danny, I can't do it anymore." He stifled a sob. "Even if I did make it through tomorrow, what good would I be to her now? What good would I be to anyone?"

"Dundas, you've got your whole life ahead of you once we're done with this place."

Dundas tilted his head to the side, a dark expression clouding his boyish features. "No, Danny. Don't you see?" He waved the pistol in the air. "We'll never be done with this. This war will never let us forget."

"Dundas. No," Daniel said, holding his hands up.

The pistol shook in Dundas's hand.

"Dundas, come on. Put down the gun. Before you know it, we'll be going home. Come on, now. We made a pact, remember?"

Dundas gave a small smile. "I'm sorry, Danny. I'm not going home."

The pistol swung up to Dundas's temple, and he pulled the trigger.

Daniel dived forward. "No!"

The pistol slid from Dundas's grasp as his arm fell by his side and his body stilled. Daniel dropped to his knees, rocking back and forth, covering his face with one hand.

Phonse scrambled from the dugout. "What in the name of Jesus . . . ?" He knelt next to Dundas. "Danny, what's happened?

Daniel staggered back until he hit the trench wall next to the dugout's opening and slid down. He drew his legs up to his chest and wrapped his arms around them, staring at the boy's lifeless body. He rubbed his cheeks and looked at his hands, now smeared red.

Frankie appeared behind Phonse, and then Winter.

"Sweet Jesus, Dundas," Winter said, running his hand through the boy's hair. "What have you done?"

"He's lucky," Frankie said. "It's finally over for him."

He walked back inside the dugout.

twenty-five

July 1, 1916
Field Hospital C

EMMA RETRIEVED A BOX OF BANDAGES, BALANCING THEM ON the three boxes she already had. She backed out of the supply tent and bumped into something.

"Very sorry, Miss Tavenor," Sergeant Watson said, catching the top box before it tumbled into the mud. "Do you need a hand?"

"No, I'm—"

The ground shook beneath her feet, and a split second later the rumble vibrated through the air. Emma turned around, looking for the source.

"That's a big one," she said. "What's going on?"

Watson faced the horizon. "I suspect it's started. We've already been warned to expect casualties this morning. You best get those bandages to the ward. Won't be long now."

Emma's stomach lurched at the mention of casualties. It had been two weeks since she'd seen Daniel, and some days it was all she could think about, even when she was caring for a dying soldier or stitching up a wound. All she could see was Daniel's face and his eyes, how he had looked at her that night. Her face grew warm. Would they go back to Middle Tickle? Would he even survive the day to face that question?

Emma made a number of trips to the supply tent before the first casualties rolled in. The hospital buzzed. Everywhere she turned, people were talking about what they would do once the war was over.

Maisie bounded into the supply tent. "Have you heard the news?"

Emma nodded. "Yes, it's started."

"Miss Tavenor." The matron waved her over. Her apron was covered in blood, and her hat was tilted to the right. Loose pieces of hair hung in her face. "Please come, you are required in triage. You, too, Miss Parsons."

Emma dropped what was in her hands, and she and Maisie followed her outside. Medical vehicles came from every direction, and the wounded were pouring from them like water from a kettle.

The matron clutched Emma's arm and moved her forward. "Standing around with your mouth gaping wide won't help anybody," she said, batting at the flap of the triage tent and moving them inside.

Triage ran on a strict system. An initial assessment was completed, usually by medics, but sometimes by nurses. If there was a chance to save a man, he was tagged, made comfortable with morphine, and seen in priority order. The nurses or VADs did whatever rudimentary work could be done to clean their wounds.

But the flood of wounded overwhelmed the system this morning. Men were strewn everywhere in all shapes and conditions. Emma ran from man to man until she realized she was moving in circles, seeing the same ones over and over. She fell to her knees and looked down at her once white apron. Medics and nurses yelled and cursed over the wailing of the wounded in a cacophony of chaos. The room spun.

She fought her way outside, moving against the crowd pushing its way in. She grabbed her stomach and gasped for air. Bodies lined the fields around the hospital grounds as far as the eye could see. She ran her hands through her hair and wondered for a second if they were all German soldiers. Could the attack have been that successful?

Maisie appeared next to her with wide eyes. She too was covered in blood.

"I need volunteers!" Major Briggs shouted. "Nurses, VADs, medics! I need you all!"

Emma turned toward the major's voice. He stood with his hands up in the air, signalling for staff to come to him. Sergeant Watson hurried outside the resuss tent, wiping his hands. Maisie was tight behind him. She followed them to where the major stood, and soon other medical staff began to congregate. Thomas appeared next to her, a strained look on his face.

"What's happened, sir?" Sergeant Watson asked.

The major ran his hand over his face. "It's a bloody big mess, is what it is, Sergeant."

Sergeant Watson's face fell. "Sir?"

"We're being cut down out there. The first and second waves of the 29th Division were mowed down in the first five minutes. The entire Newfoundland Regiment was just decimated."

Maisie reached out, and Emma clutched her hand and closed her eyes. Her heart sank. Her biggest fears had come to pass. Daniel was probably dead, along with Frankie and Phonse. She had just found him again after all this time. A hand rubbed her shoulder, and she looked into Maisie's eyes.

"He'll be okay," she whispered. "Our fellas are strong, Emma."

Emma nodded as her eyes filled, and she squeezed Maisie's hand.

"What can we do, Major?" Maisie asked.

"Can you drive?"

"Yes, sir, I can," she replied.

"Good. I need ambulance drivers."

The major turned on his heel, and a string of medics and nurses followed.

Maisie took Emma's hand again. "Come on. If you want to help Daniel, this is the best way."

Emma wiped her eyes with the back of her hand and took a deep breath. She joined a group that hurried through a field and down the Sunken Lane until they reached a dirt road just outside the town of Auchonvillers. A long line of medical vehicles with the big red crosses painted on them were lined up and already running. Men ran back and forth, unloading supplies from carriages, and an assembly line had formed to load the ambulances.

"Where are we going?" Emma asked Sergeant Watson.

He picked up a crate of supplies, tossing it in the truck. "As close to the front as we can get. Here." He handed her a helmet. "Put this on. It's going to be dangerous where we're going."

Thomas placed his hand on her arm. Her heart raced, and they locked eyes. "You don't have to do this. You can stay here. You're a help no matter where you are," he said.

She nodded, placing the helmet on her head. "Yes, I do." She gave him a quick hug.

"Stay safe," he whispered.

"You, too." She pulled away just as Maisie called to her from the driver's seat of a medical truck.

"Emma! Come on!" She was already wearing a helmet.

She ran toward Maisie and jumped into the vehicle beside her friend just as shells exploded on the other side of the ridge.

"You ready?"

Emma reached in the pocket of her dress and pulled out Daniel's handkerchief. "As I'll ever be."

She ran her fingers over the raised letters, praying to anyone who would listen that he was okay.

Daniel winced, shifting to take the pressure off the sharp object pushing against his face. There wasn't enough strength in his arms to push his body from its unnaturally folded position, and he breathed hard through his nose. His legs were pinned tight, and he reached with his one free hand to push it away. It was hard and round, and as he patted farther down, his hand groped something soft and wet. It was the squishy sound that made his stomach roll, as he realized the first thing he'd touched was a helmet—the other, whatever was left underneath. He wanted to scramble away, not wanting to know what else he shared this space with, but every limb screamed in protest.

What was he trying to get away from? The dead? The dead couldn't hurt him. It was the living to be wary of. He relaxed against the ground, his face resting once again on the protrusion. He touched it, preferring the cold, hard steel to his previous discovery. It wasn't the sole cause of his discomfort, not by a long shot, but it was unbearable. How long had he been unconscious? Hours? Days?

Daniel's eyes fluttered as he pried his heavy lids apart. It wasn't day or night, light or dark, but the purplish hue of a strange twilight in between. A grey haze curled around his body and clung to the crevices of the small crater. It was like the thick blanket of fog that often swallowed them as their small boat sliced through the waves at home, and his heart fluttered. He would give anything to be sailing into the damp fog on the cold North Atlantic now. Tears stung his eyes as the memory faded and he laboured to breathe through the putrid film that clung to him in no man's land.

A heavy weight settled on his chest, and a wet gurgling sound forced a cough. He coaxed up whatever was making it difficult to breathe, but a sharp, shooting pain stifled it. His lungs burned. A burst of frantic shouting broke out, and his pulse raced. He longed to join in the chorus, but his lips were caked together with mud and debris. Apart from a couple of deep groans, he couldn't find his voice or even open his mouth to use it.

How far did he get?

There was shouting all around him now. He couldn't move, but every nerve ending in his body still connected to tissue jolted to life. Daniel felt around until he touched the steel butt of his rifle. A small wave of relief washed over him. He was still armed—not that he could do much about it in his current state. He blocked out the pain for a fraction of a second and strained to hear the voices. Amidst the torturous shrieking, the cries for mothers, and the general saving of souls, he understood every spoken word. The lack of gunfire and commands confirmed his worst fears. He had not reached enemy lines.

Daniel slunk back against his shelter of debris and the remains of his comrades and listened to the sorrowful pleas around him. Jesus, where was Frankie? He hoped he and Phonse had gotten through the wire and rained down a fiery hell on those German bastards. He almost smirked, but his lips were so dry the painful movement was akin to ripping off a scab.

Would he feel better if the voices were German? The end result would be the same, but at least he'd die knowing he'd reached his objective. This was the graveyard shift, the cleanup crew on his own side of the battlefield. He hadn't gotten far at all. His hand slipped off his rifle, partly from exhaustion, partly from disappointment.

He should at least stand up now and be counted, be a man and admit his defeat instead of letting them look for him. Bending his shoulder forward, he mustered what little strength he had to heave his body away from the jagged crater, which had been his bed, and thrust himself onto his back. He groaned as something snapped, and searing pain shot through his leg. Black spots danced behind his eyelids, and his stomach lurched.

The overpowering smell of rot was worse than normal, and his guts rolled. Until now his young life had been spent in a boat with his father and the smell of rotting fish guts. As bad as it was in the dead heat of summer, it couldn't compare to this. The spark of coherence faded, though he fought against it. Daniel's fingers fumbled the front pocket of his tattered uniform for the photo of Emma. He kept it near his heart, and it was the only thing that kept him sane. That and his memories of her, his memories of their night two weeks ago, and his thoughts of what the future might hold for them.

He squeezed his index finger and thumb together and shoved them inside his pocket, but he couldn't feel the smooth paper. He couldn't feel anything. His pulse quickened, and he ripped his mud-caked lips apart, gasping for air.

She was everything good about life before he'd marched into the darkest days of humanity. He dragged his thumb over the familiar tattered corner and sighed, slowly sliding it out as his breathing slowed to normal. Daniel's head bobbed toward his chest, and he drifted off while something nibbled at his leg.

Emma closed another soldier's eyes and leaned back on her knees with her head bent low. Her shoulders ached and she was thirsty, but she couldn't stop. She had stayed at the casualty clearing station while Maisie drove an ambulance back and forth all day. Emma did what she could as the wounded and the dead piled in from the front only two miles away. She raised her head and scanned the hundreds of bodies in the crimson field. A new group had just arrived, and she got up and stumbled toward the medics who were laying them out.

Thomas laid a hand on her shoulder, and she stood and faced him. "Emma," he said, "You must come back to the field hospital for some rest before you collapse. You've been going all day." He brushed some loose hair from her face. "I'm going back with the next ambulance. You can ride with me."

She shook her head. "But there's more to be done."

He placed his finger under her chin and lifted her head to look into her eyes. "There's nothing to be done for these boys, Emma. They're long gone."

She bit her lip and nodded, knowing she couldn't leave without checking the tags on the last group.

"Just a few more minutes," she said.

He nodded. "I'll be back in ten, and I'll carry you out of here if I have to. Mabel would never forgive me if I let anything happen to you."

He squeezed her shoulder and walked away.

Emma picked up a lantern someone had given her earlier and walked among them. Young men, cut down in their prime. She shone the lantern up and down the lines of bodies. After all day, they looked the same. She took another step forward and stopped, stepping back again, shining the light on the body at her feet. She crouched down and pulled out the tags from beneath his collar.

Gasping, she laid the lantern on the ground and leaned over his body. She touched his cold face and wiped some hair off his forehead, feeling the matted blood at his temple.

"I'm sorry," she whispered. "I'm sorry this happened to you."

A cold fear crept into her bones as she sat on the ground. They were inseparable. Could Daniel be here among the dead? Based on what she had seen today, she could no longer cling to luck and kind fates, for what had happened was criminal.

She ran down the line, flashing the lantern over their faces, reaching for tags when faces weren't enough. Satisfied he wasn't among the dead, she came back and kneeled by the soldier's body, wringing her hands.

"Sleep well, Frankie," she said. "Sleep well."

Thomas found her there, and just as he promised, he lifted her off the ground and carried her to a medical van waiting to take them back to Field Hospital C. She dozed off and on during the ride back, but she overheard the men talk about Maisie's fearlessness. They said Emma was brave, too, for being this close to the front. She didn't feel brave. She was just searching for one man. What would she do if she found him dead?

How brave would she be then?

"Shot o' morphine over 'ere."

A voice sounded near his ear. His head bobbed before rolling to the side, and he felt like he was flying. This was it, he was dying. He didn't see any white light, and nobody spoke to him. Father Hennessey was probably laughing at him now, because if he'd paid more attention in catechism he'd know what came next. The angels were here to take him away from earth. The old folks always looked up to the sky when they talked about heaven, and pointed down below for hell. So, where was purgatory located in proximity to heaven and hell?

He and Richard had served mass for Father Hennessey almost every Sunday when they were younger, and Father had told them one day they needn't worry, they were going straight to heaven. He said they couldn't have done anything wrong in their young lives to warrant going to hell. That was for people who did bad things. When he'd confirmed the purity of their souls, he hadn't yet realized they drank the leftover wine from the chalice when they cleaned up the sacristy after Mass.

Only those who did bad things.

What would Father Hennessey consider bad? Daniel had seen too much, done too much. Not that he had much choice, orders are orders, but it probably meant a bit of a side track from the direct line to heaven. Sounded like he might be in purgatory for a long while until his fate was decided, but if what he heard was correct and they had morphine there, it mightn't be all that bad.

Was Dundas in heaven? He hoped so.

Daniel drifted, but when his body lurched to a sudden halt, he groaned.

"It's all right, Private, we've got you."

Damn it if even the angels weren't British.

"Jesus H., he's a mess," a tired voice said.

"Yeah, all right, Private. 'Ow many times? They're all a mess. It's all one bloody big mess, isn't it?" said a sharp voice with a heavy British accent.

"This might hurt a bit," the tired voice said, ignoring the other one.

"Are you serious, Private? Look at 'im. Do you think your poxy needle would hurt him after what 'e's been through?"

Daniel listened, eyes half opened. He didn't care if he was going to heaven or hell; right now all he felt was relief.

twenty-six

July 2, 1916
Field Hospital C

A SLIVER OF SUN HAD APPEARED IN THE SKY BY THE TIME EMMA arrived back at the field hospital. A smoky haze hovered over the ridge, and the smell of gunpowder was strong. Thomas helped her from the vehicle, and they walked toward the VAD quarters.

Maisie ran to meet them. "Emma! I've been looking everywhere for you," she said. "Have you been out there all this time?"

"I had to tear her away," Thomas said, with one arm around her shoulder.

Emma nodded. "I found Frankie. Daniel's friend."

She hadn't the energy for grief.

Maisie squeezed her hand. "Come with me," she said.

"Miss Parsons, I think the best place for Emma right now is her bed," Thomas said.

She raised her eyebrows at him. "And I will take her there," she said. "But first she needs to come with me."

Thomas threw his hands in the air. "Very well."

He released Emma into Maisie's care.

Maisie winked at him. "Don't worry, Corporal. I'll take good care of her," she said, leading Emma to a tent.

Emma put a hand on her head. "He's right, Maisie," she said. "I'm shattered. I can't think straight. I can't even see."

Maisie urged her forward. "You'll see this."

She opened the tent flap, and they stepped onto the ward, which was as full now as it had been twenty-four hours ago. Maisie led her to a sleeping soldier and lowered her onto a stool next to the bed. One of his legs was bandaged, and it hung from a traction line, indicating it was broken. He was bandaged from head to toe. As if sensing her presence, he opened his eyes and reached for her hand. Her eyes scoured the rest of his body until they came to rest on his face.

"Emma," he whispered.

Her eyes widened. Just when she thought she couldn't shed another tear, they flooded her cheeks.

"Daniel," she whispered back.

Concern filled his eyes. "Are you all right?"

She probably looked a right sight. A small laugh escaped her lips. "Am I all right? Yes, I'm fine," she said, placing her hands on either side of his face. "I'm more worried about you, my love."

He gave a small smile. "I'll be fine."

She looked up at Maisie, as if to verify his diagnosis.

Maisie nodded. "It's true. Sergeant Watson took some shrapnel out of his leg, and it's broken. He's got a lot of cuts and scrapes, but he'll make a full recovery."

Conscious that he ached all over, Emma placed her face close to his. He brushed his lips across her cheek, and she straightened up, studying him. She pushed his hair off his forehead and kissed him there. When she looked into his eyes again, they were moist, and he nodded at Maisie, who came forward and placed something in his hand.

"Emma," he said.

"Yes, my darling."

He opened his hand to reveal a small, gold band. "Would you do me the honour of becoming my wife?"

She placed one hand over her mouth. "Oh, Daniel," she said. She took the band from his palm and looked into his watery blue eyes. "Of course I'll marry you."

She slipped the ring on her finger, and he took her hand and kissed it, nuzzling his face into her hand. She leaned forward, kissing him full on the lips. When she drew back, a contented look had crossed his face, and she caressed his cheek as he fell into a deep sleep. A small smile settled on his lips, and Emma stared at him, unable to believe how lucky they were.

"Miss Tavenor." Sergeant Watson appeared on Daniel's other side with a piece of paper in his hand. "Someone you know?"

"Yes, sir. My fiancé." She smiled and held up her hand.

His eyes flickered, and his mouth opened and closed. "Well, well. You never said."

"You never asked," she said, still smiling.

He handed her the paper. "I guess I can give this to you."

Emma blinked and took a step back. "I thought he was going to be okay," she said.

"Oh, he is, but that leg will need physical therapy, so he must go to England. If he's lucky, by the time his leg has healed this bloody war will be over and he won't have to come back here."

A nurse called for Watson to help with a patient experiencing extreme convulsions. As he walked away, he called over his shoulder, "Don't look so sad. Do you know how many around here would give their right arm for a Blighty Ticket? Literally."

Emma looked at the Blighty Ticket she held in her hands. She was happy he would be transferred to England to convalesce and get the care he deserved, but it meant she would be staying here at the front.

Alone.

⌒

"I was just speaking with Sergeant Watson," Emma said. "He's heard from St. Augustine's, and Daniel's physical therapy is going well. He says Daniel will be coming back soon."

Maisie sighed. "I'm glad he's doing well, but I had hoped we would all be going home rather than Daniel returning," she said.

Emma had had the same thoughts, but she couldn't deny a part of her was desperate to see him, even if it meant him returning to France. Instead of hearing news of the war's end, it dragged on. The Battle of the Somme had taken thousands of lives and was waging well into its second month with Allied forces gaining little ground.

Emma swallowed hard, pushing down the bile rising in her throat. "Excuse me, Maisie," she said, covering her mouth as she pushed the tent flap to the side and ran out into the crisp fall air.

"Miss Tavenor, there is no running permitted—" But the matron's words were lost in the sound of Emma heaving her guts up at the woman's feet.

When Emma looked up, a deep frown had settled across the matron's face.

She wiped her mouth with the back of her hand. "Forgive me, Matron," she said, stifling the urge to vomit again. "I don't know what's come over me."

By this time, Maisie was standing beside her, pulling her away.

"It's all right, Matron," Maisie said. "Terrible stuff. I had it myself a few days ago. I'll get her cleaned up."

They left the matron standing with her arms folded, staring after them.

Maisie felt Emma's forehead and cheeks. "Are you all right?"

Emma nodded. "I don't know what's wrong with me," she replied. "It's been a couple of days of this. I get very dizzy and overwhelmed, and my stomach is queasy. It's the third time I've vomited today. It's worse in the mornings, but as the day goes on, it gets better."

Maisie ushered her behind the mess tent near a wooded area and stepped back, sizing her up. She ran a hand over Emma's belly, her eyes resting on her breasts.

"What?" Emma asked.

"Well, I'll be damned," Maisie said.

"Is it some kind of stomach ailment?"

"In a matter of speaking, yes, I suppose."

"How long will it last?"

Maisie laughed. "Oh, I'm guessing about seven more months."

"What?"

"Looks like you'll be getting your Blighty Ticket soon, too, missus." Maisie slapped Emma's bottom as she walked away. "You're a dark horse, Emma Tavenor. Full of surprises."

April 14, 1917

"Keep moving!" Second Lieutenant Winter yelled as they advanced from the safety of their position near the village of Monchy-le-Preux.

A deep rumble gathered momentum in the distance, and the earth beneath Daniel's feet shook. There was no time to brace for it and nowhere to go. A German shell slammed into the ground, cutting through everything in its path. Daniel was propelled skyward, with dirt and shrapnel chasing close behind. Somewhere between the shell's drone and the groan of the earth tearing apart, he heard the strangled cries of

Harry Winter and the others he'd been standing beside just a few minutes before.

"Phonse! Harry!" He yelled their names before he hit the ground and everything went black.

The intense shouting overhead jarred him awake. The voices were clipped and sounded more like Morse code than any language, but he'd been in this war long enough to know it was German. He opened his eyes and looked around the crater, which also held Winter, Phonse, Private Cahill from Carbonear, and what looked like Lieutenants Grace and Abbott. They had all begun to stir, except Abbott, whose chest was blown clear open.

"Daniel." Winter's voice was barely audible.

Daniel sat up, and pain shot through his leg. Goddamn it if it wasn't the same leg he'd broken nine months ago at Beaumont-Hamel. Wincing, he slid toward Winter, who was straining to lean forward from his slumped position against the crater wall.

"Harry, how bad is it?" Daniel unscrewed the cap from Winter's water canteen and poured some into the man's mouth.

Winter coughed and spat out blood. Breathing heavily, he leaned back against the crater wall. "I don't know, Daniel."

"Don't worry, Harry, we'll get out of here." He patted Winter's shoulder as he scanned the man's body for injuries. Winter was in better shape than Abbott, who still hadn't moved, but he was pretty busted up. There was shrapnel sticking out of his right side and his left leg, which he may lose.

"Phonse, you with me, buddy?"

"I'm here," Phonse said.

"Good stuff. You hurt bad?" Daniel asked as he slid away from Winter and toward his old friend.

"Nah," Phonse said.

"What about you, Gracie?" Phonse asked the lieutenant.

"Yeah, I'm all right," Grace said. "A few cuts, and I think my arm's broke, but—" He stopped and looked over at Abbott. "—I'll be okay."

"What about you, Cahill?" Daniel asked.

Before the young soldier had a chance to answer, two Germans jumped inside the crater. Daniel, Phonse, and Lieutenant Grace scrambled back against the wall. Cahill reached for his rifle.

"No!" Daniel yelled at him to stop, but it was too late.

The older of the two Germans aimed his rifle and shot Private Cahill clear between the eyes. Cahill slumped across Phonse's arm as the German soldier pivoted toward Daniel, rifle cocked, and a wild look in his eyes that said he'd give little thought to pulling the trigger again. Daniel's heart thudded in his ears, and he placed his hands in the air. The soldier moved his rifle around the crater, taking aim.

"*Kapitulieren jetzt!*"

The other German stood beside him, holding his bayonet ready and scanning their faces. He couldn't have been more than sixteen or seventeen, just a few years younger than Daniel. The fear in the boy's eyes belied his actions. He wasn't ready to bayonet any of them, not that Daniel thought they should risk it.

"Whoa! No need for that!" Phonse shouted, but made no sudden movement. The soldier with the rifle stepped forward and cracked Phonse across the head with it. Phonse's head snapped back against the crater wall, and the sound it made when the rifle connected with his skull made Daniel's stomach roil.

"*Kapitulieren jetzt!*"

"They want us to surrender," Winter said.

"We don't have much choice in the matter," Grace said, following Daniel's lead and placing his hands in front of him.

"*Geben Sie uns Ihre Gewehre!*"

"Give them your rifles," Grace said, as he slid his toward the German's feet. Daniel followed suit and reached for Phonse's to pass over, while his friend groaned and cursed and held his head in his hands.

The older German said something to the younger one, who bent down and retrieved Winter's rifle.

"*Offiziere hier unten!*"

Several more German soldiers jumped into the crater.

"*Aufstehen! Aufstehen!*" they yelled, kicking at the injured men's feet.

Phonse and Grace jumped up, and the Germans hoisted them from the crater. Daniel tried to stand on his good leg, but two pairs of hands tossed him up like an empty water can. He landed with a thud on his injured leg and clenched his jaw in pain. Winter fell next to him and groaned. Abbott was tossed out with as much care as a piece of garbage. He rolled still, and Daniel checked the man's battered body for any sign of life. A faint pulse beat beneath Daniel's fingers, and he prayed for Abbott's sake he was too far gone to know what was happening.

"What's next?" Phonse asked, breaking the half-hour silence in the back of a German ambulance. "We going to end our days in a German work camp?"

"Probably," Grace said.

"Well, at least we'll all be together," Daniel said, looking down at Winter, who was sleeping against his good leg.

"No," Grace said. "Officers have their own camp."

They drove at least thirty miles to a nearby *truppenverbandplatz*, the German equivalent of a regimental aid post. As they exited the ambulance, the scene around them was chaotic, and it was clear they were in German territory now.

Lieutenant Grace and Phonse lifted Winter, followed by Abbott, from the ambulance and laid the men on the ground. Daniel sat next to Winter and propped the man's head against his good leg again. A German medic appeared and noted something on a clipboard.

"He needs a doctor," Phonse said, pointing at Abbott, who had not shown one sign of consciousness since the explosion.

The medic was expressionless as he stared at Phonse for a moment, his lips in a tight, straight line. He joined a group of German soldiers a few feet away and pointed to where the Newfoundlanders were. Three German soldiers broke away and strode over. A tall, bulky man, with a cigarette hanging from the corner of his mouth, stood over Abbott and kicked him a few times. He took one last draw on his cigarette and flicked it to the ground. He drew his bayonet and sliced down through the lieutenant.

"No!" Daniel yelled, and Phonse jumped to his feet, but it was Grace who pulled him back.

The German soldier withdrew his bayonet and whirled around, waving it in Phonse's face.

"You son of a bitch!" Phonse yelled.

The medic appeared and pointed down at Winter. As much as it hurt to stand, Daniel got to his feet and stood over Winter's fragile body, shielding him from whatever was about to happen.

"No!" he yelled.

The German soldier glared at him and stepped toward Daniel with the bayonet raised.

"Stand down." The accent was heavy, but he spoke English.

"No. We have surrendered to you. I'll not stand by while you kill my friends. If you kill him, you'll have to kill me, too!"

"This is easy," the German said in clear English. "We have already killed many of you today. What is one more?"

Grace pulled him away from the German's face. "He's his batman. His servant. He'll take care of him. Lieutenant Winter won't be a problem. His wounds aren't bad," Grace said.

The German soldier and Daniel locked eyes for a moment longer. Shouts came from another group huddled about twenty feet away. A shot rang out, and the German turned his head toward the sound and began to move away. Before he did, though, he took one more look down at Abbott and spat on his dead body before moving on. Grace kept a tight grip on Phonse's arm as the man squirmed to free himself.

Daniel put his head in his hands. "Jesus Christ! What the hell just happened?" He scrubbed his hands up and down his face.

"They didn't want to waste any time moving him elsewhere. They were going to do the same to Winter. You just saved his life, Beresford," Grace said.

Daniel and Phonse stared at Grace.

"I know it's a tough thing to see, fellas, but the same thing is done on our side. I'd like to think we're a little more humane about it, but we are at war."

"*Beweg dich*." Another German soldier appeared before them. "Come," he said. "What is it you British say?" He scratched his head and raised a finger in the air. "Ah, yes. Get a move on."

Grace, Phonse, and Daniel pulled Winter up and walked him to the medical truck waiting to take them to a *lazarett*, a German casualty clearing station, to attend to their wounds. Daniel stole one last look behind him at Abbott's body on the ground. What would become of him? What would become of any of them?

As the truck rumbled to life, they were silent as they drove toward whatever fate held for them. A deep sense of regret settled over Daniel like a cloud. He hadn't returned any of Emma's letters in the last four months. The guilt crippled him now, but he didn't know what to say. In the last two years he'd seen the worst of humanity. He'd lost friends and brothers, and there was no end in sight to this war. He didn't know what he was living for anymore, but he couldn't put that on a piece of paper. He should have written to her before, because now he couldn't. He was now a prisoner of war.

All hope was lost.

A SPLENDID BOY

∾

Plymouth, England
April 27, 1917

Emma sat in front of the large window overlooking the estate's grounds. Unable to focus, she had abandoned the knitting hours ago and laid it on the table next to a cup of cold tea. She held on to the white handkerchief Daniel had given her when they were still in Middle Tickle. She rubbed a hand over her protruding belly, feeling a faint kick. The glowing skin, which had come with the pregnancy, had since given way to a sick and paltry look, as was evident by the bags under her eyes this morning. She ate for the baby's sake, but tasted nothing. Time stood still as she waited and watched, hoping for news of Daniel.

Maisie had been right, of course, and Emma had little choice but to tell the matron about her condition. Even though she had signed a contract that specified service until the war's end, pregnancy was one circumstance warranting immediate discharge. The matron gave her a disapproving look the day she signed her discharge papers, but Emma didn't care. In a few hours she would be in England, and finally able to tell Daniel about the baby. She didn't feel right about sharing this news in a letter. Besides, she wanted to see his face when she told him, and they had much to discuss.

What she hadn't counted on was Daniel returning to France early, which she found out at St. Augustine's Hospital the night she arrived. He had left a note telling her how sorry he was. The last she had heard from him was in a postcard at Christmas, but it had now been close on four months without any correspondence.

"Emma, darling," Mrs. Evans called. "You have a visitor."

A hand touched her shoulder, and she looked up into Mabel's

warm, brown eyes. Her friend kissed her on the cheek. "Emma, my dear friend, how are you?"

Emma straightened her shoulders and tried to get up, but Mabel touched her arm. "Don't get up for me."

"Have a seat, Miss Purcell," Mrs. Evans said, before leaving the room. "I'll bring some tea and biscuits."

Emma saw the woman throw a hopeful look in Mabel's direction. Mrs. Evans was worried about her, and she loved the woman for trying to bring her out of this funk, but only one thing could do that.

Mabel sat in the chair next to Emma. "Have you heard from him?"

Emma shook her head, rubbing her fingers over the handkerchief. "Nothing. I've asked my cousin Helen's husband, George, with the War Office, to see what he can find out."

"Maybe he's not in a position to write." Mabel smiled and squeezed her hand. "From what you've told me, he's a resourceful young man. Sometimes they get separated from their units for periods of time and have to go into hiding until they can reach their own lines again. Thomas said it happens all the time."

"For four months?"

"It's quite possible, Emma. The fact that you haven't heard anything means there's still hope." She smiled at Emma.

Emma wondered if Mabel believed any of what she'd just said. She certainly didn't. She had considered every scenario and couldn't think of anything to keep Daniel from at least writing her a quick note to say he was alive. Unless he wasn't.

Mrs. Evans opened the door. "Well, my dear, 'tis the day for visitors," she said, as she set the tea service off to the side. "Do come in, Mr. Whitby."

Emma pushed herself up from the chair as George entered the drawing room and removed his hat. Mabel stood, too, but Emma forgot all form of manners as he came toward her.

He leaned in and pecked her cheek. "Emma, my dear girl. How are you?" he asked, nodding in Mabel's direction.

"Hallo," she said. "I'm Mabel Purcell, a friend of Emma's."

He held out his hand. "Happy to meet you, Miss Purcell. I'm George Whitby. I'm married to Emma's cousin Helen."

Emma's stomach knotted, and she wanted to scream as she clutched the handkerchief and listened to their pleasantries.

She searched his eyes. "George, have you come with any news?"

He faltered, his eyes darting to Mabel's and then Mrs. Evans's. "I'm sorry, Emma. I don't know quite how to tell you this," he said, looking around the room. His eyes came to rest on hers. "It appears Daniel is missing and presumed dead."

His words wrapped around her heart and squeezed until she thought she would suffocate. Mabel and Mrs. Evans led her to a nearby chaise longue.

"How long ago?"

"That's the unusual piece, Emma." George furrowed his brow and took a seat in the chair adjacent to her. He turned his hat over in his hands several times. "The Battle of the Somme continued well into the fall. Daniel rejoined his unit in late September, and in early October the Newfoundland Regiment joined an assault on the enemy on the out-skirts of Gueudecourt about five miles from Beaumont-Hamel. There were some challenges, and—" He stopped, his eyes glued to her swollen abdomen. "It's not important, but they almost single-handedly held off the Germans and managed the farthest advance of the Somme offen-sive. It was heroic, Emma." There was a hint of excitement in George's voice.

"Five miles from Beaumont-Hamel," she said.

"Yes. You see, they achieved what others could not."

Emma's laugh was bitter, and it wiped the smile from his face.

"He is a war hero because it took three months to inch five miles," she said, looking between Mabel and Mrs. Evans. "Does anyone else see the madness in this?"

Mrs. Evans rubbed her back. "This whole war is madness, my darling."

Emma ran her hand through her hair. "But you said he survived?"

"Yes," George continued. "The Regiment incurred heavy losses there, but he made it out alive. What I can't explain is why you didn't hear from him after."

"Are you telling me he's only recently gone missing?" Emma's eyes widened as she rubbed her shaky hands over her skirt. Mabel squeezed her hand.

He nodded. "I am, yes. It seems he held his own up until a few weeks ago. The Regiment joined in the Battle of Arras, which brought them to the outskirts of Monchy-le-Preux, a village about five miles southeast of Arras. They suffered heavy casualties. The Germans had them surrounded on all sides in what was an impossible situation." George smiled, shaking his head. "In the end, nine men from the Royal Newfoundland Regiment were responsible for holding the ground the Allies had gained, while making the Germans believe there was a full battalion of men fighting." He bent down on one knee and took one of her hands. "It seems Daniel, like the rest of the men from Newfoundland, is made of stern stuff, Emma. You should be proud of him."

Emma's shoulders shook as the gravity of George's words sunk in. He leaned in and embraced her. When he pulled back, he slipped a letter into her hand.

"The original has been sent to his family, of course, but I've managed to get a copy for you." He rose and spoke with Mrs. Evans in hushed tones as she walked him to the drawing room door.

She opened the letter and doubled over as an ungodly sound filled the room.

"I think you'd better ring for the doctor, Mrs. Evans!" Mabel yelled.

twenty-seven

November 1918
Compton House, near Plymouth

EMMA STOOD IN THE GARDEN WATCHING A ROSY-CHEEKED AMELIA run after the puppy, who was taking great sport in grabbing the child's stuffed rabbit from her hands, running away, and glancing back to ensure the child was following.

"Emma!"

Thomas Purcell raced toward her, carrying a newspaper in his hands. "It's over! The war is over!"

Hearing his voice, the young girl abandoned her quest to catch the puppy and ran to him, grabbing on to his pant leg.

He scooped the toddler into his arms and planted a big kiss on her cheek. "There's my little sweetheart." He leaned over and kissed Emma. When he drew back, his eyes sparkled with excitement. "It's over, darling."

Just hours after she learned of Daniel's death, Emma gave birth to their daughter, Amelia. Thomas had come to see her within a few weeks and held her hand while she mourned for Daniel and lamented what would become of them. In the end, he shocked her with his revelation that he had been in love with her since they first met. He understood her feelings and her sadness and said he would never diminish them, but he also told her he cared too much about her to let her raise Amelia on her own, without a father. A few weeks later, he convinced her to marry him.

Amelia nuzzled his cheek, and Emma watched them together. A tremendous guilt crept in and clutched her heart. As she watched her husband with her little girl, she imagined it was Daniel holding her, and she hated herself for it. Thomas was a good man, and he cared for them both, but one day she would have to tell Amelia the truth.

"When?" she asked.

"An armistice was signed at five o'clock this morning. By eleven o'clock, hostilities on all fronts will cease. Lloyd George will make the announcement himself in half an hour. Isn't it marvellous?"

Emma ruffled Amelia's hair. Finally, some good news. It had been a terrible month. The first casualty from the Spanish flu at her grandfather's estate had been a young housemaid. Two days later, Emma's mother had succumbed.

When Emma returned from the war in 1916, there had been a noticeable difference in Rose Grey. She had wasted away to nothing, driven mad by the drink. She had withdrawn from everyone and rarely came out of her room.

In the weeks since her mother's death, three more servants had died, and the epidemic was spreading throughout England at an alarming rate. Thomas had moved them to his parents' place in Compton, just to be safe. Mrs. Evans was coordinating with the servants' families on burials and leading the disinfecting of the house. Closing up the house for a few months to let everyone return to their families seemed like the right thing to do until the terrible ordeal was over. Mrs. Evans would reside with them at Compton House once all matters were seen to.

Thomas set Amelia down, and she ran after the puppy again. His arms came to rest around Emma's waist, and she leaned back against his chest.

"What will happen now?" she asked.

"I imagine it will take some time for the news to reach everyone," he said. "But as they retreat, the army will pack up and send everyone home. It will take a few months, of course."

Emma nodded. Her mind started down the same old path it did from time to time. What if Daniel had been in hiding all this time, like Mabel had suggested two years ago? What if he had deserted? Once the war was over, he would be free to leave. Free to come home. To find her.

But she wasn't free.

Amelia squealed as she fell into the carpet of green grass and the puppy pounced on her and licked her face. Emma watched her daughter. She had Daniel's blue eyes and brown hair. When her husband turned her around to face him, she looked at him for the briefest of seconds. Her face reddened, and she turned away. The hurt in his eyes said he knew what she had been thinking. He squeezed her shoulder before walking back up to the house.

The war was over. They had nothing to fear anymore. She had a wonderful husband who loved her very much and was a good father to Amelia. She should be happy. But she wasn't. All she could think of was Daniel. After two years, anyone would tell her these thoughts were crazy, that there was no hope, but she didn't think so.

She didn't believe he was dead.

He stepped off the train at Weymouth and asked for directions. He had a notional idea of where the Grey estate was from listening to Emma talk about it. A uniformed man told him it was five miles down the road and offered him a lift by horse and carriage, but he declined. It wasn't a long walk. His leg wasn't what it once was, but the walk would give him time to think. Not that it would help much. There was no way he could think of to minimize the shock Emma would get when she saw him. He just hoped it would be followed by extreme happiness.

A few minutes in, and already his leg throbbed. It had healed well from the first wound at Beaumont-Hamel, but after he'd injured it the second time at Monchy-le-Preux, it hadn't really mended properly. It was bad enough the German doctor had removed the little metal fragments from the exploding shell by simply reaching inside his wounds with his bare hands and rooting around until he found them, but it was done without even a sniff of anaesthetic.

After spending some time at a *lazarett* near Douai, Grace and Winter were shipped to Holzminden, an officer's camp in Germany, and he and Phonse were sent to Friedrichsfeldt, a work camp near the Belgian border. They spent the next year working in a nearby salt mine under the harshest of conditions. They knew nothing of the war's end until they got up one morning to find the Germans were gone and the gates were wide open.

In the distance, a large building came into view. He knew Emma's family was well off, but as he got closer he saw just how big the house was. The land stretched on forever. The whole population of Middle Tickle could live there and never even run into each other. He thought there would be more people about for a place so large, but it was quiet. One motor car sat in the drive, and he scanned the grounds, walking up the shrub-lined path to the enormous house. He stepped up to the double wooden doors and knocked.

He was just about to turn away when a man in his early twenties opened the door. "May I help you?" he asked.

Through the open doors he spied a wide staircase laid in red carpet. It was a grand house, for sure. He couldn't take his eyes off the stairs, hoping she would bound down at any minute, as if somehow sensing he was there.

"Sir? May I help you?"

"Hmm? Sorry," he said. "I'm looking for Emma Tavenor. Would she be at home?"

The man stiffened and stepped back. "She . . . I . . ." He stopped. "I'm afraid we've evacuated the Grey estate for the time being."

He stepped out and closed the door behind him, motioning down the driveway. They walked away from the house.

"Forgive me for showing up like this. My name is—"

The man stopped to face him. "I suspect I might know who you are. It's Daniel, right?"

"Yes," he said, reaching out his hand. "And you are?"

He hesitated before taking Daniel's hand. "Thomas. Thomas Purcell."

Thomas jerked his hand back and rubbed it.

"Nice to meet you, Thomas. I'm looking for Emma. Is she here?"

"No."

"Do you know where I can find her?"

Beads of sweat broke out on Thomas's forehead, and his face reddened. "You're supposed to be dead," he said. "I mean, she thinks . . ." His hands fell to his side. "She thought you were dead."

Daniel winced. Of course she would think that. He had vanished without a trace. Even though as prisoners they were owed the right to make contact with their families through letters, those German bastards took great pleasure in denying those rights. In fact, if they found you with any paper at all, a heavy punishment would be doled out. He'd seen more than one man tied to a post in the middle of the camp for days on end.

He understood this man's hesitation. He was probably a close relative of Emma's and wouldn't want to cause her any more distress than necessary. Maybe if he talked to her mother first, she could explain it to her daughter. The last thing he wanted to do was startle her into some kind of hysterical fit. He'd seen enough of that to last a lifetime.

"Is her mother here?" Daniel asked.

"No."

"Where is Emma?"

"As I explained, Daniel. The estate has been evacuated."

"Yes, but, you see, I need to speak with her. She needs to know I am alive."

"I'm afraid that's not possible."

"But why not?"

Thomas dragged his hands through his hair, and his eyes moved beyond Daniel toward a meadow on the far side of the property. Daniel followed his gaze and spotted a white cross in the distance. His vision blurred, and his breath caught. He broke into a run.

"No! Daniel! Come back."

Thomas ran after him.

Daniel ignored the shooting pain in his leg. Breathless, he fell in front of a pile of evenly spread dirt and looked up at the white cross standing watch. Thomas arrived behind him, gasping for breath. After a few minutes, when their breathing had returned to normal, Daniel spoke.

"How?"

Thomas hesitated. "Spanish flu."

"When?"

"Three weeks ago."

Daniel closed his eyes and leaned forward. He had been so close. His shoulders shook. He wasn't a religious man by any stretch, but he said a prayer. The last four years flashed through his mind. Bern, Frankie, Dundas. The war had robbed them of so much, taken their youth, their innocence, millions of lives.

And for what?

He picked up a handful of dirt from the grave and placed it in his pocket. He took one final look before wiping his eyes. He got to his feet. With hunched shoulders, he dragged himself down the drive and toward the train station.

As heavy as his injured leg felt, it wasn't nearly as heavy as his heart.

twenty-eight

June 1981
St. John's, Newfoundland

DANIEL LAID HIS CUP ON THE TABLE AND LEANED BACK IN HIS chair. "I arrived back in Newfoundland in February of 1919," he said. "And that was that."

Penny was still as she sat across from him. "Did you ever marry?"

He shook his head. She was quiet as the seconds ticked by.

"You okay?" he asked.

"I don't know what to say."

"Why do you have to say something?"

"You've just told me this gut-wrenching story, and I feel like I should have something to say to you. Something profound. Something to make you feel better."

"I feel fine."

"Daniel. You missed out on a whole life with the woman you loved," she said, her eyes becoming glassy. "Marriage. Children. It's so tragic."

"It was sixty-five years ago, Penny. I lived my life."

"But not the way you could have. Not the way you wanted to."

He considered what she said. "You don't miss what you never had."

He had kept up a brave front for this long. There was no way he would break down now.

"Well, it's settled, you have to go."

"I don't have to do anything," he said.

She smiled. "Have you always been this contrary?"

"For about the last sixty-five years."

Her eyes flickered. "I bet you were quite charming in your youth."

"What makes you say that?"

"Well, Emma sounds like she was a remarkable woman. So, she must have seen something redeemable in you."

Emma had thought he was charming. Her photograph looked up at him from the Formica-covered tabletop. Over the last few days, he'd removed the box's contents, bit by bit, and all the articles were laid out, partially organized by the way he had told Penny his story.

He picked up the *Wipers Times,* a trench magazine British soldiers had published after they found several abandoned printing presses. The name Wipers had come from their mispronunciation of the Belgian city Ypres. It was a play on words, in line with the magazine's purpose. The publication was chock full of poetry, ironic lines, and stories relating to the war and the position they were all in. At first, the military's highest ranks had been apoplectic about the publication, but they were later convinced it was a coping mechanism that could do them all some good. He flipped the pages, and a photograph slipped out that made the corners of his mouth curl.

"That's me, Phonse, and Bern." His shaky finger pointed at their youthful visions. "This here is Frankie, with the lopsided grin on his face. It was taken at Aldershot, before we left for Gallipoli in 1915."

Penny placed a hand on his arm. "Do you ever think about what it looks like in France now, after two world wars?" she asked.

One time he knew the North of France like the back of his hand, and when he left it was a pile of rubble. The French could only have just finished rebuilding when they were forced into the Second World War. How a people could endure such ruination of their cities, their landscape, and their spirit, he didn't know. He often wondered over the years what it looked like now.

"Newfoundland Memorial Park is really quite stunning. I've been there a few times. It's a beautiful tribute. Aren't you even curious?"

After the war was over, Thomas Nangle, the Regiment's padre, helped the Newfoundland Government purchase the land near the communities of Beaumont and Hamel. He'd seen photographs of the caribou looking out over no man's land.

"I bet nobody has ever visited Frankie's grave," she said.

Boy, she was really pulling out all the stops. "Those graves are well kept up by the Commonwealth War Graves Commission," he said.

"Keeping up a grave and visiting it are two different things, Daniel." She patted his hand. "After all these years, wouldn't you like to visit his grave and say goodbye?"

"It's a long way to go to say goodbye."

She smiled. "Might do you some good." She reached over and touched his chest just above his heart. "In here."

A moment later, Penny stood and gathered her things.

At the door, she laid her bag down and hugged him. As she pulled away, she kissed his cheek. "I do wish you would change your mind," she said.

"It's a long way for an old man to go by himself."

Her eyes widened. "I can go with you. You wouldn't be alone. Fly to London, and I'll meet you at Heathrow."

He stammered and glanced back at the table, at all his reminders from the Great War—photographs and postcards, letters and his soldier's field guide—articles that represented a few short years in his otherwise long life, but that had affected him more than anything else had.

"Say you'll come. I'll take good care of you," she said. "I promise."

"I never responded to the invitation. It's too late now."

"It's not too late," she said. "When I get back to the hotel, I will contact the organizers and arrange all the details. You have a passport, right?"

"No."

"Okay, well, that's the first thing we need to do. I'll be back for you in the morning." She lifted her bag, an excited fire in her eyes. "You won't regret this, Daniel. I'm sure of it."

She climbed into her grey Dodge Pinto and backed out of his driveway.

He shuffled into the kitchen and sat down at the table, picking up the photograph of the four of them again.

"Frankie, old buddy, looks like I'm coming to see ya."

"This is a lovely old hotel, isn't it?" Penny asked.

"Hmm," he murmured.

What had struck him the most was how little the place had changed. The decor was different, of course, designed to meet modern-day standards. Otherwise, it was much the same as it had been in 1916, when he had stood in the lobby with a heart full of dreams.

"I've rented a car," Penny said.

"You have?"

She held up a blue pamphlet with an attached single key on a ring. "They've dropped it here at the hotel for us. It's just around the corner in a parking lot. Now, I know there's a bus taking Canadian veterans around. There's a couple of British buses, too. I'm sure you would be most welcome on any of them. But the last time you were here, you were on someone else's timetable." Her eyes twinkled when she smiled. "I figured you might like to be on your own this time."

"That's thoughtful of you, Penny. I quite appreciate it," Daniel said.

"I suppose you're tired. You've come a long way in twenty-four hours. Would you like to have a lie-down?" she asked.

He looked at his watch. It was just after one in the afternoon. "No."

"Okay, we can get something to eat, if you'd like. The dinner isn't until eight o'clock tonight." She pointed to the right. "I think the hotel restaurant is that way."

"No. I'm not hungry. If it's all the same to you, I'd like to go and visit Frankie."

"Oh. Of course," she said. "The bellman can take our bags to our room, and we can leave whenever you're ready."

"I'd like to pay my respects before I do anything else," he said.

"It's about a forty-minute drive, isn't it?"

"I don't know," he said, looking her in the eye. "Last time I was here, I walked it."

They stepped outside the main hotel doors and moved aside for a young woman to enter.

"Penny?" the woman asked.

"Hallo, Sarah. Of course I should have realized you'd be here," Penny said. The two women embraced like old friends.

"Yes, I've been volunteering with the logistics team for the week's activities. I started about six months ago. I wouldn't miss it. I have actually interviewed the VAD they're honouring tonight." She leaned in close to Penny. "She has a remarkable story. Truly remarkable. I must tell you all about it when we get home."

"Danny, Sarah is an old friend from grad school. Sarah, this is my friend, Danny," Penny said. "He has a pretty remarkable story of his own."

"Hello," Daniel said.

"Oh, hallo, Danny. Pleasure to meet you." Sarah stuck her hand out, and Daniel accepted.

"Danny's being honoured tonight, too," Penny said.

"How lovely. Well, congratulations, Danny. I'm sure you've earned it. I must run, Penny. Let's catch up soon," Sarah said, as she hurried away.

They stepped onto the cobblestones of rue Porion, and he turned his head, hoping that, whatever else had been destroyed here during the First and Second World Wars, the Amiens Cathedral had survived.

"What an amazing piece of Gothic architecture," Penny said, digging into her purse for a camera.

He followed her as she rushed toward the magnificent structure. Penny snapped photos while she talked.

"Oh my, and I thought the flying buttresses on Westminster Abbey were something, but look at these." Using her hand as a visor, she squinted and looked down the street. "Did you know the hotel shares its foundation with the church? The canons of the cathedral used to reside in the Priory."

Penny was animated in a way he'd never seen before. Daniel didn't know if Gothic was fit to eat. He knew the cathedral was a church, and a little older and fancier than most churches in Newfoundland, even the Basilica, which was a pretty grand church. Though he wasn't a religious man by any means, he did feel a connection to the Amiens Cathedral. He and Frankie had taken refuge there a few times, and he would admit he spent some of that time praying.

He wouldn't have had as much patience with anyone other than Penny, but she was a dear young girl, and he appreciated all she had done for him. So, he listened to her animated description as she went on about the cathedral. Her passion for most things historical came from a history book and a longing to remember a time she would never understand. He was happy she couldn't. She hadn't known the times he'd lived through, and she was better off for it.

She probably didn't even know the people of Amiens had feared the cathedral would be destroyed during the war, so they had removed the precious stained glass windows and placed sandbags high in the cathedral's nave to protect it from damage.

The car park was close to the church, and they found their blue Fiat Brava and climbed inside.

"You must buckle your safety belt, Daniel," Penny said as she start-ed the car.

"Why? You a bad driver?" he asked.

"No!" She laughed. "It's the law in France."

"You sure you don't want me to drive?"

"Do you drive a manual?" she asked.

"No, but at least I don't drive on the wrong side of the road."

She chuckled. "I think I'll be okay. At least as long as there are cars coming at me." She winked and pulled out into the street.

Daniel mumbled something and reached for his seat belt.

He closed his eyes and rested his head against the window as the car inched its way deeper into the Somme Valley. When he opened them, he was surprised once more by the land. It had returned to a state fit for farming, and the trees had grown quite high again. To anyone who hadn't had the misfortune of living here during the war, they probably wouldn't even notice the signs of a ravaged landscape. They just didn't know where to look.

His eyes drifted to a field, and off in the distance he imagined the full battalion of the Royal Newfoundland Regiment marching through these fields on its way to the front lines. He looked down on them like a bird soaring from high above. They were as sharp as ever in their khaki uniforms, with their kits on their backs and their rifles slung over their shoulders. Their arms swung back and forth in sync as Private Billy Connolly sang "It's a Long Way to Tipperary" at the top of his lungs.

"Won't be long now," he said.

Penny cast a quick glance in his direction and back to the road. "I was getting worried," she said. "There hasn't been a sign in ages."

"I don't need any signs," he said.

Every now and again, he thought he recognized something, but it was a fleeting thought. There was peacefulness and a beauty about the place now, but he knew they were getting close to Beaumont-Hamel, not so much by the landscape but by the intensity of pressure he felt welling deep within his heart. It was like an internal compass drawing him closer, and even if Penny had blindfolded him and thrown him in the middle of one of these fields, he would still find his way. He was drawn to it by his friends and comrades, the ghosts of the past.

Only a few miles to go.

"You okay?" Penny asked.

"Yeah."

They slowed and turned left into a parking lot backing onto a field, and Penny turned off the car. Daniel's eyes were peeled to the park's entrance, and he got out and walked toward it. Penny closed his door and followed behind him.

"Hello. Bonjour. I'm the caretaker of Newfoundland Memorial Park," said an older gentleman. "Welcome. May I offer you a tour?"

"Hello," Daniel said. "I don't believe there is much about this park, as you call it, I don't know already. But thanks for the offer," he said, and kept walking.

He looked to the right, the direction they had just driven from, and where he had marched first from Louvencourt and then Albert, in 1916. He crossed the road and veered to the left of the park's entrance.

Penny shrugged at the caretaker. "I'm very sorry, sir. He would prefer to be on his own."

The caretaker smiled. "Most of them do." He held up his hand in a gesture of understanding.

She started after him. "Daniel," she said, placing a hand on his arm, but he kept moving, like a magnet being pulled toward its force field. She fell in beside him and remained quiet.

He pointed. "This is where we waited the night of June 30, 1916. We called it St. John's Road. It was a support trench, you see."

The winding, man-made vein they had dug into the earth was still at least six feet deep after all these years, but its current purpose was vastly different. The last time he'd seen this trench, it was a mud pit. Now, hummocks of green grass grew, and the duckboards were clean. Each side of the trench was lined with wire stanchions to contain the curious.

He climbed down into the trench and walked a few feet before kneeling. "This is where Dundas died." He touched the grass and bowed his head.

Using the top of a stanchion, he hoisted himself up, and Penny stood beside him. He walked through the trench, which skirted the left perimeter of the park, and toward a cluster of trees. To his right was all farm fields and blue sky as far as the eye could see. The birds sang, and a rabbit ran across the path in front of him. The trench was winding, and as they rounded a bend, the massive bronze caribou monument sitting atop its rocky outcrop came into view on their right. Its head was high, watching over the sacred ground.

Daniel followed the caribou's gaze and walked a few more steps before he stopped. The sun had shifted in the sky, casting a long shadow over no man's land. The green grass and the grounds were well-manicured. A neatly kept graveyard full of colourful flowers lay in the distance, but that's not what he saw. He saw mud and debris and craters and bodies. He blinked away the terrible images and the moisture gathering in his eyes.

Penny slid her arm through his. "You want to keep going?"

He nodded.

They walked about one hundred and fifty feet and stopped next to a sign that read "Danger Tree."

"That's an odd name, and not much of a tree, either," Penny said.

He was hardly listening. His mind was transported to a few nights before they went over the top in 1916, when the night sky was all alight with German flairs. Frankie had stood by his side and covered him while he took aim, picking off as many of the enemy as he could. When it was over, they had retreated here to a small copse of trees to assess the damage.

His mind flashed forward so fast he almost buckled from the shock of his own powerful memories. It was July 1 at 9:15 a.m. when the CO raised his ash stick to signal the advance. They barrelled over the top and waded into no man's land under a constant stream of heavy German gunfire. Men dropped all around him, and he couldn't avoid walking on them as he tried to cross the one-mile stretch of land.

He lifted a shaky hand and touched the ragged piece of wood, which had been made to look like a damaged tree, void of branches or leaves.

"There was a cluster of trees here," he said. "The Regiment used it as a landmark. I don't remember a lot about the first of July. I was taken down pretty fast, as we all were, but this is where most of us got caught up." He held up his hand and pointed to the cemetery on the eastern border of the park. "We were just trying to get over there, but they had the perfect vantage point and picked us off one by one."

Penny's jaw dropped. "When I think of a battlefield, I tend to think of something much bigger than this."

"Hmm. You'd never think it would take so many lives to gain two hundred feet of ground, would you?" He linked his arm with Penny's and led her toward Y-Ravine Cemetery. "Come on. There's an old friend waiting for me."

"Your name, sir?" asked a middle-aged woman seated at the registration table outside the hotel's banquet room. Hundreds of people were assembling inside.

"Beresford," he answered, looking at the woman for a second before peering back inside the ballroom. He cast a side glance at Penny and coughed, leaning close. "In case you were wondering, I don't do crowds well."

"I would never have guessed." Penny laughed. "How about we make an exception for tonight?"

He grumbled under his breath.

The woman scanned her list again and picked up another clip-board. "Oh!" She stood up and thrust her hand out to shake his. "Mr. Beresford," she said, "there are some people who are anxious to meet you." She came out from behind the table and slipped her arm around his back, leading Daniel inside the banquet room. "Come with me and I'll show you to the VIP table."

His eyes widened. "What have you gotten me into, Penny?" he grumbled.

She grinned and squeezed his arm. "You deserve this, Daniel. Lord knows, if anyone does, it's you."

The woman led them to a long table at the front of the banquet room. "Mr. Tissier," she said. A tall gentleman in his mid-forties, look-ing smart in a dark blue suit, looked up from the podium, where he was rifling through some notes. "Allow me to introduce you to Mr. Daniel Beresford. Mr. Beresford, this is Donald Tissier, the chairman of the Great War Veterans Reunion Association."

Mr. Tissier's eyes lit up. "Mr. Beresford, I am delighted to meet you." He stepped forward to shake Daniel's hand. "You've come a long way to be here."

"I have, yes."

"Is this your first time in France since the Great War?"

"It is."

"We are happy to have you here for this. You might even find some old friends from the war here."

"Doubtful, sir. All my old friends are dead," Daniel said.

"That is unfortunate, Mr. Beresford. The Great War took a terrible toll. It may be long overdue, but we'd like to honour you here tonight. I do hope you can take some small comfort in that."

Daniel glanced at Penny again. He was already beginning to regret being here, and he knew she could see it in his eyes.

"Let's get you seated and a drink down your neck." She swooped in and turned Daniel toward the table.

"That's the best idea I've heard all night," he said, as she pulled out his chair and helped him down. Patting Penny's hand, he peered into her youthful eyes framed by a mane of bouncy strawberry curls. "You're too good to me."

She put her arms around his shoulders and squeezed him tight, much as he imagined a daughter would. "I'll be right back." She had wormed her way into his heart in the few weeks he'd known her. He was going to miss her when he returned home.

She was back in no time with a drink for him and a glass of red wine for herself. She winked as she laid it in front of him. The lights dimmed, and Mr. Tissier stepped up to the podium. A large screen behind him held a still photo of the inscription in every commonwealth war graveyard: *They Liveth Evermore.*

"Welcome, everyone. Tonight we gather from all corners of the world to commemorate the sixty-fifth anniversary of the Battle of the Somme. It gives me great pleasure this evening to award two very distinguished people with honours they earned during the Great War, but who have never been properly acknowledged until tonight.

"Women played a significant role in the war effort and were an integral part of the military. They served as nurses, ambulance drivers, and VADs. Tonight we honour one such woman, a VAD, who, on the opening day of the Battle of the Somme, left the safety of the casualty clearing station to work within a few feet of the front line. She worked tirelessly for twenty-four hours, helping hundreds of wounded soldiers and holding the hands of the dying, before she was forced back to the hospital, no longer able to stand due to shock and exhaustion."

Daniel sipped his whiskey. Alcohol made him so sentimental, and as he listened, his thoughts drifted to Emma and what she had seen that day and all the days of the war.

"It is my sincere honour to award the British Red Cross War medal, earned sixty-five years ago, to Mrs. Emma Purcell, who is with us tonight from just across the channel, in Plymouth, England."

A chair scraped the floor to his left as a woman seated at the lower end of his table rose. Applause filled his ears, and the whiskey, which had just slid down his throat, threatened a quick return. He gripped the table end with both hands and leaned forward to watch the woman identified as Mrs. Purcell approach the podium. She stood tall and faced the crowd as Mr. Tissier opened a small rectangular box, removed the medal, and pinned it to the woman's chest.

Daniel blinked a few times. The name Purcell sounded vaguely familiar but did not match what was running through his head. Emma served at the front on July 1, 1916, and she was from Plymouth. This could not be a coincidence. Even though the lights were dim, he could see her plainly. Her hair matched her grey eyes, but she had the same graceful presence she always had. Pale skin, with hardly a wrinkle. She was still beautiful, and she was standing a few feet away from him.

"Daniel," Penny's voice sounded in his ear. She reached for his shaking hand, and he turned to her. The look on her face told him he wasn't crazy.

"Daniel, is that Emma?" she whispered.

His mouth trembled, and he nodded, unable to communicate.

"My word!" Penny gasped, her eyes filling.

Applause filled the air again. Mr. Tissier shook Emma's hand and embraced her warmly before she turned back to her seat. Daniel pushed his chair back and stood.

"Our next honour of the evening belongs to a man who is with us tonight all the way from Canada."

Daniel stepped away from the table and turned in her direction. She was still smiling, looking down at the red box in her hands as she made her way back to her seat. He walked toward her slowly.

Mr. Tissier continued. "This courageous man, now the last living member of the famous Blue Puttees, one of the First Five Hundred, who volunteered their service to the British Army as the distinguished Royal Newfoundland Regiment, risked his life to save an officer in the field before becoming a prisoner of war. He was later shipped to a German work camp near the Belgian border, where he remained a POW for the duration of the war."

When Emma heard the word "Newfoundland," she raised her head. Her eyes fluttered and locked on his. The rest of Tissier's words faded into the background. Daniel opened and closed his mouth several times. He raised a shaky hand and touched her cheek. It was soft and warm and full of life.

"Emma?" he whispered.

Her breath hitched, and she closed her eyes, nodding. She reached for his hand and pulled him toward her. Her body shook as he held her, and they stayed that way for a long time, neither willing to pull away. He was aware the room had quieted, but neither of them dared break their connection. He had dreamed of this so often over the years, he thought he might be in the middle of a dream now.

"Daniel, is it really you?" she asked, pulling away just enough to look up at him, but holding his hands tight.

"It's me."

"But—" Her eyes held so many questions.

"Mother." A woman appeared next to Emma, her face deeply creased with concern. "What's happening?" She looked at Daniel carefully.

As if one surprise wasn't enough for the night, he stared into the face of a woman who reminded him so much of his mother it was unnerving. He caught the glint in Emma's eyes, and she squeezed his hand, nodding. It was everything he needed to know. He reached for the woman's hand. She raised her hand to his slowly. A look of confusion crossed her face, and her eyes widened in surprise as understanding seeped in.

"Amelia," Emma said, reaching for her daughter's other hand.

"Mother. Is this . . . ?" Emma nodded, letting out an uncontrollable sob.

"I'm Amelia," she said, smiling through her tears. "I believe I'm your daughter."

The three of them stood holding hands, their physical connection being the only thing keeping Daniel steady on his feet. It had occurred to him none of this was real, but when he saw Penny with her wide blue eyes and her hand over her mouth, he knew it was very real.

Sarah, the young woman they'd met earlier in the day, appeared with Mr. Tissier in tow, and ushered them through a side door into a smaller room with a couple of couches and chairs. Sarah and Penny moved to the back of the room, their heads bent low in deep conversation.

Daniel talked to Emma and Amelia for hours, and somewhere along the way, Amelia had left them alone, allowing her parents to revisit a time in their lives only they could truly understand. The next morning, Penny and Amelia drove them back to the Somme, to the place that had not only bonded them for life but had also driven them apart. As the scarlet sun prepared for its evening retreat, a long bugle sounded the "Last Post" a few miles away.

Daniel took Emma into a warm embrace. "It's always been you, my darling. It's only ever been you," he whispered in her ear. Arm in arm, they trod lightly over no man's land, through these now green fields of France.

The bloodstains of yesteryear had long been washed away.

epilogue

"What ever happened to your father?" Daniel asked.

Emma frowned. "I never saw Father after I left Middle Tickle in 1915. He was a stubborn man."

"So that's where you get it from." Daniel gave her a slight grin.

She smiled. "His sister, Ethel, wrote me just before the war ended and told me he had run the fishing firm into the ground and was bankrupt. He was apparently wrought with guilt after I left, and moved into St. John's with her. He died of a heart attack in 1920."

"And what about Thomas? Was he good to you?" Daniel asked.

He stood in front of the wall of windows in the grand library of the Grey estate and looked out over the gardens. His eyes were locked on the slope of land that led to the small graveyard on the hillside, remembering the one time he had been here in 1919. The memory was so vivid he could smell the damp earth from the freshly dug graves. The hurt crept through him as he played the scene over in his mind, and he turned away from the windows to find Emma standing behind him.

"Yes. Thomas was a good man." She smiled. "He did something most men would never have done, marrying a woman pregnant with another man's child. Postwar England was no place to raise a baby alone, even if I did have money. The stigma would have ruined me." Her eyes were glassy.

The bitterness seeped into his aching bones. A good man could never have stolen another man's life. Their eyes locked, and she took his hands in hers.

"I knew you weren't dead," she said. "I knew. Don't ask me how. I can't explain it, but when the letter came that day . . ." She shook her head. "I never believed it." She looked past him, into the garden, a sadness settling around her. "Thomas always believed he was competing with a ghost. He never said it, but I knew. I saw it in his eyes from time to time." She looked wistful. "I suppose, in a way, he was." She met his eyes again. "He knew I wasn't over you and I never would be." Her brow furrowed, and she swallowed, casting her eyes downward. When she looked up again, her eyes were glassy. "What I don't understand is why you never came for me." She searched his face for answers.

Somewhere deep inside, a flood of emotion surged, and he pulled his hands away, breaking the connection between them. Silently, he cursed Thomas. He had been here! He had walked the five miles from the train station, all the while imagining the look on her face when she saw him for the first time. Alive. He imagined a life with her, a family, children, but Thomas had robbed him of everything. He rewound through the last sixty-five years, through the nightmares, depression, and loneliness. It could all have been so very different if Emma had opened the door that day, but she hadn't. He opened his mouth, but stopped.

"What is it, Daniel?"

"I came."

Her mouth gaped. "When?"

He trod carefully. "It took some time for news of the war's end to trickle into the work camps. We were eventually rounded up and shipped back to England. Some of us required medical treatment, others needed a few square meals. Some of us just needed to know we were free and the whole thing was finally over."

"You were here in England?" Her eyes widened.

He nodded. "Yes. I did six weeks at Wandsworth. They still thought there might be something they could do to heal my leg after it was damaged the second time. I wasn't fit for much. I needed . . ." His voice trembled. "Some time." He swallowed hard. "When I felt well enough in January, they released me. I took the train to Weymouth and walked here one morning."

Her hand covered her mouth. "We had closed up the house and gone to Thomas's family home." She stifled a sob and shook her head in disbelief. "You were here. You were so close to me, and I didn't know. I should have been here!"

Pain stabbed his heart. "No, Emma, you did the right thing. The Spanish flu was a terrible ordeal. You couldn't risk harm to yourself, or Amelia." This he truly believed.

Spanish flu had spread across Europe like a flash flood, and the soldiers just back from the front were mostly to blame. They weren't the healthiest after four years of living in a trench, half-starved and only half sane.

She stopped, her eyes slowly meeting his again. "But we came back within six months. Why didn't you return?"

He watched her face. "I had no reason to."

Her hands dropped to her side. "I don't understand."

"I thought you were dead, Emma."

She raised an eyebrow. "Why would you think that?"

"That morning, I ran into someone here at the house. He made it sound like you were all dead, and I saw the freshly dug graves." She let out a pained cry, and he reached for her hand. "I was broken-hearted, naturally. I went back to Weymouth, and from there to London. The Regiment shipped us home in February. I never left Newfoundland again until a week ago."

"But," she said, "it doesn't make any sense. Surely whoever was here knew it had been Mother, cousin Helen and her daughter, and a few servants who passed. I was fine. I was sick for a few days, but it passed."

The anger and resentment Daniel felt toward Thomas began to evaporate. While Emma had spent her life with another man, she had never stopped wishing it was him. Daniel had always been there between them, and Thomas knew it. He died knowing it. She stared at him a minute longer, and a look passed between them.

He placed his hands on either side of her shoulders and stared into her grey eyes. "What's done is done, Emma. I've spent my lifetime loving a memory. For whatever time we have left, let me love you."

Acknowledgements

The seeds of this book were sewn by chance one night, with a colleague, over a glass of wine. I jokingly said, "I have a great idea for a miniseries, set in Newfoundland, England, and France at the outbreak of the First World War. We could even recreate the old streetcar running through Water Street!" Later that evening, a visiting colleague, who overheard our conversation, tapped me on the shoulder and asked, "Whose story is this?" I said, "Nobody's. I was only kidding." We talked about it for several hours, and he said, "Can you do it?" I replied quite honestly, "I don't know." It only took me three years, with a small break to have my twin girls, but I finished it. Thank you, Mike Prince.

But before all that, I must acknowledge the unwavering support of my friend April Traverse, who indulged my crazy ideas, read my ramblings, and talked me into taking a writing course several years ago, with local writer Paul Butler, who advised and commented on some early chapters in the manuscript. It was there I met a kindred writing spirit in Debbie, a.k.a. Kate Robbins, whose enthusiasm for writing was infectious. Over the last eight years we've been critique partners, kicked each other's asses, and spent many a night "story-storming." Together, we founded the Scribe Wenches, a powerhouse group of talented female writers in St. John's—Victoria Barbour, Valerie Francis, and Lesleyanne Ryan—and these women are a constant source of support, advice, and a tremendous force to be reckoned with. LA, thank you for your early read of the manuscript and for your military advice and expertise, and most of all your years of service.

To Frank Gogos—the most dedicated and passionate historian of the Royal Newfoundland Regiment. You've uncovered so much about these soldiers' lives, significantly adding to the Regiment's narrative. We've been on a remarkable journey together over the last three years, travelling side by side to England, France, Belgium, and Turkey, these places that are the backbone of Newfoundland's First World War story. You're a vast wealth of knowledge and you've willingly shared yours with me repeatedly and without hesitation. For your advice, encouragement, and friendship, and for suffering through "the scene," thank you.

To my loyal and supportive friends, Renee Ryan, Debbie Marnell, April Traverse, and Nancy Burden, who commented on early drafts and partial chapters, thank you for your excitement, feedback, and belief in me to tell this story. Dave Adams, thanks for the early read and suggestions, and Jim Prowse, for all the times you answered my numerous military questions and for making sure my French was bon—merci. To my family, John and Bill Broderick, who answered my nautical and fishery questions, and to Libby, such an unassuming talent and a generous friend, thank you for talking me through obstacles, the self-doubt, and for your eagle eyes when it counted most. Also for your healthy respect for commas, a trait we don't share, but I will try to do better next time.

A big thank you goes to Marjorie Doyle for her sound advice and for giving me the confidence to move forward with this story. Thank you to my editor, Robin McGrath, who fixed all my venial sins and took the time to explain them, but mostly for understanding what I was trying to do and making it better. Lastly, thank you to Garry Cranford of Flanker Press for taking a chance on this novel and on me.

I was determined to finish this manuscript while on maternity leave with my twin girls. On countless winter afternoons, I bundled them up and strapped them in car seats. A quick stop for coffee and a twenty-minute drive to the end of the continent, and I'd park in front of the ocean and write as much as I could before they stirred. On other days, especially when I put the big push on to finish, I relied on my family. This book would not have been possible without my mom and dad, Pauline and Leslie Martin, my in-laws, Margaret and Bob Clarke, and my aunt and uncle, Jacinta and Bob Sinnott, who offered to sit with my girls—and I know they loved every minute of it—enabling me to escape to the basement office or the quiet lull of a coffee shop to finish this story. There were times I felt so guilty about leaving them, but I feel less so now.

Last spring, I very unexpectedly lost my father, and while I miss him every day, I am thankful for the time he spent with my girls. They may not remember it . . . but I do. And to my mom, thank you for encouraging me to explore my creative side and for helping me understand that being different isn't bad. It's actually quite good!

To my husband, Kris, who bought me a laptop nearly ten years ago and told me to stop talking about writing and just do it, thank you for your patience and the reminders to stop overthinking and for occupying the kids over the last six months as I've repeatedly said, "I'm almost finished." To my girls . . . my most unexpected and beautiful girls, Katelin and Khloe, you are my finest accomplishment. Someday you'll understand Mommy felt the same away about these characters as you did Elsa and Anna from *Frozen*. I love you guys!

The main characters of this novel, Daniel Beresford and Emma Tavenor, are fictitious. Any resemblance to real persons, living or dead, is purely coincidental. Several historical figures do make an appearance, and in some cases I took artistic licence to place them there. They were heroes, men and women, and all are the essence of who we are as Newfoundlanders and Labradorians. If I gave them a fictional voice, if even for a few pages, they deserve it. Any factual errors are mine.

A note about the title: Several years ago, while researching for this book, I came across a quote by King George V. He wrote, "Yesterday, I gave the V.C. to Private Thomas Ricketts, Newfoundland Regiment, who is only seventeen and a half now, a splendid boy."

Over the last three years that quote has stayed with me. These men who served in the First World War—weren't they all splendid boys?

PHOTO BY FRANK GOGOS

Melanie Martin was born on the west coast of Newfoundland and Labrador but spent her formative years in Northern Manitoba. She has a master's degree in Newfoundland history from Memorial University and has contributed to historical journals, websites, anthologies, and educational textbooks on significant events in Newfoundland and Labrador's turbulent social and political history, specifically around resettlement and the industrialization attempts during the Smallwood years.

Her interest in Newfoundland and Labrador's role in the First World War has been ongoing since her first visit to Newfoundland Memorial Park at Beaumont-Hamel, France, in 2006. Since then she has visited all the sites significant to the Royal Newfoundland Regiment in France, Belgium, and Turkey. Melanie works for the Government of Newfoundland and Labrador and leads the First World War commemorations file, Honour 100. She resides in St. John's with her husband, Kris, their twin girls, Katelin and Khloe, and their dog, Dyson, who mourns for the days when his mother didn't write and he was an only child.